CHRISSY'S ENDEAVOR

ISABELLA ALDEN

LIVING BOOKS®
Tyndale House Publishers, Inc.
Wheaton, Illinois

Visit Tyndale's exciting Web site at www.tyndale.com

Tyndale House Publishers edition 1997

Living Books is a registered trademark of Tyndale House
Publishers, Inc.

ISBN 0-8423-3189-1

Printed in the United States of America

04   03   02   01   00   99   98   97
8   7   6   5   4   3   2   1

CONTENTS

WELCOME

by Grace Livingston Hill

As long ago as I can remember, there was always a radiant being who was next to my mother and father in my heart and who seemed to me to be a combination of fairy godmother, heroine, and saint. I thought her the most beautiful, wise, and wonderful person in my world, outside of my home. I treasured her smiles, copied her ways, and listened breathlessly to all she had to say, sitting at her feet worshipfully whenever she was near; ready to run any errand for her, no matter how far.

I measured other people by her principles and opinions, and always felt that her word was final. I am afraid I even corrected my beloved parents sometimes when they failed to state some principle or opinion as she had done.

When she came on a visit, the house seemed glorified because of her presence; while she remained, life was one long holiday; when she went away, it seemed as if a blight had fallen.

She was young, gracious, and very good to be with.

This radiant creature was known to me by the name of Auntie Belle, though my mother and my grandmother called her Isabella! Just like that! Even sharply sometimes when they disagreed with her: *"Isabella!"* I wondered that they dared.

Later, I found that others had still other names for her. To the congregation of which her husband was pastor she was known as Mrs. Alden. And there was another world in which she moved and had her being when she went away from us from time to time; or when at certain hours in the day she shut herself within a room that was sacredly known as a Study, and wrote for a long time, while we all tried to keep still; and in this other world of hers she was known as Pansy. It was a world that loved and honored her, a world that gave her homage and wrote her letters by the hundreds each week.

As I grew older and learned to read, I devoured her stories chapter by chapter, even sometimes page by page as they came hot from the typewriter; occasionally stealing in for an instant when she left the study to snatch the latest page and see what had happened next; or to accost her as her morning's work was done with: "Oh, have you finished another chapter?"

Often the whole family would crowd around when the word went around that the last chapter of something was finished and going to be read aloud. And now we listened, breathless, as she read and made her characters live before us.

The letters that poured in at every mail were overwhelming. Asking for her autograph and her photograph; begging for pieces of her best dress to sew into patchwork; begging for advice on how to become a great author; begging for advice on every possible subject. And she answered them all!

Sometimes I look back upon her long and busy life, and marvel at what she has accomplished. She was a marvelous housekeeper, knowing every dainty detail of her home to perfection. And a marvelous pastor's wife! The real old-fashioned kind, who made calls with her husband, knew every member intimately, cared for the sick, gathered the young people into her home, and loved them all as if they had been her brothers and sisters. She was beloved, almost adored, by all the members. And she was a tender, vigilant, wonderful mother, such a mother as few are privileged to have, giving without stint of her time, her strength, her love, and her companionship. She was a speaker and teacher, too.

All these things she did, and *yet wrote books!* Stories out of real life that struck home and showed us to ourselves as God saw us; and sent us to our knees to talk with him.

And so, in her name I greet you all, and commend this story to you.

Grace Livingston Hill

(This is a condensed version of the foreword Mrs. Hill wrote for her aunt's final book, *An Interrupted Night*.)

1

THE WAY IT BEGAN

FOR eighteen years the endeavor of her life had been to have a good time. At least, tradition said that she was less than a year old when she began with vigor to try to have her own way and to make as much happiness out of it as she could.

Of course, she had her own peculiar views at that age, and later, as to what happiness really was, and to say that she sometimes came to grief by the very road which she supposed led to paradise is to admit no more than falls to the lot of mortals older and wiser than herself.

Neither did she acquire so much wisdom by experience as those looking on thought she might have done; and on this day which marked her eighteenth anniversary, she was still eagerly engaged in the same endeavor.

It was the keeping of this idea uppermost which had been the apparent cause of her coming to the pretty mountain village of Western to pass the summer of 1885. There was a certain Professor Forman who did not know of her existence, and who thought principally about bugs and birds and blossoms, and who was nevertheless a link in the chain of events which brought her there.

It began in a careless conversation with her friend, Grace Norton.

"We must go to the seaside, of course, on Mamma's account; she thinks it agrees with her there better than anywhere else; and she likes Sea Rest better than any other resort because of the class of people who go there. They seem to me to think of nothing but what dress they shall appear in next; and I detest Sea Rest. The very name is a falsehood; the sea never rests. I don't like the ocean, anyway; great roaring monster, always hurrying up the beach after somebody. I can never get away from the feeling that the only reason he doesn't swallow me at one swoop, and be glad over it, is because he can't quite get me; and he is everlastingly trying. I just hate the ocean!"

"Where would you like to spend the summer?" Grace Norton had asked as soon as the voluble voice ceased.

"Oh! I don't know; anywhere almost, except where I have been. I like change, especially when the thing I have had doesn't suit me. I am not so very hard to suit, either. Honestly, Grace, you wouldn't like Sea Rest any better than I do. Louise likes it, of course, because Horace Burton is there, and they can wander along the beach for miles without appearing queer, and the ocean will roar so, all the time, that nobody but their two selves will know what they are saying. But I don't care enough for anybody to walk miles of beach with him, only Papa—and he never has time to walk on the beach or anywhere else; if he should undertake it, somebody would be sure to choose that occasion for 'getting beyond his depth.' They are always getting beyond their depth at Sea Rest. I think that is because they have so little depth of any sort; or else they would get carried off by the undertow and take every bit of Papa's time to bring them back again. It is dreadful to have a physician for a father; he never belongs to you for but two minutes at a time, and you are not sure of him then. That's one reason why I don't like Sea Rest—we all pretend to have so many things there that we don't have. When I grumble a little about going to the same old place every summer, Mamma looks reproachfully at me and says: 'One would think, Christine, that you would prefer to go to a point where your father can reach us so conveniently. Only two hours' ride; he can run down every few days and often spend the entire Sabbath with us.'

"Now, between you and me, that is a pretty little fiction of Mamma's with which she stays her heart, year after year. As a matter of fact, Papa doesn't get away more than three times during the entire summer; and then, as I say, some accident is sure to happen which takes all his time and strength. Of course, he is glad to be of service, and I am in full sympathy with Mamma when she says: 'What a providence it is that your father was here tonight; he has saved that girl's life.' It is almost always a girl, Grace, who does some silly thing at the seashore and gets herself in trouble. It is all very nice to have him there, but all the same it is not having a visit with Papa. And as for Sundays, just as though people were going to wait until after Sunday was over before they fell sick and sent for their favorite physician! On the contrary, one would suppose they took special pains to begin all scarlet fevers, and pneumonias, and things of that sort on Sunday mornings just as the bell is tolling for church!"

Grace Norton laughed merrily. "What a wild little creature you are to talk!" she said.

"Wild!" said Christine, with a wider opening of her great brown eyes. "That's not wild, that's just the truth; but, of course, there's no use in talking; Mamma is just devoted to that part of the world. You see, she meets old friends—they come year after year, the same people—and it seems to them like getting home. I can understand how it is."

"But I don't see why it doesn't work in the same way for you," persisted Grace. "Some of your old friends must return 'year after year.' Why are not you just as glad to see them?"

The silvery laugh with which the answer to this question began showed that the young girl's grievances were not deep.

"No, they don't; not one of my friends returns, but my enemies do, and that is one reason why I don't like the place."

Silence for a few minutes; then Chrissy, with a face into which a touch of gravity had stolen, said:

"I don't quite know what is the matter with me, Grace. It seems to me I must be different from other girls. I don't mean that about 'enemies,' of course, but honestly, I haven't any friends there, though I meet the same girls year after year. They don't think as I do about an earthly thing, or I don't think as they do, which would perhaps be a more modest way of putting it. If one were not so tired of it all, it would be comical, the certainty with which we will disagree; even about so trivial a matter as a new way of wearing the hair, we cannot talk five minutes without quarreling; or, at least, disagreeing so thoroughly that we all feel stuffy and uncomfortable. Now, I am not a particularly belligerent individual, as a rule. How do you account for it?"

Grace laughed again.

"It must be laid to the charge of incompatibility, I suppose," she said, feeling as though she liked the brown-eyed girl better at that moment than ever before.

Her next question was born of this thought:

"Have you really no plan which you would like to carry out for the summer?"

"Oh! dozens of them; but nothing on which I have set my heart. I don't mean that my heart shall have a thing to say in the matter; it's of no sort of use. I would like ever so well to join the Willards; they are going to the mountains. I always thought I should like the mountains; they keep still, you know; I don't like a thing which is forever going after something and never getting it, like the sea; besides, Professor Stuart is a cousin of the Willards, and he is going to be with them all summer and go out botanizing with the girls; if I have what Mamma calls a 'strongly defined taste,' I think it lies in that direction; but Papa doesn't like the Willards, so I have told myself to keep still about that plan."

"What if you would come to Western for the summer? We have grand mountain scenery; and if you like botanizing, there is an excellent opportunity. You know Professor Forman? I mean you have heard of him, of course? He spends his summers at Western; his brother lives there. He goes on long walks with his nieces, hunting queer flowers, you know, and talking them over. His nieces are lovely girls—friends of mine; they always invite half a dozen of us to join them, and we have lovely times."

Then impulsive Chrissy put both arms around her

new friend and kissed her rapturously while she declared that she was the "dearest girl in the world" and it was a "perfectly lovely plan." Of course she knew Professor Forman—at least Papa did—and only last week he said to her that if she could have him for a teacher, there would be some sense in her picking flowers to pieces to see how they were made. Oh! if she could only go to Western for the summer instead of to that poky old Sea Rest, she would be the happiest girl in the world. But then, of course, she couldn't. How could she? Mamma never would consent to her going to a place where she was an entire stranger and spend the summer at a boarding-house all alone.

Whereupon had followed much planning and many conferences between Chrissy's new friend and Chrissy's mother, which had ended, or more properly speaking so far as results were concerned, had begun in the decision that Chrissy Hollister should spend the summer in Western and board with Grace Norton's aunt, who usually opened her large old-fashioned country house to summer boarders.

No plans had ever given Chrissy greater pleasure. Her aversion to the seaside resort where her family regularly spent the summer was much more deep-seated than she had allowed to appear; and in the prospective delight of not being obliged to endure a single fashionable evening in the seaside parlor, she bore the railleries of the family in regard to her becoming an independent female with unfailing good humor.

So it came to pass that on the afternoon in early summer of which I write, Miss Christine Hollister, better known among all her friends as Chrissy, stood before the cottage mirror in a pretty little room in

Western and rearranged the frizzes of her brown hair that had been demoralized by travel, looking about her all the while with an interested and admiring gaze.

Does not the room where a young girl proposes to pass her summer deserve a word of description? It was a very simply furnished room; calculated in dollars and cents, the contents of a small pocketbook would cover the expense; but if one added brains, and skill, and artistic design, and could coin them into money, the result would make a difference in his bank account.

Matting on the floor—white, with just a touch of blue, almost like a thread hinting at color, instead of a defined stripe. White curtains at the windows—very simple ones—looped back with bands of flowered satin, of which the groundwork was blue. A cottage bedstead, bureau, and toilette set, all in white, with the daintiest decorations in hand-painting that Chrissy's beauty-loving eyes had ever seen. She looked lovingly at the plump bird, who swung on a spray of goldenrod on the mirror frame.

"You lovely little darling," she said, "I can't believe that you are made of nothing but paint! You look as though you couldn't help bursting into song this minute. And as for the goldenrod, it waves in the wind, I am sure of it. Grace!"

She raised her voice for this last word and waited for the answer from the room across the hall before she asked her question:

"Who painted these flowers and birds? Aren't they just too lovely for anything?"

"It is my work," Grace said. "I dressed your room myself after I came down here. Aunt Maria couldn't get any furniture for it that suited her, so we just put our heads together and made some. Doesn't it look cool and pleasant?"

She had come to the room door to finish her sentence and stood for a moment admiring the picture with the addition of pretty Chrissy in a white dressing sacque, with her wavy hair floating about her. Then, her name being called, she departed, not waiting for Chrissy's admiring sigh.

"It is all just as sweet and cool and charming as it can be. All blue and white; there isn't another color in the room," she continued, talking to herself, or to the birds and butterflies, who strayed even over to the mirror.

Presently her eyes rested on the blue satin pincushion, covered with white lace. Across it lay a ribbon—a badge of some sort. Chrissy laughed as she noticed that even the ribbon, which had evidently been dropped there by accident and forgotten, partook of the general character of the room, being of white satin and bearing on its surface, painted in delicate tints of blue, five mystic letters: *YPSCE*. Chrissy studied them curiously, admiring the graceful curves of the rustic work but wondering much what those letters could represent. Then, as she heard the familiar step in the hall, she appealed again:

"Gracie, what is this badge lying on the cushion? What do the letters represent?"

"Oh! did I leave that there? Why, it is our young people's society, you know. I'm coming, Auntie"; and Grace had vanished down the long flight of stairs.

Chrissy considered the letters, dropping her hairpins right and left as she bent over the cushion and studied.

"Young people's society," she murmured; "yes, of course, but the question is, What do *C* and *E* stand for? I thought I was acquainted with all the societies in the country belonging to young people. If it were

CC, it might mean chess club—Young People's Social Chess Club. Why wouldn't that be a good idea, by the way? Have a regular club, organized on business principles, and have champion players who would go out to play with other clubs. I wonder if they do it? If chess were not so uninteresting to many people, I might start one at home. Papa would enjoy it, and I'd like it well enough if I could always play with him; but I can think of people with whom I wouldn't spend a whole evening playing chess for a kingdom. And those are the very ones with whom I would have to play; that's the way things work. But *CE*—I'm sure I don't know what they can mean. Let me think. Young People's Society for—Carved Esthetics. How would that do?" with a bubble of laughter over her own folly. "Really, I don't like to give it up. They must mean something, and I ought to know what. Grace Norton always spends her summers in this little town; I shouldn't think she could know many things that I had not at least heard about. She said: 'Young People's Society'—so much matches. I must find a use for that C and E. Young People's Society of Classic—what? I wonder what may strictly be called *classic?* It if were only *B,* it might be twisted into a Browning Club, somehow— they are very fashionable—or it might be Bores or Blunders. I certainly can't think of a word that begins with *E.* Young People's Social Card—what? Yes, that's the question. If I could make that troublesome *C* into a *P,* I could read it without any trouble: Young People's Society for Progressive Euchre. But *YPSCE* is going to be too much for me, I am afraid. Wait! I have it at last: Young People's Society for Catching Eels; that fits exactly." Whereupon she went off into a succession of silvery little giggles.

Then, with a determined set of her pretty brown head, as she pushed the last hairpin into place: "Now, see here, Chrissy Hollister, it would be well for you to concentrate your wits, if you have any, in a determined effort to discover what those letters represent. If there is a new idea under the sun for the entertainment of young people, so fully fledged that they have hand-painted satin badges, and you can't tell what they mean when you see them, it shows that your education is defective. I mean to guess this riddle without other help than that afforded by my eyes and ears. If they have a club of some sort, it is altogether probable that they are enough interested in it to talk about it. If I don't learn before I'm many days older what *YPSCE* stands for in Western, and without inquiring in so many words either, then my name is not Chrissy Hollister."

And she shook out her pretty robes and went down to supper.

2

CHOICE ENGLISH

IT WAS several days before she had opportunity to begin her study of the puzzling initials. Getting acquainted with new people and places so occupied her mind as to keep her curiosity in regard to them in the background.

As they sat, one evening, chatting together in the after-supper twilight, a group of young people of which the pretty stranger was the center, a chance remark recalled to Chrissy her resolution.

"Oh goodness!" was the sudden exclamation of Miss Nellie Tudor, accompanied by a little squeal and a sudden drawing back of her masses of drapery; "there's an apple-tree worm! If there is anything that fills me with perfect horror, it is one of those worms."

Stuart Holmes came promptly to the rescue and, as he disposed of the offending worm, said with an amused smile: "I congratulate you on the absence of our critic."

"Oh dear! what an escape," said Miss Nellie, glancing about her with an air of mock terror; "though, after all, there is an unselfish way of viewing the matter. I think the critic is of the opinion that he would have to retire from office if I did not furnish him material."

In answer to Chrissy's look, Grace Norton explained:

"It is one of the outgrowths of our society; we have a critic elected to serve six months, who reports at our monthly meetings the inelegancies of speech which he has chanced to overhear from the members. A few of us have the honor of appearing in every report."

"Especially Nellie Tudor," added that lively young lady. "I really meant to be very careful all this month, but I can't help it, an apple-tree worm is horrid, anyhow."

Amid the general outburst of laughter at her expense, Chrissy pursued her investigations by questioning Stuart Holmes.

"What other exercises do you have at your society meetings?" she asked, a satisfied light shining in her fine eyes. She believed that, thanks to the worm, she had solved the mystery of the initials: Young People's Society of Choice English. That was what the letters represented, of course. She wondered she had not thought of it before. This disposed of the troublesome *C* and *E* in an entirely legitimate manner and was a very suggestive name for a society. "It is an excellent idea," mentally commented Chrissy. "I mean to organize one as soon as I go home and get Belle Parkman to join it with her 'Just horrids!' and her 'Perfectly awfuls!' about the most trifling things." She had held her first meeting and elected officers before she realized that Stuart Holmes was answering her question.

"Our rules are quite flexible. We have a committee on program appointed at each meeting to serve at the next one, and under certain general restrictions they are at liberty to arrange any exercises they choose. Sometimes we are very musical, at others almost entirely literary. It depends, you see, very largely on the character of the leading spirits for the hour."

"I understand," said Chrissy, very happy over her discovery and much pleased with this new idea. She had already thought of two unique entertainments which she would get up in the society she was going to organize at home. "I think it is an excellent arrangement," she said aloud.

"Oh yes! It is quite an enjoyable feature of this society," said Stuart. "We find that in this way certain people can be reached and gradually drawn in who at first have no other object than that of being entertained."

They were interrupted. A quick knock sounded on the open hall door near which the group was gathered, and a clear voice said: "Good evening, all. Is Stuart Holmes here?"

"He is here," answered Stuart, rising without waiting for further summons and joining a young man in the hall. He was followed by a chorus of voices urging him not to allow himself to be called away from the company under any pretext whatever. He returned after a few minutes' conference and addressed Gracie:

"Barnard has sent me word that his charge is not so well tonight, and as he is suddenly called in another direction, it falls to me to look after matters for a while."

"Oh!" said Grace. "We are sorry, but of course—"

"Certainly," he said with a smile, answering her unspoken words. "By the way, did you receive my message about the flowers for Saturday? Miss Lambert said she could furnish all that would be needed, but the young ladies would have to call for them—her

Jimmie is away. She was particular that you should understand that fact, and how glad he would be to serve you if he were at home. Also, Miss Potter told me they would have to depend on your committee for music tomorrow. You knew that, I presume?"

"I surmised it," said Grace, smiling. "There is certainly no present danger of our growing careless for the want of something to do; all of which reminds me that I had orders to tell you that the new clerk in the white goods department at Hall & Eaton's needed looking after."

"At Hall & Eaton's? I hadn't heard of him. What name, please?"

He drew a little brown book from his vest pocket and scribbled rapidly in it, Grace furnishing him a name and one or two other particulars, and Chrissy listening in puzzled silence. What were those young people about? While she puzzled, her mind went off to Sea Rest and called over the names of the young ladies and gentlemen who were probably at this moment lounging in the parlor of the boardinghouse with which she was most familiar, and she smiled as she contrasted the probable conversation with what was going on about her. These people were certainly very different. She wondered what made the difference. It could not be a difference which had to do with culture, for these young people were all well bred and well dressed. They belonged evidently to the educated and refined portion of the world.

"And as for conversation," said Chrissy as she closed this rapid mental review, "if one doesn't see more evidence of brains here in five minutes than could be found in an entire evening at Sea Rest, then I'm not a judge. But that is not saying a great deal.

Those people know they have no brains, I suppose; at least, everyone else does."

Meantime she was giving critical attention to the matter at hand. While Stuart Holmes wrote, he glanced about the room.

"Where's Dunlap?" he asked. "I thought I saw him here."

Then, catching sight of him at that moment, said:

"Look here, Dunlap, you are booked for tomorrow at the Rooms. Did you know it?"

"I did not. How is that? Tomorrow won't be my regular evening."

"No, it is your special evening. Aren't you a substitute for Sayles? He is called out of town—telegram from home."

"Is that so? I've received no notification."

"Why, yes, you have. I'm notifying you to the best of my ability. You will receive the formal one by the morning mail, I presume; this is only to prepare your mind."

And then with a smile and bow he departed.

"What is it that calls him away?" Chrissy asked, a note of disappointment in her voice. She was sorry to have lost the presence of this alert, appreciative young man.

"He is on the relief committee," Grace explained, as though relief committees were part of the regular program of polite society. "This poor fellow who is sick has no relatives in town except us, so of course we are bound to look after him. Stuart is chairman of the committee and has more than his share of work occasionally."

"What benevolent people you must be here!" Chrissy said, her handsome eyes opening wider than usual. It was so very new to her to hear young people talk about "relief committees" and duties.

"Oh no!" said Grace quietly. "We are only brotherly and sisterly."

But Chrissy was following out her own train of thought.

"You seem to be so busy," she said, "and so systematic. What was all that about flowers, and music, and I don't know what else? Have you each a special niche, or a dozen of them, which you are expected to fill?"

Grace laughed.

"We are rather busy, it is true," she said. "I never used to realize that there was so much in the world to do. Perhaps we are unusually busy just now; but I don't know; each season seems to have its specialties. Still, as you say, we are very systematic; so the burdens are not heavy, because there are many shoulders to bear them. The chairmen of committees have to keep their wits about them to save unnecessary steps, as well as time. What did you ask me? Oh! the music. It is for a funeral service—a little child belonging to a very poor family who live away up by the tannery. Such a sad case, Chrissy; you would be interested in them, I am sure. There is a very sweet little child. Oh! that reminds me—I must tell Nellie Tudor something. Nellie!" raising her voice, "I have two new names for your Saturday calling list."

"Horrors!" said Nellie.

There was a general laugh, in the midst of which a voice was heard to say:

"Do, somebody, take notes here for the benefit of the critic!"

The conversation became somewhat critical, giving Chrissy opportunity for indulging in her own thoughts.

"What queer people they are! For young people, I mean. One would think they were their grand-mothers; yet they are merry enough. But I don't see what looking after the sick, and attending funerals, and all that sort of thing can have to do with choice English. I suppose I am trying to mix several things that were not intended for mixing. They probably have a literary society and a benevolent organization of some sort, and some of the same persons belong to both. The literary society must be real fun. I mean to get their ideas and adapt them to our young people at home."

In pursuance of ideas, she questioned again: "Are you reading some special author in your society?"

"No," Grace said, "they had not done so as yet. The plan had been discussed and almost adopted; but since they could have only monthly readings, some of the members had thought it too long to wait for con-nected works, and they had been making each eve-ning's program complete in itself."

"By the way," she added, "we must have some recitations from you. You will help us, will you not?"

"Why, yes," said a gratified Chrissy, who knew she recited exceptionally well; "while I am here I have no objection to helping in any way that I can."

"That will be lovely," said Miss Tudor, who was listening to this conversation, and who now added her eager afterthought: "Miss Hollister, you will join our society, will you not? Oh, yes indeed! We take transient members, and you are going to be here all summer; we can get ever so much help out of you in that time. You don't know how skillful we are in making people work. Once you let Grace Norton and Stuart Holmes get control, it is a hopeless case; you have to work whether you want to or not. I know it by bitter experience." She said this with a merry little laugh. Then a trifle more soberly: "Besides, our aim is to spread ourselves. Grace tells me you have no organization in your city; we expect you to become so much attached to us that when you go home, the first thing you will want to do will be to organize; just keep us in remembrance. That is the way the thing works. I shall tell Stuart Holmes I have another victim for him."

Grace Norton smiled on the chatterer as she said: "It is fortunate that we all know you so well, Nellie; if you do happen to commence a remark that sounds as though it were going to be sensible, you spoil it before you reach a period."

"You see how it is," said Nellie with mock dignity, still addressing Chrissy; "that is the sort of tyrant I am under; but I endure it for the sake of the cause."

"I shouldn't wonder if I should do just as she said," Chrissy told herself late that evening, in the privacy of her own room as she unbound and brushed her hair. "I know I shall miss them when I go home, and if their society is what makes them so different from most of the girls of our set, I shall certainly organize one the first thing I do. They are just as pleasant as they can be. I don't think I ever met a company of young people who had such nice times together. I am glad they invited me to join their literary society instead of the other one; I don't think I should like to be mixed up with funerals and things of that sort. They certainly seemed to mix them wonderfully, though—the literary part and the other. How that Stuart Holmes did go on! One item of business seemed only to suggest another. I hope he is not so absorbed in his benevolent schemes as to have no time for the Society of Choice English. He certainly uses very choice English. I wonder if I have discovered the true name of the society? I think it must be that; the two things match, and the idea is a real splendid one—so much better than 'Browning Clubs'; for the fact is, I suppose we do use just horrid English."

With which elegant English sentence Miss Chrissy retired for the night.

3

BEWILDERMENT

HER first Friday evening in Western, the occupant of the white room was in a bustle of preparation for the first meeting of "our society."

"It is rather strange they haven't asked me to take any part tonight," Chrissy said, talking to herself after her usual fashion. "I suppose they thought I would prefer not to do so at their first meeting, since I am an entire stranger. But I would just as soon as not, if they needed it. I don't feel like a stranger; it seems as though I had known them always. I mean to be ready, so if any of their program should fail, I could help them out. Let me see, what shall I choose? Something bright and sparkling and not very long. I wonder how it would take here to do the caricature of 'Bingen on the Rhine'?"

Springing up with one pretty foot still in its slipper, the other encased in a trim French boot, she posed as an awkward giggling schoolgirl and hurried through the familiar words: "A soldier of the legion lay dying at Algiers," without so much as a comma between the sentences and accompanied by a running fire of the most absurdly inappropriate gestures, always introduced a half minute behind time. The recitation reached its climax in a distressful wail, broken by convulsive sobs, over the three-times repeated line: "For I was born"—Then came a howl of despair as the would-be reader realizes the fact that she had forgotten her piece. Chrissy broke off to laugh over a pleasant memory of the bursts of applause which had greeted her last happy rendering of the burlesque, and to wonder whether Stuart Holmes had ever heard it, and whether he would think she did it well.

"I shouldn't like them to think I could do nothing but burlesque," she said as she buttoned her other boot; "but something gay and unpretentious is the thing for a first appearance. If they encore me, I'll show them, perhaps. Nothing lengthy tonight, of course; but I'll put a little heart into it."

Then she turned suddenly to another question of interest.

"I wish I knew whether I was going to be too much dressed for this evening. I'm sure white ought to be simple enough for any occasion. But this is a good deal trimmed. Grace said she meant to wear the buff muslin she has worn all the afternoon. But then she is the same as at home here, while I am an entire stranger. Of course I would be expected to be carefully dressed. I believe I'll venture it. I'll put these gloves in my pocket until I find whether the girls wear light gloves or not. Of course if I recite I shall need them. This dress doesn't look badly on me, I must say."

Whereupon she swung herself gracefully around, tipping the little mirror to its utmost to get a view of the soft, lace-covered folds that fell in elegant waves about her.

"Mamma would say it was too white and insist upon

a sash, or at least a few knots of ribbon of some bright color. But Mamma does not understand the sort of society one meets at Western. I think elegant simplicity is better; I am naturally quiet in my tastes. I wonder why. Louise, now, is just as different! I believe I should like to live in a pretty village all the year round."

There was no denying the fact that our pretty Chrissy was very well satisfied with her appearance and surroundings. She pushed a bouquet of delicate moss rosebuds into place, assuring them that they gave just the touch of color which she needed and smiled back on the vision in the mirror as she arranged her dress hat, whose long, white plumes touched the lace-covered shoulder.

Now for her fan—a dainty, down-fringed beauty, in itself a conspicuous thing—and drawing on the gloves which were to be replaced on occasion for the flesh-colored ones in her pocket, she pronounced herself ready.

"It is ridiculous," she said to the mirror as she gave it a parting glance, "but for some reason, I feel a good deal dressed. I don't know what Mamma and Louise would think to hear me say so. I suppose it is because Western is such a little place. But party dresses are worn to literary gatherings sometimes, and this is certainly not a party dress."

The young guest's interest in this particular gathering had been on the increase since the day before, when Grace Norton had met her in the hall with her hands full of dainty notes and had said:

"Here are invitations for all the young people in the house to Mrs. Warder's lawn tennis party. And don't you think, it is to be tomorrow evening? Isn't that a pity?"

"Why?" Chrissy had asked, handling the delicate

notes with the genuine pleasure which a cultured taste has in all pretty things.

"Because we are engaged; it is our society night, you know."

"Oh! Can't we go to the tennis party and get round to the society in time?"

"Oh! No, indeed; they are not to serve tea until seven o'clock, and our meeting opens at half past seven."

"Oh!" said Chrissy again; then, after a moment's pause: "I thought perhaps we might go to the society a little late; but if you do not think so, of course I want to do whatever is best."

She spoke somewhat regretfully. She was very fond of lawn tennis and had a charming new costume which as yet there had not been opportunity to wear; but she dismissed her regrets complacently at last, with the following reflections:

"They must have splendid times at their society. There doesn't seem to be a question in the minds of any of them which to give up. A literary society of the study of choice English, which can be managed in such a way as to become a successful rival of a lawn tennis party, is worth studying."

It was a shadow of this thought which had made her choose her dress with great care, because, of course, such a gathering as this must be, to have assumed such importance, would surely admit of a handsome evening costume.

In the hall, just emerged from her own room, was Grace. Did she, or did she not, give a little start almost of dismay as her eyes rested on the lace-robed vision of loveliness waiting for her? For herself, she wore the pretty buff suit that had been her afternoon dress during the week. Her brown and buff hat, which matched the suit, was the one that belonged to her daily walks. Neat she was, certainly—Grace Norton was never otherwise; but Chrissy could not help saying to herself:

"She might be going to a prayer meeting instead of to a gathering of young people, to judge from her dress."

However, neither young lady feeling on sufficient terms of intimacy to venture unasked a verbal criticism of the other's toilet, the white lace dress followed the plain buff one in silence down the stairs.

"The others are gone," Grace said, quickening her steps as they reached the street. "I hope we are not late. Stuart Holmes is to lead this evening, and he is hopelessly prompt. Oh! There he is! Then we are not late. I am glad."

By the time the sentence was concluded the young man in question had crossed the street and joined them.

"The very person I especially want to see," he said genially. "Grace, I want to ask a favor of you, to the effect that you will take special pains to be good to Charlie Stone tonight."

"To be good to him!" Grace said smiling. "Wouldn't that indicate that I am sometimes bad? How am I do to it?"

"I may safely leave the *how* to you," he answered lightly. Then, more seriously: "He is having a hard time and is a good deal discouraged; I have been anxious about him all the week. I am glad of this opportunity for mentioning the matter, because I shall probably not be able to see you after the meeting. I have those two little girls in charge who live over on the North Side—the Boltons, you remember. Their mother says the difficulty in that way of their attending the meetings regularly has been that they are not sure of company home; she objects to their going alone. Very properly, too, in my judgment. That is that next thing we ought to do, I believe—contrive some means by which those young ladies on the North Side and those who live on Spring Street might always be sure of proper escorts home from the meetings. I wish we owned a society omnibus, or something of that sort; we could keep it busy most of the time."

The words were spoken half laughingly, but there was a gleam in the young man's eyes which said that he did not think the idea a bad one; and those who knew him would have hinted that he would be very likely to try for it. After this he gave attention to Chrissy. He had heard with pleasure through their friend, Miss Tudor, that she was willing to join the society. She would join as an active member, he hoped.

"Why, yes," Chrissy said with a bright little laugh; she would like to be connected with the society while she remained in Western. And as to the "active" part, she believed she had the name of being active in all directions. Mamma often told her there was nothing passive about her.

By this time they had reached the entrance door of the church parlor, and Stuart Holmes had gone promptly forward like a man who had business waiting for him. Chrissy, meantime, had lost herself in wonderment as to why these young people were so very eager to have the people from the North Side and from every side attend their meetings.

"I wonder what the motive power is," she said to herself for the dozenth time. "I shouldn't be surprised if there was a rival society in town, and each was striving to take the precedence in numbers and interest. That would account for the sort of intense way in which they go about everything."

It will be observed that this young lady was fond of finding out things for herself, and took some pride in her ability to do so.

The large parlor was more than half filled with young men and maidens. Some of them quite young—"mere children," Chrissy called them—with a sprinkling of some so much older that she felt justified in whispering to Grace: "Those people on the third seat don't consider themselves young, I hope!"

Grace had only time to smile back on her and murmur, "Young in heart," when Stuart Holmes, rising from his seat at the desk as if to call the society to order, gave the guest an added surprise. What he said was, "Let us pray."

Chrissy bowed her head with the others, but in truth she did not hear much of the short, earnest prayer which followed, being absorbed with the novelty of this way of opening a literary gathering of young people.

As usual, her thoughts went to Sea Rest. She tried to fancy the boarders in the parlor gathered for an evening's entertainment and commencing with prayer.

"But then," she told herself, her lip curling the while, "I don't suppose these young people would open a dance with prayer; and as that is the only way in which the boarders at Sea Rest are capable of entertaining themselves, it is not fair to compare the two."

Then she became aware that the prayer was concluded and that the whole company had burst into song. Words and melody alike were new to her, but the opening lines fastened themselves on her memory and stayed with her through the coming days:

> *I've found a friend in Jesus; He's everything to me;*
> *He's the fairest of ten thousand to my soul;*
> *The lily of the valley. In Him alone I see*
> *All I need to cleanse and make me fully whole.*
> *In sorrow He's my comfort, in trouble He's my stay;*
> *He tells me every care on Him to roll;*
> *He's the lily of the valley, the bright and morning*
>   *star;*
> *He's the fairest of ten thousand to my soul.*

From that moment, on through the hour, Chrissy Hollister may be described as in a bewilderment of surprise. Nothing was as she had planned that it would be. That it was a society of some sort was apparent, for certain notices were read pertaining to "lookout committees," "flower committees," and the like, but for the most part, it was song, and prayer, and words of encouragement or experience in the Christian life.

The roll of membership was called, but no society with which Chrissy was acquainted was in the habit of responding after the manner of these young people in this new world to which she had come. For instance, Nellie Tudor answered to her name by saying, in a clear, firm voice:

"I will pay my vows unto the Lord now in the presence of all his people. I believed, therefore have I spoken; I will walk before the Lord in the land of the living."

Before Chrissy had recovered from the sensation caused by hearing this merry young lady's voice in such a connection, the familiar name, Grace Norton, was read, and she replied:

> There's a wideness in God's mercy
> Like the wideness of the sea;
> There's a kindness in His justice
> That is more than liberty.
>
> If our love were but more simple,
> We would take Him at His word;
> And our lives would be all sunshine,
> In the sweetness of our Lord.

The very next name was that of Charlie Stone, whom Chrissy remembered to have been reported as having a hard time. He sat with head bowed on the chair in front of him, and there seemed to be a moment of hesitation on his part, during which time that curious undertone to sympathy and anxiety which on occasion takes possession of an audience, could be distinctly felt in the room. At last he raised his head, and his voice, low and slightly tremulous, broke the stillness:

"Hitherto hath the Lord helped me."

"Thank God!" broke in low tones from the pastor who sat near him, and who had evidently waited in great anxiety. Instantly Stuart Holmes began to sing, and fifty voices joined him without hesitation:

> He all my griefs has taken,
> And all my sorrows borne;
> In temptation He's my strong and mighty tower.
> I have all for Him forsaken,
> And all my idols torn

*From my heart, and now He keeps me by His
   strong and mighty power.*

*Though all the world forsake me
And Satan tempts me sore,
Through Jesus I shall safely reach the goal;
He's the lily of the valley,
The bright and morning star;
He's the fairest of ten thousand to my soul.*

Poor Chrissy's surprise and bewilderment became
so great as to almost unnerve her. She had felt so sure
that she understood the entire matter and had done
so much unconscious planning as to what the program would probably be, that to have it develop in this
way was overwhelming. At times the ludicrous side of
the subject presented itself. She imagined herself going forward in party costume, with the addition of
those flesh-colored kids in her pocket, and following
the singing of some tender hymn, or the earnest words
of prayer, with her proposed burlesque of "Bingen on
the Rhine."

"Suppose I should!" she said to herself in that hyster-
ical condition to which some persons find themselves
victims on occasion. "Suppose I really should stand up
and recite that thing in the midst of this meeting!
Wouldn't that be too dreadful for anything? What
would they think of me?" And then she giggled out-
right—not a very loud giggle, though it sounded loud
to her, and it brought a flush to Grace Norton's face.

After that, Chrissy bowed her head and did not
raise it again until the meeting was concluded. The
very last exercise, preceding the benediction, hushed
her into a gravity which showed a pale, almost
startled face when she raised her head. It was the

proposal of new names for membership, and among them was her own! Membership in what? What was this gathering, and what had she in common with it? Run over her list of accomplishments as she might, nothing about them fitted such a place as this. Why had she been so foolish as to promise to join them? What would they think of her when she told them she could do no such thing?

Stuart Holmes came directly toward them, speaking to her:

"Miss Hollister, here is the active-membership pledge, which we would like to have you sign. Didn't we have a good meeting?"

"I'm afraid," began Chrissy; "I—that is—I am sure there is some mistake; I did not think—I mean I did not know—"

He did not even hear her but broke in upon her stammering words with an abrupt:

"I beg your pardon. Grace, don't let Charlie Stone get away without speaking to him, please; it is very important. And there go my little girls; I must run. I'll explain all your perplexities the next time I see you." This last, with the bow and smile, were for Chrissy; then he made a hurried dash after his "little girls."

4

SEEKING STANDING GROUND

IT HAPPENED that Grace walked homeward in earnest conversation with Charlie Stone, and Chrissy was joined by Nellie Tudor and her brother. There was no chance for any words with Grace. Nellie Tudor's head was full of the hymn which had been sung for the opening, and she hummed strains of it: "He's the fairest of ten thousand to my soul," breaking off to say:

"That is a lovely tune. Don't you think the harmony is exquisite, especially on the chorus, when that heavy bass comes in? But the words half frighten me. Sometime I don't know whether I ought to sing, 'He's the fairest of ten thousand'; that is saying a great deal. Do you ever feel that way?"

"What way?" They seemed to be the only words at Chrissy's command.

"Why, half scared over the words you sing, lest you might be claiming more than you have any right to. Perhaps you never have any trouble; I dare say you don't. You are probably good, like Grace, and Stuart Holmes, and those. But I am such a giddy, silly thing, you see, that half the time I don't know whether to sing or to keep still, for fear things won't match. Do you ever feel that way?"

"I don't know what I feel," Chrissy said, with a half laugh, yet by no means sure that it would not end in a burst of tears. She was still in a tremble of excitement and was crumpling the innocent bit of pasteboard in her hand into a shapeless mass, wondering the while what dreadful pledge she was expected to sign and assuring herself that she would do no such thing.

She made very incoherent *adieus* to her companions when they reached home, drawing Grace away in nervous haste, instead of lingering with her in the parlor, as was their custom.

"Come to my room," she said in an eager, half-breathless way. "I want to talk to you."

But once within the privacy of her own room, the door closed and locked, Grace looking at her with pleasant eyes of mild inquiry, poor Chrissy suddenly burst into an apparently uncontrollable paroxysm of laughter, which continued, despite Grace's puzzled and pained look, until it spent itself in a burst of tears, as causeless, from Grace's standpoint, as the laughter.

"Why, Chrissy!" she said at last, in tones full of anxiety. "What in the world is the matter with you? I never saw you act so strangely!"

"Sit down," said Chrissy, mindful at last of her duties as hostess. "Take the little rocker and sit where I can see you. I want to talk to you."

As she spoke she perched herself, schoolgirl fashion, on the bed, having first drawn the rocker directly in front of it and motioned her companion to be seated. Her pretty face was flushed, her eyes shining through tears; there was a curious tremble of the lips which might develop either into tears or laughter at a moment's notice.

"Where have I been tonight?" she demanded.

"Where have you been?" repeated Grace. "Why, to the regular Friday meeting of our society, of course. And I thought—"

"What society?" interrupted Chrissy. "I never saw or heard of such a society as that before; and it wasn't in the least like what you described, or at least it wasn't like what anybody could have imagined from—"

She could not finish any of her sentences, because her truth-loving conscience reminded her that she had evolved the description of this meeting from her own brain, assisted by a few initial letters.

After a moment's reflection, she began again:

"Whoever heard of a literary society being just a prayer meeting?"

"But we are not a literary society. Why did you think we were? We have a literary department, with meetings once a month, just as I told you, but that is not the most important one, by any means. This, tonight, was our regular Friday meeting. Don't you remember I told you so yesterday?"

"But why do you have such a meeting at all? I mean, what has a meeting of this character to do with choice English?"

"With choice English!" said Grace, greatly puzzled in her turn; "Something, I hope; at least, I wish we all used it on such occasions, if not always. But why do you think of that in connection with our organization?"

"Why, because you told me, or—that is—isn't that the name of the Society?"

"Isn't what the name?"

"The Young People's Society of Choice English. I don't see what on earth it can be then," for now Grace was laughing; "those words fit all the letters on that white ribbon, and nothing else fits that would make the least bit of sense."

"You dear child," said Grace, speaking gently, "what a bewilderment it must have been to you! I don't think much of our talk could have fitted your idea; we were so busy, you see, that we forgot to be careful about the English. Why, it is a Young People's Society of Christian Endeavor. I thought you knew, of course."

"Christian Endeavor!" echoed Chrissy. "How *should* I know?" Then she thought of that pledge she was expected to sign and shivered. "I never heard of such a thing. Where did you get your idea?"

"Why, Chrissy Hollister, you have surely heard of the Christian Endeavor societies; they are springing up all over the country."

"I can't help it; I never heard of them. What are they for?"

"Just what the name indicates. We are young people, and we are Christians; as such, we endeavor to do what we can in the service of Christ. It is really a very simple matter, as you will find when you join us. Didn't Stuart Holmes give you a pledge card? Is it that little wad of paper you have in your hand? I think he will have to give you another to sign. What made you treat it so cruelly? If there is enough of it left to read, smooth it out and see how simple and matter of course it is."

"There is no use in my reading it," Chrissy said after two whole minutes of silence, during which time Grace looked at her and waited.

"Why not?"

"Because I—why, I'm not that kind of a girl; I never did such a thing in my life!"

"Such a thing as what?"

"Any of it," said Chrissy with a half laugh and an undertone sigh. Then she smoothed out the crumpled pledge card and read the heading aloud.

"'Active-membership pledge!' The idea of my telling that young man that I was always an active member of everything! What must he have thought of me? Grace Norton, what made you let me go to such a meeting in this ridiculous rig? I shall never be able to endure the sight of this dress again, and it is my prettiest white one. 'Trusting the Lord Jesus Christ for strength, I promise him that I will do whatever he would like to have me do.' The idea of my signing such a pledge as that!"

"Why not, Chrissy?"

"'Why not!' I wouldn't do it for anything in this world!"

"But I want to know, Why not?" persisted Grace's quiet voice; and Chrissy found, as many another had done, what a difficult thing it sometimes is to answer a very simple question. She made an effort to do so.

"Because it is a perfectly dreadful promise! Awful! I don't see how anybody could dare to make it."

"But, Chrissy, let me understand. Aren't you a member of the church?"

"Of course I am. What has that to do with it?"

"A great deal, I should think. Does that pledge on the card cover any ground that you have not already been over with covenant vows?"

"Oh! Well now, Grace Norton, you know that is a very different thing."

"I don't, really. Haven't you made just such a promise as you find on that card? How is it different?"

"Because it is," said Chrissy, with that delicious disregard of logic which is sometimes found in people older than she.

"Very different, indeed. Signing your name to such solemn words! Listen to this: 'As an active member, I promise to be true to all my duties; to be present at, and take some part in, every meeting, unless hindered by some reason which I can conscientiously give to my Lord and Master, Jesus Christ.' Grace Norton, I think that is a perfectly terrible promise to make! I wouldn't be bound by it for anything in this world. Think of my taking part in a meeting! The parts I am accustomed to take don't match."

A vision of the proposed recitation floated through her mind again. She saw herself at that prayer meeting, struggling through the burlesque she had planned, filling her audience, not with admiring laughter, but dismay, and she burst into a nervous laugh.

Grace Norton sighed as she watched her. This was, to her, an entirely new development. She had dealt before with young people—church members—who objected to joining the society on the plea that school duties, or home duties, or social duties, or invalidism, or something, prevented their doing what would otherwise be agreeable; but never before had one frankly said to her: "I think it is a perfectly terrible pledge, and I wouldn't be bound by it for anything in the world!" Was this what all those other excuses had meant?

"Well," she said, rising as she spoke, "I am sorry you feel as you do; we had looked forward to having your help all summer. I thought you would be a splendid helper, and I told the girls so. I don't understand your objections in the least. It does not seem to me that, in taking this pledge, I have done more than to renew my church covenant, in a convenient form for frequent reference. But, of course, we must not urge you beyond your convictions of what is right. You must tell

Stuart Holmes as soon as possible. It was he who proposed your name of active membership, and if he must withdraw it, he ought to hear from yourself the reasons for doing so."

The next evening was Chrissy's opportunity for explanation. It chanced that she and Stuart Holmes were alone together in the music room, Grace having just left them in answer to a call. You may have observed that Grace Norton belonged to the class of young ladies who are always being called to help somebody.

Stuart turned toward Chrissy with a businesslike air and smile as he said:

"May we claim our new 'active member' for active service at once? I have a bit of work on my mind which I am somewhat impressed that you can accomplish better than another."

She interrupted him eagerly: "Oh! Mr. Holmes, I am glad you have spoken of it; I wanted to explain, and, indeed, to offer an apology for the trouble I have made. There has been a misunderstanding—a very curious one on my part. I was as stupid as an owl, I suppose; but, indeed, I cannot join your society at all. I must ask you to absolve me from my promise to help."

He was very sorry to hear it, he said, treating the subject with exceeding gravity. Might he be allowed to ask the reason for this decision? She very much wished that he wouldn't, but he waited courteously, and she attempted her explanation.

"Why, I—as I said, there was a misunderstanding. I thought it was simply a literary society, and that the help desired would be in the line of recitation, and music, and matters of that sort. I had not heard the name of the society, and I thought—it was—was something else, something very different from what it is. There is no one to blame but myself, of course; I ought to have inquired before I made any promises. But you will release me, please; I cannot join an organization like the one your pledge belongs to."

"There is still a 'misunderstanding,' so far as I am concerned," he said, smiling gravely. "Am I to understand from this that you are not a Christian?"

"Why, no," said Chrissy, her confusion deepening. "I am a member of the church, if that is what you mean."

"That is, of course, the outward pledge of what I mean. In that case, may I ask why you cannot belong to our organization? You have seen that the pledge we use is simply the Christian's covenant set down in black and white, for us to look at."

"It doesn't seem so to me," said Chrissy desperately. "I think it is a terrible pledge. I told Grace that I wouldn't sign it for anything in the world, and I wouldn't. Why, it would affect everything one did and said—talking about people, and everything! I wouldn't dare to sign it, Mr. Holmes; I wouldn't, really."

The smile which answered her was still very grave. This Christian worker was older than Grace Norton. He understood human nature better. He knew that this young, professing Christian did not realize the import of the confessions she was making. Was it not part of the work of their organization to endeavor to help people to see plainly the ground on which they stood?

How should he help her? Someone came into the room in search of a piece of music. Chrissy went to help find it. It proved to be a work of time. Piles of sheet music were gone over in a vain search, during which time Stuart Holmes was engaged in writing rapidly on a card which he had drawn from his pocket.

The messenger finally departed, and he drew his chair near to the seat Chrissy had taken.

"Miss Hollister, I want to get at the root of this matter if I can," he said. "I understand you to say that you will not sign our Christian Endeavor pledge. You have read it carefully, I suppose?"

"Oh! indeed I have," Chrissy assured him. She had read it several times, each reading making her feel more certain that she must not sign it; that, in fact, she would be a hypocrite if she did so. And if there was one thing more than another that she wanted in life, it was to be always perfectly sincere. She thought that people who signed that pledge must be either very good indeed—better than any persons she had ever known or ever expected to know—or else they were hypocrites or prisoners, and she did not want to be either. She was honest, certainly, and was insisting on trying to occupy neutral ground. Stuart Holmes thanked her in his heart for her frankness; it made his way clearer.

"Then let me read to you this card which I have written and ask if you are willing to sign it: 'I promise the Lord Jesus Christ that I will *not* strive to do whatever he would like to have me do; that I will *not* pray *nor* read the Bible; and that just so far as I know how, throughout my whole life, I will endeavor *not* to lead a Christian life.'"

He read the words slowly, with deepening gravity and with solemn emphasis on the negatives, Chrissy meantime regarding him with wide-eyed wonder, not to say horror.

"Mr. Holmes," she said at last, "I think that would be wicked."

"To sign this card, do you mean? Why, of course, the signing of it is merely the expression for the convenience of others of a deliberate conviction and line of action. Whether I put my name to it or not does not alter the facts, you know, as they stand revealed to the Lord Jesus Christ. If I have honestly and deliberately resolved to try to do whatever he would like to have me do, there can surely be no objection to my writing it on paper for the purpose of letting others know where I stand, and of winning them to know with me."

"But isn't there a very great difference between not promising that one will do a thing, and promising not to do it?"

"In sound, yes. In practical life, what degree of difference do you think there is? The trouble is, Miss Hollister, we do not reason about these matters in a commonsense way, as we do on other subjects. Suppose, for instance, I ask you to promise to walk with me in the park this evening. No, you will not promise, but I have a very special reason for desiring you to do so. I offer what inducements I can and ask if you will promise to try to arrange so that you can do as I wish. No, you will not promise. But I urge the matter. Will you not make a little effort in the direction of my desires? No, you will promise nothing.

"What would I be justified in concluding? If, for the purpose of illustration, you can conceive of yourself as having previously pledged to order your life in accordance with my wishes, what opinion would I be likely to have of the pledge? Miss Hollister, what must the Lord Jesus think when his pledged friends are not willing to renew their promise to try to please him in their lives? Is it not equivalent to saying that they do not mean to try?"

"But one might change one's mind," said Chrissy faintly.

"And the pledge I have written is for a lifetime, do

you mean? I see your point. Very well, let us change the wording. I will date the card for tomorrow. I will erase the words *my whole life* and make it read: 'So far as I know how, throughout this week I will endeavor not to lead a Christian life.' Are you willing to sign that?" he asked.

Chrissy lifted great, troubled eyes to his face and answered with intense gravity:

"Not for the world, Mr. Holmes. I should not dare to do such a thing; I think it would be very wicked."

"But, my friend, one must stand somewhere! Either you are willing to try to please the Lord tomorrow, or you are not willing; there is no middle ground. All I am asking of you is to tell me on paper which it is."

There were steps on the piazza outside, and the sound of merry voices drew nearer. The young people were moving toward the music room. Stuart Holmes arose to go. He was in no mood for merry talk. He laid two cards in Chrissy's lap: One was a new, clean, Christian Endeavor pledge card; the other was the card on which he had written. He bent over her, speaking low and earnestly:

"Indeed, Miss Hollister, I would not unduly press you, but this is my Master's business, and I feel that I ought to know where you stand. If you will sign either the one card or the other, whichever emphasizes your deliberate conclusion, and give it to me tomorrow evening after service, I shall know on which side to look for you for one week at least."

5

"THE WORLD, THE FLESH, AND—"

I BELIEVE every hour, and almost every moment, of that fair June Sunday is distinctly photographed on Chrissy Hollister's mind. I know that afterward she could say of it, "Just six months ago at this hour I was sitting in my little rocker by the window" or "Just a year ago at this time I started for the young people's meeting—that Sunday evening, you know."

As to earth and sky and flower and bird, the day was perfect. But the strangest turmoil her young life had ever known was going on in Chrissy's heart. Her unrest showed itself outwardly in an irritability that was as foreign to her nature as it would have been to a bird's; and Grace, who knew nothing about the two cards, or the disturbed conscience, and was herself as quiet and as well poised as a lily, looked on in a sort of maze at the apparent transformation in her heretofore sunny friend.

"I'm not coming," Chrissy said, irritably, in reply to Grace's call at her door that the family were gathering in the east parlor for morning worship.

The door was ajar, and Grace ventured to push it

open and peep in a face full of solicitude. There stood the young woman by the window, apparently engaged in nothing more important than gazing out on the lawn. She did not even turn her head as Grace spoke:

"Pardon me, Chrissy; I was afraid you were sick. Why are you not going down, dear? The service is very brief, and you will enjoy it. Miss Patterson always sings with us on Sundays."

"I do not wish to go down. I wish you would not wait for me, Grace, for I certainly don't intend to go."

Still Grace stood irresolute. At last she said in the gentlest tone:

"Chrissy, dear, I'm afraid you are not feeling well; I wish you would tell me, and let me do something for you. Don't you know I promised your father that I would take excellent care of you?"

Then Chrissy turned toward her a haughty face. "What an idea!" she said. "I am perfectly well, and do not need any care. I simply do not wish to go downstairs. It is quite an unusual experience to me, anyway, to be invited to family worship in a public boardinghouse. I presume there is no compulsion about it, is there?"

"Certainly not," said Grace, and I think she may be pardoned for speaking with a touch of dignity. "I thought you would enjoy it."

Then she went away—went downstairs slowly, so slowly that by the time she reached the door of the east parlor, Chrissy came flying after her and went into the room with her hand slipped through Grace's arm. But if Grace had known how the hymn that was being sung smote on the soul of her friend, she might have understood her nervous mood better.

'Tis done, the great transaction's done;
I am my Lord's, and He is mine;
He drew me, and I followed on,
Glad to perceive the call divine.

Those were the words with which the air was pulsating as they entered and crossed the room to Grace's accustomed seat near the organ.

"No, it isn't done," said Chrissy to her conscious, and she shivered at the thought. "Nothing is done. Not any of the things that I thought settled long ago." She looked at Nellie Tudor with a curious wonder as to how those words affected her. The bright young face was as serious as was in keeping with her nature, and she was singing heartily. "I wonder if she feels that 'He is hers,' and I wonder how that feels, or ought to feel? And I wonder if I know nothing about it, and never did?" These were the tormenting questions which haunted her. She paid no attention to the reading, or the prayer, but went on with her unprofitable thoughts. The unreasonable irritability grew upon her. At first she decided that she would not go to church. She did not want to hear any more from these fanatical people; they were different from any people she knew, and she had nothing in common with them. The pastor was a fanatic, too; she could tell that from his prayer the other evening. She would stay at home and read Howells's new book. She had brought it down with her to help beguile the time; this was just the day for it. And tomorrow she would write to Papa and tell him she was bored to death, and ask him to let her come and keep house for him in town, and go back and forth with him to Sea Rest. Or, if he wouldn't consent to that, as of course he wouldn't, she must make up her mind to endure Sea Rest, and the teasings of Louise and Harmon. Anything would be better than the discomfort of the last few hours. Then she grew angry at Stuart Holmes. It was all his fault, she assured herself. All this discomfort grew out of his unwarrantable interference. What business had he to write out a horrid card of his own making up and ask her to sign it? Wicked it was, too. They needn't call him such a good young man when he could think the thoughts on that card! She had never pretended to have a very great amount of goodness herself, but she wouldn't dare to think such things, to say nothing of writing them. Of course she wouldn't sign his old card, not the other, either. What right had he to give her cards to sign? What business was it of his, she should like to know, where she stood?

She would just get away from them all, as quickly as she could. She did not belong among such people. The thoughts ended almost with a sob. She was back in her own room now, where no one could hear her. There came over her a pitiful feeling that she did not belong anywhere; that there were no people with whom she assimilated. "I thought they were going to be so nice," she murmured; "they seemed to have such lovely times together; and now it is all spoiled! I don't know why it is, either. I don't understand why I care so much. Suppose he was rude. People have been rude to me before, and I lived through it and really cared very little about it. Why can't I give him back both his cards tonight and tell him I have no use for either of them, and that I decline to appoint him as my father confessor, and then just go on and have a good time, without taking any further notice of him?"

A few moments more spent over this new thought, and she started up with energy:

"I'll do just that thing," she said frankly; "it would be too babyish for anything to allow that officious young man to spoil my entire summer. I'm not going to stay at home from church, either. I don't believe I like my own company well enough for that. Besides, Grace would ask a hundred anxious questions and want me to take quinine and telegraph for Papa. Dear little Grace, how cross I was to her this morning! I don't see what made me. She is not to blame. I'll go to church with her, and I'll wear the very prettiest suit I have and astonish the villagers."

To carry out this last enthusiasm, she devoted the next two hours exclusively to the business of dressing. Twice she changed her mind entirely as to which suit should be worn, necessitating much unfolding and folding away again. Then when the momentous question was at last settled, because she liked the ruffles in the pale gray dress better than she did the ones in the blue silk, she ripped, and basted, and rearranged generally. After that, it pleased her to set the flowers in a different position on the hat that matched the blue suit, and finally to remove them altogether, and substitute a cluster which was in a box at the bottom of one of her trunks. In this absorbing occupation she chose to make herself believe that she was getting the better of her questioning anxieties; to further prove it to herself, she hummed a strain of music over and over, stopping in the middle of a bar as she discovered that the melody was one she had caught on Friday evening, and the words which fitted the line she was humming were, "He's the fairest of ten thousand to my soul."

"Sometimes I don't quite know whether I have a

right to sing such words," that giddy Nellie Tudor had said.

Chrissy tried to curl her lip over the memory of it.

"Little simpleton!" she murmured. "Of course she had no right. As if anybody could sing them, really meaning just what they seem to say! It is just poetry."

But this was dangerous ground on which she did not mean to stay. She dismissed all hymns abruptly from her thoughts and hummed a strain from the last opera she had heard. She would not have sung the words—that was her concession to the Sabbath; but the music, she told herself, was "divine" and had no troublesome associations.

The very butterflies might have envied the young lady who finally moved down the aisle of the pretty village church. A trifle late she was, for Chrissy had discovered at the last moment that the gloves at hand were not of exactly the right shade and had dived after her glovebox for another pair. It was not that she was gorgeously dressed; she had exquisite taste, but her choice had been quite as bright as the day and occasion would allow, and the entire costume showed that careful attention to minutest details which exceedingly well-dressed people always show to initiated eyes. Chrissy knew she was making a sensation; and the thing which would ordinarily have annoyed her, on this particular morning gave her satisfaction. She even rejoiced to see that Nellie Tudor's thoughts evidently wandered quite away from the words she was singing and fastened themselves upon the beauty of the lace which trimmed her dress. The truth is, when one sets out to feed one's heart with husks, very mean and moldy husks will sometimes suffice. I do not know that Chrissy realized at the time that she had entered upon a deliberate attempt to stifle the voice of an accusing conscience.

The first thing about the service which attracted her attention was the text. In truth, it might have surprised a more careless heart than Chrissy's that on this particular morning the pastor should have chosen for his text the words, "Choose ye this day whom ye shall serve." But the surprise only added to her irritation.

"Everything is about choosing," she muttered. "As if one were to be driven into making decisions! It is a queer coincidence, to say the least, that such a verse must be forced upon me just now. If I thought that was some more of Stuart Holmes's interference, I would never forgive him in the world. Not that I mean to forgive him, anyway. He had no business to meddle with my affairs. It is that which annoys me so much. Of course I am not disturbed about the other matter; why should I be? I settled it long ago. I told him I was a member of the church."

Whereupon her thoughts took a swift journey to the city church where, in her "long ago," which meant just three years back on a fair June Sunday, much like this one, she stood before the altar, with a large number of others, and acknowledged her determination henceforth to be the Lord's. She remembered it all vividly. She could even recall some of the sentences the minister used. "Renouncing the world, the flesh, and the devil," sounded the rich, full monotone, and the words seemed to echo themselves along the spacious aisles. She remembered at the moment she was thinking how queer it was that the girl who happened to be standing just at her right was Jennie Humphrey, who worked for her board somewhere and went to school and always wore such odd dresses

that looked as though they had belonged to somebody else and the seams had been taken in hurriedly
to make them answer for her. She had one on then,
the color of which did not suit her complexion, and
the style of which did not fit her form.

"She looks like a dowdy," Chrissy had thought;
"she always does, poor thing! The contrast must be
rather striking between us."

And when Chrissy remembered that, as she had
looked down complacently at her own rich robes,
there had come to her the feeling that all this was very
wicked indeed; that she ought to be giving careful
heed to what the minister said. She tried to listen, but
those words, "renouncing the world, the flesh, and the
devil," were still repeating themselves in her mind; she
remembered wondering how it was to be done. She
lived in the world, and ought to live in it; in fact, must,
whether she would or not. How could she renounce
it? Then that statement about the "flesh" was queerer
yet. Suppose it possible for a person to move about
without any flesh; how one would look! Over this
idea she had nearly laughed, and then had brought
herself up with a sharp rebuke and had tried very hard
to keep her thoughts from wandering, but had not
succeeded well. When next the solemn words which
had puzzled her recurred to her, she told herself that
those were theological phrases which persons so
young as she were not expected to understand.

It was wonderful how vivid was the memory of the
entire scene. It did not give poor Chrissy the satisfaction she thought it ought. She was hunting through
her mind for some proof that this important question
was quite settled, and these poor rags of thought were
all she seemed able to produce. She understood the
"theological phrases" but little better now than she

had three years ago. And here was this preacher bringing it into his sermon; not exactly the same words, but
a good deal about the world. It made Chrissy very
cross to hear him.

"What does he mean, anyway?" she muttered. "I
wonder if he knows, himself? He needn't preach to
me; I hate the world. Haven't I run away from Sea
Rest just because there is such a silly, hateful world
there all the time that I couldn't endure it?"

"Ah, but, Chrissy, pretty Chrissy, you know that is
not because it is the world, but because it is a little
piece of it that you don't fancy. You are perfectly well
aware that there is a very rose-colored world of your
own, with which you are much in love at this
moment."

"Well, why shouldn't I be?" she said angrily, when
she became conscious that something like this
thought was claiming her attention. "What particular
religion is there, I wonder, in going through the world
with a long face, and hating everything in it except a
Bible and psalmbook?"

The above is a fair specimen of the train of thought
in which she indulged during that entire service. By
two o'clock of that summer afternoon she had been
to dinner; had declined curtly, not to say rudely, two
earnest invitations to accompany Grace to Sunday
school; had declared her determination not to go out
of the house again that day; had thrown aside, in
reckless confusion, the pretty plumage of the morning, and, attired in a loose, white wrapper, her hair
tucked unceremoniously into a net, had propped
herself up among the pillows, Howells's last book in
her hand, prepared for an afternoon of enjoyment.
Her last act, before settling herself on the bed, had
been to set the door of her room ajar to catch the

breeze from the hall window. The book was opened to the page which had engrossed her at her last reading; but instead of the familiar names "Marcia" and "Bartley," in whose affairs, "Marcia's" especially, she had been deeply interested, she seemed to see the name of Stuart Holmes. She seemed to hear his earnest voice saying:

"Whether you sign the card or not will not change the facts as they stand revealed to the Lord Jesus Christ."

What were the facts of the case as they stood revealed to him? In the very midst of the long sentence gotten off by that remarkable person, Bartley Hubbard, Chrissy found herself asking this question: What did it all mean? Why was she not willing to join this society which seemed to be such a pleasant thing to these young people? Why was it that a simple invitation to sign their pledge had thrown her into such a turmoil? Was she not, after all, a Christian? Then, what had that June day meant three years before, when she stood in the great church and made those promises about "the world, the flesh, and the devil"?

"I didn't know what they meant then," said poor Chrissy, "and I don't now; but I know I thought then that I loved Jesus. Don't I think so now?"

With her fingers marking the line she had last read in the book, she looked away from it, and her heart almost seemed to her to stand still as she tried to answer that solemn question and realized that she could not be sure whether it gave even a feeble, fluttering yes in reply.

It was perhaps an hour afterward; at least I know the boarders were returning from Sunday school, and the sound of their voices as they neared the house floated upstairs to Chrissy's ears; but it was not their voices that roused her to action. Her first movement was toward the door, which she closed and locked, even slipping the bright little bolt into place after she had turned the key. Then she took the book with its tragic story of Marcia and dropped it into one of the lower trays of her trunk, closing and locking the trunk and carrying the key over to her dressing case in a mechanical sort of way, not as though she realized what she was doing but as though she fully realized that the time had come when something must be done.

6

THE "VALLEY OF DECISION"

I AM sure you feel anxious about this young girl. I am sure you realize that she had come to a place where two roads met; that she was called upon just now to make a deliberate decision as to which one she would take, and that the decision she would make probably involved her interests, not for time only, but for eternity. I am sure that, had you been dealing with this soul in peril, you would have turned white and caught your breath in quick gasps in your effort at self-control, even as Stuart Holmes did, when a white-robed figure came toward him that evening in the dusk of the church vestibule and, without speaking a word, placed in his hand a card, then turned and moved swiftly away.

This had been a hard Sunday for the young man. Whether you realize it or not, this Christian worker knew that he was dealing with one in danger. He understood that for one to deliberately parley with a question regarding one's soul meant a deliberate parley with the Holy Spirit. And a soul in peril was to Stuart Holmes a terrible thing. He had not lived close to his Lord for the past four years without coming to realize something of the importance of souls.

Much of his leisure time that day had been spent in his room on his knees. He had watched the pretty face in church that morning with an anxious heart, seeing nothing there which gave him a hope that earnest thought was being given in the direction he asked. He had questioned Grace with an eagerness that he could not control as to her friend's whereabouts during the Sabbath-school hour.

"She is at home," Grace said, shaking her head mournfully. "She would not come with me, though I coaxed her as much as I dared. She says she is not going out of the house again today; that once a day is enough for meetings. I don't know what to think of Chrissy. I never heard her talk as she did the other evening about our prayer meeting, and she has not been herself since."

Mr. Holmes turned away with a heavy sigh, and carried home with him a burdened heart. To add to his anxiety, a haunting fear of his own act came to torment him. At times he had assured himself that he had done very wrong; that he should not have spoken to a girl of Chrissy's type in the way that he did. He ought to have waited until he knew her better, and to have tried to gain an influence over, and lead her gently, by degrees, to a consideration of these subjects. Above all, he should not have written and given to her that terrible card. What if she should sign it! What if he had, by his unwisdom and his precipitancy, hurried her into talking a step which he and she must regret forever!

It was a day to be remembered. All he could do was to murmur on his knees again and again that he had meant right, and to implore that the Master would overrule the folly and ignorance of his workman and not let harm, because of this, come to one for whom he had died.

Is it any wonder that he felt himself grow pale and knew that he was trembling when that white, silent spirit handed him a card and slipped away? Is it any wonder that he went home alone with long strides and went to his room in nervous haste, yet held the match in his hand unstruck, while he dropped once more on his knees and murmured a trembling word of prayer?

At last he turned on the gas and looked. It was the familiar printed pledge that met his eye, with its strong opening words: "Trusting in the Lord Jesus Christ for strength, I promise"—and below in the fairest and firmest of characters was the name:

Christine Gordon Hollister

As for Grace, she had her share of anxiety that June Sunday. If it was not so deep as that borne by Stuart Holmes, it was because she did not know the special occasion and had no personal accusations to make. She had supposed that Chrissy was, like herself, a Christian, and had urged her coming to Western for the summer, more for the purpose of pleasure in her company and the hope of having her efficient help in some of their many schemes, than because she had any idea that the young girl needed help herself. Grace Norton was, in a peculiar degree, one of those persons who suppose that others who make the same profession with themselves are at least quite as far advanced as they; and the fact that Chrissy was, and had been for three years, a professing Christian, had settled for her, without argument, the belief that they should find in her a kindred spirit. While I write this sentence, I am conscious of your wondering comment.

"Were there not young people, members of her own church," you want to ask me, "who were not in the least in sympathy with aggressive Christian work of any sort? Had such an efficient young woman as this lived in the world so long without discovering that there are Christians and Christians?"

How shall I answer you? In the first place, yes; she had come in contact with young people whose names were on the same church roll as her own, who would take no active part in any Christian work. In the second place, do you not know people who stop before each new exhibition of character, which is unlike what they had reason to expect, and regard it with a bewildered air, as a development that they do not understand and cannot explain; and then, after a moment's pain, rally and dismiss it from their thoughts and go on believing and expecting as before, until they are brought to another halt? If you have observed that phase of humanity, you understand my friend Grace. It is a question, perhaps, whether such characters are to be pitied or envied.

But Chrissy pained and puzzled her friend. She could not dismiss her from thought, because she had begun to love her and count upon her as one of their choice number. She had planned many ways in which to secure her help.

"I do not understand her," she said anxiously to Nellie Tudor that evening after church. She had not seen Chrissy after the one o'clock dinner, until she came down to a lunch just as the bell was ringing for evening service. "You see I have changed my mind," she had said with a smile as she lifted a glass of milk in her gloved hand. "I said I was not going out again, but I am."

Grace had assured her she was glad, but there had been time for no more words; they had been somewhat late again, though this time, it was not Chrissy's fault and had walked rapidly; Grace with her Aunt Maria, and Chrissy going on ahead with a little ten-year-old daughter of one of the boarders. On the homeward walk, a young worker who had numerous questions to ask in regard to his calling list for the week had absorbed Grace's attention, and Chrissy had walked home in almost total silence with Aunt Maria; she was not given to much speaking and was perfectly willing to foster the quiet mood of her young guest. At the door Chrissy had paused only long enough for a quiet "Good night, Grace," and had flitted away up the stairs. Five minutes afterward, when Grace had followed her, anxious for a few minutes' talk, she was just in time to hear the little bolt of her door slip into place. It was then that she had turned away with a pained and puzzled air and had said to Nellie, who was on her way to her room:

"I do not understand her; she hasn't seemed like herself today; nor, indeed, for several days."

"Are you sure you know what 'herself' is?" was Nellie's shrewd question. Then in answer to Grace's puzzled look, "I mean, are you well enough acquainted with her to know that this is something unusual, or is she a person subject to moods?"

"She is the most sunny-hearted girl I ever knew," Grace said earnestly; "I have seen her when something had occurred that I knew very much annoyed her, shake it off in a few minutes with a resolute air, and be her sunny self again. This secluding herself all the afternoon in the way she had and refusing to go to Sunday school is as unlike her as possible. She is always ready to go anywhere, and not especially fond of being alone. What could have occurred to annoy her?"

"She has seemed to me today a little like a person whose conscience was ill at ease," Nellie said.

But Grace looked unenlightened.

"What could trouble her conscience?" she asked again.

But Nellie shrugged her shoulders and shook her head.

"I don't pretend to say," she added after a moment. "I have so many things to trouble my conscience, and it is so constantly giving me stings that I suppose I have a habit of thinking something of that kind must be the matter. I thought of it this morning in church when I looked at her. In fact, I thought of it before church, when I heard her humming an opera; and again this afternoon, when I passed the door on my way to Sunday school and saw her cuddled among the pillows with Howells's book in her hand. I know I used to have a way of doing little reckless things like that when my conscience was giving me a particularly disagreeable set of pokes; things of which I wouldn't exactly approve at another time, you know."

But poor Grace did not "know"—did not understand this phase of human nature in the least.

"Why should one whose conscience is troubled do that which would in the end only add to the trouble?" she asked with a face full of perplexity. "I do not understand."

Nellie laughed.

"Of course you don't," she said, with a loving caress accompanying the words; "I knew you wouldn't. You are good. But I have an idea that Chrissy Hollister and

I are kindred spirits in wickedness, and I don't believe she is one bit satisfied with herself at this minute."

Now, the fact in the case was that Chrissy Hollister was at that moment on her knees.

She called to Grace as she heard her footstep in the hall next morning. It was early; very few of the boarders were yet astir. Chrissy, in a white dressing sacque, with her brown hair falling about her like a veil, was leaning from her eastern window watching the sunrise.

"Come and look," she said to Grace, who had opened the door in answer to her call; "it is a new sun, made on purpose for this day. I never saw its like before."

"The view from this window is very lovely," said Grace, coming close and bending to get a clear vision of the glory. "It is why I chose this room for you in preference to that larger one across the hall. Mrs. Andrews, who occupies it, is never awake at sunrise, and I knew you would enjoy it."

"There was never such a view from this window before," said Chrissy, with a sort of bright solemnity in her face, if I may use such a term. "For me, I mean," she added, in answer to Grace's wondering look; "yesterday's display was gorgeous, but nothing like this. It is a new world. Grace, I want you to forgive me for being so horrid to you yesterday. You needn't say I wasn't," she added, as Grace looked surprised and a trifle embarrassed; "you can't, you know, because it wouldn't be true, and you are always true; it is what attracted me to you in the first place. I am sorry I was so horrid, Gracie, but I couldn't seem to help it. It wasn't that I was vexed with you; I was so utterly bewildered over my own self that I hadn't room to think of anybody else; and I couldn't seem to get the consent of myself to be decent to anybody. Did you know, Gracie, that yesterday was a wonderful day to me?"

"I knew that there was something which made you very unlike yourself," said truthful Grace.

Chrissy nodded significantly.

"I don't think I was myself part of the day; I think Satan entered into me and managed me pretty much after his own fashion and to his entire satisfaction. But I don't want to be 'myself' anymore. I don't mean to be, if I can help it. I just read that verse in the Bible, 'Yet not I, but Christ liveth in me.' At first I thought I must not say it, because that was the great, grand Paul, and, of course, I could never be like him. But then, I remembered that Christ had promised to live in my heart as surely as he had in Paul's; and it needn't be I, Paul, who was using the words, but I, Chrissy Hollister."

A sudden gleam lighted up Grace's face that was not a reflection of the sun's glory.

"You are glad, aren't you?" Chrissy said, watching her, and she stooped and kissed her.

"That is nearly all of it," she added after a moment, speaking as one who was very near to tears, though she was smiling. "When I called you, I thought I had a long story to tell, but I find it sums itself up very well in that phrase, 'Not I, but Christ.' I can tell you what it grew out of—that pledge of yours. I felt that I couldn't sign it; must not, you know, because it would not be true. Yet it troubled me that I could not. I kept wondering why I, who was a member of the church, was not able to make the same pledges as you. If it had been signed only by such persons as Nellie Tudor, I should have thought she did it as she might do a hundred other things, without thinking at all. But you are different, and Mr. Holmes is different, and it troubled me. Then he gave me a horrid card to sign—terrible! And when I told him I thought it would be wicked to sign it, he said it was where I stood if I was not willing to sign the other; and that signing a card, or not signing it, would not alter my standing in the sight of God. That troubled me still more and frightened me. I could not get away from it, though I tried hard; I never tried so hard to do anything in my life. I said Mr. Holmes was no gentleman, that he had no business to write cards for me to sign, nor to ask me such questions; I said I would write to Papa to send for me, and that I would go down to Sea Rest and have a gay summer; I said you were all a set of fanatics, and I did not want to have anything more to do with you. Oh! I was horrid. You can see it was not I; because I, when I was myself, liked you all, much better than I did other people, though I knew I did not feel as you did about many things. I would not go to Sunday school, because I did not want to hear any more on the subject. I fixed myself beautifully on the bed, to read a new book, and expected to be comfortable, and I was miserable. On every page of the book, that terrible card Mr. Holmes wrote seemed to be staring at me. At last I made up my mind that I wouldn't be driven into being wicked because a stranger had said things to me that he had no right to say. I decided to put away my book and read a good many chapters in the Bible. When I united with the church, my Sunday school teacher told me that she hoped I would read a chapter in the Bible every day; I thought, then, that I would, but, dear me! I haven't done anything of the kind. There have been weeks at a time, during the gay season, when I haven't looked into it. Then I would have weeks when all I would do would be to get a hurried snatch at some verse just as I was putting the finishing touches to my dress. I used to promise myself that I would think about the verse a great deal during the day. But I generally forgot what it was before I reached the foot of the stairs. But I used to have violent spasms of goodness, usually coming on Sunday afternoons, when I would read whole books through, genealogy, chronology, and all; hurrying, you know, to see how much I could accomplish before the dinner bell rang. Yesterday I resolved on one of these efforts; but it was of no use. I began at the very beginning and resolved to read the book of Genesis through before I stirred, but I got no further than that terrible question asked by the Lord himself: 'Where art thou?' Grace, I can't tell you with what power it came to me that I was trying to do exactly what Adam tried—hide from God!

"I don't know how to tell you the rest, though there isn't much to tell; it was a very different thing to live it from what it is to tell it. There came to me a feeling that I was not a Christian at all—never had been; that uniting with the church was all a mistake. But I was not willing to give up the belief that the matter was settled. I went back over that past experience and tried to recall just how I felt, and tormented myself as to whether I would have been likely to have felt that way if there had been nothing in it. But I couldn't get a ray of comfort; and I never was so unhappy in my life. I turned away from the book of Genesis—it seemed to be full of stabs, and I felt as though I couldn't bear any more. I kept turning the leaves nervously, wondering what I should do; no part of the Bible seemed safe, since I had grown afraid of Genesis. There came to me a suggestion that I was nervous; that that terrible card I had been asked to sign—if I would not sign the other—had unbalanced me, and I wondered whether I had not better get out Howells's book again and read it for a while until I was in a calmer mood, then I could come back to the Bible. As I turned the leaves and thought these thoughts, my eyes were caught by these words: 'Simon, Simon, Satan hath desired to have thee, that he might sift thee as wheat; but I have prayed for thee, that thy faith fail not.' Grace, it almost broke my heart. I had not cried before; it had seemed to me as though I should never cry again about anything; but when I read that verse, it was as if my heart had turned to tears. I knew as well as though he had said 'Chrissy, Chrissy,' instead of Simon, that Satan desired to have me. And when I thought that the dear Lord Jesus had prayed for Simon, there came to me a consuming desire to be so prayed for. I slipped down on my knees, and I did not begin with 'Our Father, who art in heaven,' nor any of those words; I just cried out: 'Oh, Jesus, pray for me—Chrissy Hollister! Don't let Satan get me.'"

The sun had risen now in all his glory, and a strong, full tide of light was flooding the large east window and flooding both the girls. Grace had not spoken a word, neither had she need; her face was radiant, though it was wet with tears.

"It is a longer story than I thought, after all," Chrissy said, smiling; "but it is just done—the part that can be told. I don't know how long I knelt there—a good while, I think. Twilight was coming on when I arose. But Simon Peter himself could hardly have heard the voice of his Savior any plainer than I did. The first thing I did was to get that card—the printed one—and put my name to it. I wanted to sign it. I was glad of the opportunity to put on paper my resolve to serve him all the days of my life. He had made the world over for me in that few minutes, and that is why there is a new sun shining this morning."

This last was with a radiant smile, and then her arms were close about her friend's neck.

7

TANGLES

I FEEL like lingering over the story of that happy summer. It was so unlike what Chrissy had planned, that at times when she stopped for breath she wondered in a smiling way whether she could be the girl who came to Western, because she did not know what else to do with herself, and who brought one trunk filled with the latest books with which to help her beguile the time.

Books that she did not even unpack; not that some of them were not well worth reading had she been able to spare the time for them, but the summer was so full of more important interests that she was content to let them lie in obscurity.

The truth is that before this new member of the Western Christian Endeavor Society had been enrolled two weeks, she had convinced her fellow workers that she was, indeed, a very "active" member. The schemes she thought of and planned and persisted in until they were carried to success sometimes astonished even the old workers.

"She was quite right," Stuart Holmes said one

evening, as he and Grace were discussing the situation; "there is nothing 'passive' about her. I thought that last scheme of hers would surely fail, and I believe it is going to work better than any plan we have yet tried. Doesn't she impress you as one who, in a remarkable manner, takes words to mean just what they say? Our pledge never meant so much to me as it has since I have heard her take certain deductions from it for granted. Yet the thought is there, and the meaning evident, when one stops to consider it."

I have a fancy that, were there time to linger over the story, some of the little worker's schemes, aided and abetted as they were by these wide-awake and somewhat trained young people, might be helpful, or at least suggestive, to you; but the fact is, there is not time. The summer waned while we were talking about it; the leaves of the maples turned to crimson and gold, and there came into the early morning air that delightful crispness which means that frost has already arrived, and winter is but a step away. With these changes came to Chrissy a summons home. At first, in the shape of permission to return now as soon as she pleased, followed by a few words of sympathy for her that their delay in opening the house had detained her so long in that dull little village. Then came a gentle hint that the sooner she came the better pleased would the family circle be, and much wonderment was expressed at her remaining away a day longer than was necessary. Then, as Chrissy still lingered, came an imperative summons, which she must needs obey.

"My trunks must be packed this very afternoon, and I must take the morning train without fail," Chrissy said, looking up with a sign from the perusal of her letter.

"Tomorrow!" echoed Grace in dismay. "You can't

possibly do that. You must wait until after the reunion, of course."

Chrissy shook her head.

"I can't, Grace. Impossible as it seems, that reunion will have to get along without me. I suppose they can, but I feel very important, some way." The sentence closed with a light laugh, but it was immediately followed by a sigh. Nothing was plainer than that Chrissy was not ready to go home. But she remained firm, despite Grace's coaxing and evident dismay, for there were several plans connected with the annual reunion which seemed to demand Chrissy's presence.

"I must go," she said again, decidedly. "When Mamma writes like that and calls me *Christine,* it means business. As long as she said *Chrissy,* I thought I might venture; but when she writes out *Christine* in large, strong letters, too—look, the name covers half the line—then I know that I am to go home without any more delays of any sort. Mamma is afraid I have already disgraced the family by remaining here so long without any fall clothes. She wonders what people think of me still in my summer hat, and what an extraordinary object I must have been in church last Sabbath, such a chilly day as it was, in a summer dress. I wouldn't answer for the consequences if I should tell her I wore my traveling dress. As for my hat, I don't believe anybody thought of it, do you? I am sure I didn't. Isn't custom a ridiculous thing? Why should I have to lay aside that hat, for instance, which I have grown used to, and like, and which isn't a bit soiled, and spend hours of fussing and ever so much money getting settled on a new one merely because fashion chooses to decree that the precise time of year has come when I must appear in autumn finery? It isn't that I don't like new things well enough; I like them very much—bonnets and everything. When a bonnet becomes shabby or dowdy looking in any way, I want to be done with it and have another. What I object to is being ordered by some uptown milliner as to just what day I must lay my hat away and get another."

"Are fashionable people so very particular?" Grace asked, much amused. Her winters had been chiefly spent in the seclusion of boarding school, which had scholarship as its central aim, and she knew very little about fashionable life.

"Particular! You think I'm just talking for the sake of hearing myself grumble. I'm just telling the truth. My sister Louise orders her bonnets and dresses and everything by the almanac. Let the day be ever so summery, and her summer hat be ever so becoming, she may lay it away with a sigh, but she lays it away at the precise hour when she knows other fashionable ladies will do the same and decks herself in autumn colors and styles. Oh! I must go home tomorrow without fail. I disgraced the family name last Sunday. I knew I did it at the time, but I rather enjoyed it. That isn't malicious enjoyment, is it?" she asked, with a half-anxious smile. "They were not here to be scandalized, you know, and I do get so tired of all these things. There are so many of them—one for every hour in the day."

"One what, Chrissy dear?"

"Whim," said Chrissy with energy. "Fashion. What 'they' do and wear and don't do and wear. I know who 'they' are in our city. It is a certain Madam Fijou, a French *modiste* who never saw France and whose accent is at times painfully English, and not 'choice English,' either"—with a gleam of laughter in her eyes; "but she manages us, body and head—I had almost said *soul*. She is an autocrat, and no one who hopes to have a name in society dares to dispute her decrees. I have had many a battle over her in the past and have come off victorious; her tastes and mine don't always agree, and Papa rather likes individuality, I think. But I am not going to battle about such trivial things anymore. I am going to be very good and wear green when they say green—though I look like an ash heap in it—or anything else that they want worn. There will be enough things of importance to battle over. I may well let trivial ones go."

Again there came that long-drawn sigh. It was the nearest that she came to an explanation in regard to the perplexities which she felt awaited her. She was too loyal to home to talk over its drawbacks, even with Grace.

Will you now think of Chrissy as moving somewhat restlessly, as well as with apparent aimlessness, about the cozy back parlor of a handsome town house? The date was about the second week in November, a dreary evening closing in upon what had been a dreary day. It seemed to Chrissy, in thinking it over, that the sun always shone in Western and rarely shone here. She had been at home but five days. Mrs. Hollister was lounging gracefully in the easiest of easy chairs, resting from the fatigues of fashionable calls. Dr. Hollister was in dressing gown and slippers, indulging in the evening paper. Louise, the eldest daughter of the house, in pretty evening dress, and with an air of expectancy, listening occasionally when steps were heard in the hall, occupied her waiting time in wrestling with a skein of embroidery silk, which was, of course, in a tangle. It has been my observation that embroidery silk nearly always is. Only Chrissy was restless.

Her unsettled movements seemed to annoy her mother. "Is there any method in your frequent journeys from the piano to the window or the grate?" she asked at last, a smile on her face, but just enough reproof in her tones to make Chrissy's face flush, as she answered only with a smile and dropped into a chair near her father.

"Chrissy pines for the excitements of Western," said Louise with a mischievous glance at the girl. "I believe, Mamma, that she is homesick; she had impressed me that way ever since her return."

"A girl in her own home with all the home faces about her can hardly be said to be homesick," replied Mrs. Hollister; "but I presume Chrissy does miss her friend Grace; she was always very warmhearted toward her friends."

The smile was full and sweet this time. Mrs. Hollister was very fond of her pretty young daughter. Louise was soon to be married and go out from them to a home of her own, but the mother looked to this beautiful girl, just dawning into young ladyhood, to keep the house as gay and attractive in the years to come as it had been in the past. It is true Chrissy had troubled her a little already with what Louise called "queer, old-fashioned notions," but the mother had argued that they were but the restless questionings of a naturally independent mind, untrammeled as yet by any sense of responsibility; that the duties of society, when she was obliged to take her place as eldest daughter, would soon tone her down.

"If you would settle to some occupation, you would feel less lonely, dear," said Mrs. Hollister sympathetically; "though, to be sure, I don't know what one of your tastes would find to do. It is such a pity that you are not fond of fancy work."

The sentence closed with a little sigh, reminding Chrissy that there had always been a great deal about her which made her mother sigh.

Louise gave an irritated twitch at her silk. "I wish you were fond of untangling silk," she said, "for I certainly am not. When it reels off smoothly and gracefully under my fingers, I almost love the soft, bright stuff, but when it snarls itself up in this fashion, it reminds me of a little termagant of a girl we used to have in school, who would get so angry over some trifle that she would pull her own hair. I should think you would enjoy battling with snarly silk, Chrissy; it requires so much jerking and pulling to make it behave that it would meet the demands of your energy."

"No, it wouldn't," said Chrissy resolutely. "I wouldn't like to battle with a thing to make it behave, unless the thing was worth the effort when I had conquered it."

Then, to forestall the inevitable argument as to the importance of embroidery silk, she plunged into another subject which she shrewdly suspected would lead to more argument:

"Mamma, I don't settle to any work because I thought of going out."

"This evening?" said Mrs. Hollister in surprise. "What is going on? I had an idea that we had one entirely leisure evening this week."

"Mamma, I thought of going to prayer meeting."

The pitiful question which presses itself on me at this moment is, Why should a young girl belonging to a nominally Christian home, seated with her own family circle, feel her heart beating faster and the glow on her cheeks rising to her forehead because she had made such a simple statement as this to the mother who is a member of the very church whose prayer meeting she proposes to attend? It is a very easy matter to ask questions. It is another thing to answer them satisfactorily.

Surprised silence on the part of the mother. As for Louise, she asked, almost sharply: "What prayer meeting?"

"The regular Thursday evening prayer meeting of the church, Louise."

"What a queer idea! No young people attend, do they?"

"I don't know. I thought I would go and see. Dr. Dullard gave a very general invitation to it on Sunday."

"Of course anyone attends who wishes," said Mrs. Hollister with the air of one who ought to know. "It is certainly entirely proper for Chrissy to do so whatever she chooses, but I should hardly think you would choose so unpleasant an evening for your first attempt. It is quite dark out, and looks like rain, or a storm of some kind. Besides, there is no one to go with you, and we have your father at home for the first time in I don't know how many months. I should think you might content yourself with us this evening."

There was again that curious note of reproach in her voice, to which Chrissy was greatly used but to which she was very sensitive.

She opened her lips to make reply, but Dr. Hollister forestalled her. He had seemingly been absorbed in his paper; Chrissy did not think he had heard a word of the conversation.

"So far as my presence is concerned, my dear, I shall have to tear myself away immediately. I have already lingered too long. There are two people at the West

End who probably each have had a severe nervous attack by this time because I am not there; not that they need me, but then they think they do; and for some natures that is almost as bad as though they did. As for this little girl who is aping grown-up airs, if she wants an escort as far as the First Church—it lies directly in the line of my travels—I shall certainly not object to her company."

"And what about getting home, Dr. Hollister?" said his wife, only half pleased, while Chrissy, pausing only to hear her father say he would attend to that, made all haste from the room, eager for the brisk walk with her father into the night and the darkness. Chrissy was much in love with her father, and he had little time for walks.

It was very exhilarating. Her depressed spirits came up with a bound.

Dr. Hollister was not a Christian. He had once said, half in sarcasm, that he had not time to be such a one as he should be and did not care to be one after the usual pattern; but he was evidently not displeased with Chrissy for going with him tonight, and she reached the chapel in a glow of healthful satisfaction. She never forgot the sensation which crept over her before she had been five minutes in that large, rather chilly, not very well-lighted room, wherein were scattered perhaps thirty people, sitting, for the most part, as far from one another and all of them as far from the front as circumstances would allow. They were singing when she entered. No one offered her a hymnbook, but she possessed herself of one, and by dint of considerable exertion found the place and was ready to join in the wail of sound which rolled its solemn cadence through the large, empty space:

In vain we tune our formal songs,
In vain we strive to rise;
Hosannas languish on our tongues,
And our devotion dies.

Poor Chrissy! She stopped singing before she had reached the close of the third line. Not that she did not feel the truth of the words; she felt them too keenly and was sad over it. It seemed to her that her devotion had suddenly died. Even greater was her appreciation of the next verse:

Dear Lord, and can we ever live,
At this poor, dying rate?

It seemed to her that she could not. Then followed Deacon Truman's long, slow prayer, made up of phrases so familiar to his lips that they could roll off glibly without any thought on his part. It was well for Chrissy that she knew of one redeeming feature in this exercise. Deacon Truman had a right to his name; he was a true man in every sense of the word.

Nevertheless, it was hardly possible for a young girl to be other than wearied by the smooth flowing phrases that implied so much and were spoken and listened to as though they meant so little. In a general way Deacon Truman was sincere; that is, there was no mockery, in the crude sense of the term, in his prayers. Yet he used words of whose solemn and tremendous import he had never even thought, therefore he did not use them in such a manner as to oblige others to think. There followed what seemed to Chrissy long, long silences, broken at intervals by the pastor's voice saying:

"Brother Small, will you lead us in prayer?" or,

"Deacon Jones, can't we have a few words from you?" or, "Brethren, I hope you will not let the time run to waste."

In the midst of these pauses, Chrissy seemed to hear a voice repeating in sibilant undertone:

"I promise to be present at, and to participate in, every regular prayer meeting of the society, unless prevented by some reason which I can conscientiously give to my Master, Jesus Christ."

"But this is not a meeting of our society," said Chrissy's other self.

"But there is no society here," said Chrissy's clear-cut conscience.

"Perhaps there might not be this winter. Did the spirit of the pledge teach that at all other gatherings save that one which she was now unable to attend, she might sit silent when her Master, Jesus Christ, was the theme?"

"One object in taking part in a prayer meeting," said Chrissy's conscience, continuing the argument with her, "is certainly to help others. Could I do something here for that purpose? There is Dr. Stuart's boy Rob over in the corner—the only young person present besides myself. Isn't it probable that he thinks this one of the stupidest hours he ever spent? Could I do something to make it seem pleasanter to him?"

"But oh dear!" said that other self, "could you ever, ever say anything in this great solemn meeting? It seems so grown-up—so very old, someway."

She listened to the distinct thud, thud, thud of her heart, and wondered whether she would repeat a Bible verse when Deacon Jones's remarks were over and wondered whether she might not repeat those lines of which Grace Norton was so fond—those which said:

If our love were but more simple,
We should take Him at His word.

And wondering and waiting and trembling, she, too, "let the time run to waste." But the benediction was being pronounced before she was sure that she would do nothing to help along that prayer meeting.

8

CONFLICTING "DUTIES"

IT WAS the resolve born of this dreary prayer meeting which led Chrissy, at the first opportune moment, to broach the subject of a Christian Endeavor Society in their circle.

She chose a time when the family were gathered; unwisely, it seems to me. Had I been a member of a household made up after the pattern of the Hollisters, I feel sure I should have talked up all questions of ethics with each individual member separately.

Mrs. Hollister toyed with a trifle in bright-colored wools and called it work. She was a woman who did not enjoy sitting with folded hands; she liked, rather, to busy those hands about something which was as near nothing as fashionable life could suggest. Louise was at her interminable sewing—delicate work, ruffles, and tucks, and matters of that sort. Chrissy had once confided to Grace her belief that the only time in life when a modern young woman was industrious with her needle was a few months before her marriage. The sign held good in Louise's case. Dr. Hollister sat at a side table, busy over his book of "cases," making careful memoranda of some which gave him special anxiety. This was the hurried doctor's device for spending some minutes each day with his family. If he had a few minutes after dinner, instead of retiring to his office, he established himself in the back parlor with the family, provided there were no guests present, and imagined himself to be visiting with them, while he looked over and made notes of the matters which must receive attention before he slept.

Perhaps it was a wise arrangement, since it was the best for which he could plan; for, by dint of listening to bits of talk from one and another of the group, he certainly managed to glean a more intimate knowledge of the questions which were interesting his family than he could otherwise have done.

Thinking back, I find I have not presented the two young daughters of the house to your notice.

The truth is, they were at the age when in fashionable homes it is a too common matter to ignore them as much as possible. And, although Mrs. Hollister protested occasionally against the follies of fashionable life and assured her friends that she would not live as the Wentworths and the Truesdells did for anything in this world; and although she was a member of one of the prominent churches in the city, and, judged by the rules of those who live for the world only, would not have been called a woman of fashion, yet the fact remained that in her immediate circle she was looked up to as a leader and had a great deal to do in the line of what she was pleased to call "social duties."

As for the girls, they were twelve and fourteen years of age; small for their years, and inclined to be quiet and studious, which Mrs. Hollister thought was a great comfort, especially while they were passing through the awkward period of their lives.

She herself inclined to the opinion that a good boarding school, where Sara could be taught not to grow round-shouldered, and Faye could be induced to turn out her toes, would be the best thing for them; but Dr. Hollister did not favor boarding schools, so the daughters rounded their shoulders, and turned their toes to their hearts' content, and were kindly and affectionately neglected by every member of the family circle.

I would not have you suppose that Mrs. Hollister was an indifferent or coldhearted mother. On the contrary, she was in some respects an overanxious one. The rounding shoulders, for instance, and the toes turning in gave her at times almost sleepless hours; but she had a daughter who was in a few months to make a brilliant marriage, which would place her a notch higher in the social scale than she had been as a girl, and she had a beautiful daughter of eighteen who was beginning to attract a great deal of attention in society; so the mother's hands and thoughts were very full. As for Sara and Faye, they were well, and behaved well, save for that matter of shoulders and toes, and their special time would come.

On this particular evening the girls, contrary to their usual custom, were in the sitting room; the next day was to be a holiday in the school which they attended, and the weight of books over which they nightly bent had been deserted for once.

They were not finding the evening enjoyable, however; they lounged from easy chair to sofa, yawned a great deal, tossed over piles of engravings at which they looked so often that they had lost their charm, opened and closed many books that did not attract them beyond a passing glance, and privately assured each other that they would rather study a great deal than do nothing in this stupid way.

As for the son of the house, a young man not yet quite twenty-three, he rarely honored the home with his presence of an evening, but on this occasion he was present of necessity and was being petted by reason of a severe cold which had been inclined to settle on a pair of weak and badly treated lungs. So Chrissy had full opportunity to get the views of the entire family.

Louise tried to be sympathetic but found it difficult.

"What a queer idea!" she could not help saying, having questioned Chrissy until she reached the prayer meeting feature of the Society. "I should think the general prayer meeting would be sufficient. Why do the young people want one all by themselves? Why, no, Chrissy dear, to tell you the truth, I don't believe it would take in our circle at all. We have a great many engagements now, you know; it is almost impossible to get a leisure evening. If it were not for an occasional rain, such as we have tonight, I don't think I could ever find a chance to do my work. Oh! my joining such a thing would be entirely out of the question. Whatever I might have done before, I certainly could not spare the time this winter. One whole evening a week is a great deal, especially when one hasn't any evenings."

"It is only one hour out of an evening," pleaded Chrissy, "and winter evenings are long, you know."

"Yes, but one hour breaks it up. If there were a party afterwards, or a dress concert, how awkward it would be. One couldn't go to such a meeting in full dress."

No; Chrissy remembered the incongruousness of such an attempt. The thought carried her back to that evening in June when she first attended a young people's prayer meeting. How ridiculously out of place she had felt in her white-embroidered, lace-trimmed dress! How far away that time seemed! How different things were now from then! No, that wasn't it; things were just the same—"quite the same," she said under her breath with a sigh; it was she that was different. How homesick the retrospection made her feel! If she could only see Grace Norton for a few minutes; if she could just peep into that church parlor, all unexpected, and hear the strong, young voices and earnest words. How glad they would all be to see her! Why could she not have a congenial spot in this city as well as in Western?

"I mean to have a Society, if it is a possible thing," she said aloud, in response to her own thoughts rather than because of any encouragement which she had received.

"I don't believe you will find it a possible thing," said Louise with a light laugh. "This is a very different place from Western, remember. People have a great many engagements. There's the German Club, which takes an evening each week; then we have our regular Bryant Circle; and the demands of society are constantly increasing. You are too young to realize how it is, but by the time the season is over, I fancy you will be wiser than you are now."

"It is going to be a very gay season," said Mr. Harmon Hollister, speaking hoarsely. "Foulard was telling me yesterday of several rather brilliant schemes. Oh! by the way, Louise, he has a plan for a very select social club to meet perhaps twice a month for parlor dancing—just give the evening to it, and have a good time. That might be very pleasant, don't you think, if the members were carefully chosen?"

While Louise promptly assented that it certainly might but added that she did not believe that she and

Horace would care to join because they had so many society engagements already that they never had time to visit together, Chrissy went off into one of her reveries as to the difference in people. She thought Stuart Holmes must be about the age of her brother Harmon. She tried to imagine that young gentleman spending his time as Harmon spent his. She had certainly never realized until her visit to Western that young men of culture and position could be so unlike.

As for Dr. Hollister, he had glanced up anxiously when his son spoke and, at the first pause, said: "You will need to take care of that hoarseness, my son, or your social clubs will not be of any special interest to you this winter. Do you take the remedies I gave you?"

"Occasionally, sir," replied Harmon with a careless laugh that ended in a cough. "If I have to play the role of an invalid, I can join Chrissy's society and get my fun out of that. How is it, Chris? Will you take me for a member, provided I'm not well enough to keep things spinning?"

Before Chrissy could reply, a question came from another quarter:

"Is it a society for girls like us, Chrissy?" It was Sara who asked, and her face was lighted up with eager interest.

"No," said Chrissy, promptly. "Or—why—yes; I suppose it would receive you as members." The latter part of the sentence was spoken more slowly and with almost a surprised note in her voice.

She had remembered those "little girls from the North Side" and realized that they were not older than her sisters. She looked over at the girls curiously. It seemed strange to think of them as old enough to join a society of which she was a member. Truth to tell, Chrissy did not feel very well acquainted with her younger sisters. Their summers had for the past three years been spent chiefly with their grandmother in the country, and their winters were spent in the school and study rooms, while Chrissy had been busy, since her graduation, with all sorts of schemes which did not include them.

"I would like to be a member of a regular society, and be on committees, and help plan things that were worth doing," said Sara, while Faye's face bespoke her own interest and sympathy.

"The idea!" said Louise, laughing. "Those midgets! Mamma, you will have two more grown-up daughters before you are aware. It must be a strange sort of affair, Chrissy, which admits of such incongruousness as that suggests. Imagine a society which is sufficiently flexible for Harmon and myself and Horace—you would like Horace, too, wouldn't you—and Sara and Faye?"

"Why, Louise," interposed Sara in an injured tone, "we go to church, and so do you and Harmon and Horace—to the very same church. Why don't we have a different one for us?"

Dr. Hollister glanced at his oldest daughter and smiled.

"You are being asked a somewhat difficult question, are you not, my dear?"

"Not at all, Papa. I have often thought it would be an excellent idea if children had a church of their own to attend. How can they be expected to appreciate the sermons which we older people need?"

Sara curled her lip over this and murmured something in an undertone, while Dr. Hollister stayed his pencil a moment and looked thoughtful.

"I have always fancied that the church ought to be a sort of home," he said musingly; "a family circle where father and mother and children of different ages each had their portion fitted to their needs. But I don't know much about these things, and I grant you that I think the church we attend has very little that my younger daughters can be expected to understand. In fact, I'm inclined to think we older heads are sometimes more mystified than benefited."

"Well," admitted Louise, "I think myself that Dr. Dullard is almost too deep for every Sunday, but he has the name of being the most intellectual preacher in town. I suppose one's tastes are cultivated in listening to him."

"Chris," asked her brother suddenly, "what is the object of this thing you are in love with?"

"The object of it?" repeated Chrissy slowly, more to arrange her thoughts and formulate an answer that should meet Harmon's moral nature than because she did not understand the question.

"Yes. What are you aiming at? I was reading when you first began to talk and didn't hear. Is it a charitable affair, a sort of Dorcas Society, or is it for fun or what?"

"It is to help develop one's Christian character," said Chrissy, speaking very gravely and with heightened color.

She could not help feeling how utterly foreign to all Harmon's thoughts and plans such an attempt as this would be. Harmon broke into a low whistle, which was instantly checked by a fit of coughing.

"The dickens!" he said, when he could speak again. "Then that counts me out entirely, inasmuch as I have no Christian character to develop. What will a fellow do in such a case, if this wretched cough cuts me off from the usual resources?"

The "wretched cough" had him in its possession again almost before the sentence was concluded. His father looked up once more with a distressed air and spoke in a tone of annoyance:

"I wish you had character enough to protect yourself from constant exposures. That cough sounds as though it had gotten a decided hold."

Mrs. Hollister's anxiety now came to the surface and expended itself in begging the invalid to have his feet soaked, and to take a sweat, and to drink hot lemonade, all of which suggestions he scorned.

Following this, the little girls were directed to retire at once, and Chrissy followed them, feeling that she had made no progress at all, feeling, also, distressed about Harmon.

9

"NOT PARALLEL CASES"

IT TOOK several days following this effort in her own family for Chrissy to get her courage to the right point to call on her pastor.

Not that she was in the least afraid of him. He was a very genial man, a favorite with the young people, who met him socially a great deal, and enjoyed merry chats with him almost as well as they did with persons of their own age. It was a sentence often heard on the lips of the older members of the church, spoken in very satisfied tones: "How popular Dr. Dullard is with the young people!"

And Chrissy had been one of his favorites. Yet as she sat opposite him in his study that afternoon, she began to realize that there were some subjects on which he certainly was not well posted and which he found hard to comprehend.

He looked mildly down on her from over his gold-bowed glasses and repeated for the third time, in varying language, the thought which evidently oppressed him.

"Don't you think, my dear young friend, that the

regular prayer meeting of the church could meet all your requirements in that line?"

Then Chrissy repeated her explanation, varying the language a little also.

"It isn't simply a prayer meeting of which I am speaking, you know. It is an organization for Christian work of whatever sort."

"Well, so is the church, my dear Miss Chrissy—and a very good organization it is, too. I cannot think that the time has come to supersede it."

"Oh, Dr. Dullard! You cannot think I am trying to organize something to supersede the church? I have been very stupid in my explanations if I have not made it clear that the Christian Endeavor Society is simply an auxiliary of the church, working under its direction. The pastor is always a member of the Society, and the general adviser in all matters pertaining to it. Why, the motto of the organization is, 'For Christ and the Church.' It is his name only which is put before that of the church."

"Oh! I understand, I understand all that, of course," the doctor said with a graceful wave of his hand, intended to help disclaim any need for information on his part. "You have been lucid indeed, my dear young lady—a most able and fascinating advocate of the cause you want to serve; but I am somewhat posted in regard to this matter from other sources. I am inclined to think it is a most unnecessary bit of machinery, well intended on the part of some, at least, but ill advised. In point of fact, why should the young people suppose that they need a separate organization in which to work? Why don't they take right hold in the church?"

Chrissy looked puzzled.

"That is what they want to do," she said timidly; "at

least, it is what I am talking about—an organization of young people in the church, directed by the church through its pastor, pledged to work in all ways that he shall consider wise for Christ and the church."

"Yes, but why must there be another organization for the purpose of doing it?"

A flash of a smile flitted over Chrissy's face, which she banished as quickly as possible, with a feeling that she was not being respectful, as she essayed to answer:

"I don't think I quite understand, Dr. Dullard. The Sabbath school organizes, you know, and the Missionary Society and the Ladies' Aid Society; even the Library committee has its distinct organization, with officers and subcommittees; yet they all are parts of the church, of course, and work under its direction. I suppose we want to organize in order to better to understand and accomplish our work."

Said Dr. Dullard: "My dear young friend, I appreciate your motive, but you are not dealing with parallel cases. I confess that I really fear the main tendency of this organization is to weaken the influence of the church. Take this proposed prayer meeting, for instance. I feel quite convinced that its tendency would be to draw the young people away from the regular weekly meeting. In fact, that has been the complaint brought against it in other places. I am much better posted, my enthusiastic friend, than you suppose. Don't imagine that I am inclined to quarrel with your enthusiasm, however; it is a prerogative of youth and must find an outlet somewhere, of course. But take the church in Rariton as an illustration. The pastor tells me that the young people gather to their own prayer meeting with a great deal of zeal but are never seen at the regular weekly meetings."

But Chrissy was very well acquainted in Rariton.

"Have they a Christian Endeavor Society there?" she asked, her face lighting. "I am glad; I spent two months there last winter, and I heard Mr. Parkwell—you know him; he is one of the officers of that church; I was a guest at his house—I heard him say that, as nearly as he could remember, there had not been a young person inside their prayer meeting for more than a year. He was regretting the fact that those who were members of the church were not in the habit of even an occasional attendance at the prayer meeting. That was before they had a Christian Endeavor Society; so it seems to me that the organization ought not to be held accountable for the condition of things in Rariton, unless it is better for the young people not to go to any prayer meeting at all than to have one of their own. How does the Rariton church know but that the society will, in time, succeed in educating its members to attend both meetings?"

Dr. Dullard smiled patiently on his guest and repeated in a mild and conciliating tone:

"I am in full sympathy with your enthusiasm and your good intentions, but I cannot but think that the tendency of an organization of this kind in our church would be to draw people away from the Thursday evening meeting."

"Dr. Dullard, how could it, when they are not there to be drawn away? I had a special reason for learning how it was in our church, and I have inquired carefully. I find that Rob Stuart is the only young person who attends the Thursday meeting with anything like regularity."

"That is true," said the doctor reflexively, and a shade of sadness passed over his handsome face. He took off his glasses and wiped them carefully before he spoke again.

"It is too true; I have often regretted it"—the sentence was concluded with a little sigh—"but we must not expect too much of young people. They are naturally gay—it is right that they should be—and young life in these days is crowded with a great many engagements; we must be patient and hopeful. We should certainly all welcome our young people to the Thursday evening meeting. I was very glad indeed to see your pretty face there last week, my dear Miss Chrissy; it did me good; and, as I say, I really fear that the instituting of another prayer meeting, especially for the young, would have a direct tendency toward drawing away their affection and interest from the general meeting; and surely that would be a result to be deeply deplored."

Was there any use in talking to Dr. Dullard? Yet Chrissy tried very hard. She kept her temper in admirable check and went patiently over her story again, avoiding the prayer meeting as a shoal on which her hopes might shipwreck, and earnestly describing the plans and aims of the society. In the course of the interview she produced a pledge card for her pastor's examination, and was sorry five minutes afterward that she had done so; for when he had glanced it over, he remarked that he was more than doubtful as to the propriety of pledging young persons with unformed minds to such solemn positions. In the light of her own recent experience, this sounded to Chrissy extremely weak.

Why should a middle-aged doctor of divinity make the same mistake which she had been led to see was such a foolish one for her? But when she asked, with as much respect as she could tutor her voice to assume, whether this pledge really did any more than to put into simple language and convenient form the pledges already taken by those who were members of the church, he made that convenient and unanswerable reply that he did not consider the cases parallel. After that, Chrissy went home. She passed the home of her most intimate friend and walked a square beyond before she could summon courage for a talk with her about the scheme which was so dear and growing so difficult. Before Chrissy's summer visit to Western, Belle Parkman had been the friend and confidante to whom all questions, whether trivial or important, were brought for discussion and sympathy. It irritated Chrissy now to think that she should hesitate and feel almost afraid to present the claims of the society to her.

"I must have grown cowardly," she said half aloud with a curve of her upper lip intended to express disapprobation of herself, "if I am really afraid to talk to Belle about things. Why should I suppose that she would not be as much interested as I am myself? I wonder if I have grown pharisaical also. Belle and I used to think alike on a great many points. I'll go back this minute and try her."

I think myself that it was an unfortunate movement. The truth is, Chrissy needed just then to come in contact with a stronger spirit than her own, not a weaker. If she could have curbed her impatience sufficiently to have gone to her own room, closed and locked her door, and held communion for a little while with that Master Mind who had promised to be with her "all the days," it would have been much better. Instead, she rang at the Parkman mansion and, being shown at once to the privacy of Belle's own room, was received with all the enthusiasm of the past, and found Belle's tongue as voluble as ever.

"You dear old darling! It was perfectly horrid of

you to stay in that poky little village so long—way into the winter, just think of it! You've lost ever so many nice things already. Chrissy Hollister, why weren't you at the Shermans' the other night? I supposed, of course, you would be there, and I kept watching for you all the evening. You wicked little thing to disappoint me so! Some other people were disappointed, too. Paul Browning asked me five times where I supposed you were and watched all the arrivals so closely that he wasn't a bit good company. Why didn't you come?"

Just at that moment it seemed utterly impossible to explain that she had gone to prayer meeting instead. She could only say, her face flushing the while, that she had another engagement that evening.

"Another engagement!" repeated Belle. "How queer to have an engagement that I knew nothing about! We are always invited to the same places. I believe I would cancel almost any other, though, for an evening with the Shermans. I do think they are the most delightful family. They know how to entertain so well. We had a charming time; danced all the evening, though I don't suppose you would have liked that. Have you grown any fonder of dancing than you were? What did you do all summer, anyway? Wasn't it dreadfully poky? We had just a lovely time at Long Branch. You can't think how we wished for you. I was going to write and tell you so, but we were so dreadfully crowded with engagements that there was no time for letter writing. I did write one letter, and you never answered it. Naughty girl! I told you all about the Brownings' coming, and what fun Paul and I had bathing. He said you ought to have been there, that the waves were just heavy enough for you to battle with, and that you would like to overcome them. He thinks you are a person with a great deal of courage; the most plucky girl he ever knew, he said; and when I asked him if he did not know it was always considered polite to except present company, he laughed and said that just at that moment he would rather be honest than polite, because when people spoke of you, they wanted to be very honest for the next few minutes, at least, in order to keep your name free from the breath of anything distasteful. He considered you also the most honest girl he knew. Did you ever hear such rudeness? Tell me how you busied yourself, dear, and what made you stay so long. Your mother said she thought you must be taking leave of your senses."

How was Chrissy to introduce the Society of Christian Endeavor into this atmosphere?

10

PRONOUNCED OPINIONS

NEVERTHELESS, she made a brave effort and broke into the midst of Belle's description of a donkey party which was "too funny for anything," with a statement of what she was trying to do.

"I like societies," said Belle, "and for us young people to have one all by ourselves, without any of those old boys and girls, I think would be real fun; but I don't know about the kind you speak of. Aren't they rather—well—poky? You wrote me something about them, you know, in that one letter you managed to send, and I remember I thought they seemed a little slow—well enough for summer in a country place, but I didn't suppose they were intended for cities during the season. Is that the constitution, or whatever they call it?" She reached forth her hand for the pledge card with which Chrissy was nervously toying and glanced over it. "Read the Bible every day!" was her first exclamation. "Gracious! The idea of my promising such a thing as that. It is as much as I can do to read a few verses on Sundays."

"But Belle," said Chrissy, who was by this time

much in doubt what to say or how to say it, "if you could promise that first part about doing whatever Jesus Christ would like to have you do, surely the other need not disturb you."

"Well, it would; I have promised the first, of course, in a general way—everybody does who belongs to the church. I'm not a heathen, Chrissy Hollister, please remember, if I haven't spent a summer in Western. Nobody is expected to be perfect, I suppose; and of course I try to do what is right; but to promise to read the Bible every day is quite a different matter, and this about prayer meetings is real hard, I think. What if I had an engagement on the same evening as the prayer meeting? Would I be expected to break it and go to the meeting anyhow? I don't think it is right to make such wholesale promises."

Behold! here were Belle Parkman and Dr. Dullard standing on the same platform! Who would have supposed it possible? Chrissy was more than doubtful about the propriety of carrying the conversation further, but as she seemed to be expected to answer, she reminded the questioner that the pledge gave her opportunity for excusing herself from the prayer meeting on occasion.

"I don't think it does; I think that is the horrid part of it. Think of my going to the Lord Jesus Christ about an excuse; just at though he were a mere human being! In fact, I must say such talk as that sounds to me kind of wicked."

Had she ever talked in this wild and silly way to Stuart Holmes? Chrissy wondered. It hardly seemed possible; yet something in Belle's manner carried her back to that evening when she had said to him so earnestly: "I would not dare to sign such a pledge as that, Mr. Holmes; I wouldn't really."

Yet she had not meant just what Belle seemed to mean. She had never been quite so absurd as this. She wished Stuart Holmes were here to talk to Belle; he had slipped the false foundations from under her feet so easily, she had little doubt but that he could help Belle. She wished there were anyone to whom to appeal.

"Grace goes to her pastor," said poor Chrissy to herself in a sorrowful jealousy, "but of what use for me to tell Belle to talk with Dr. Dullard?"

There was certainly no use in further talk at present, for she felt that she had no arguments which would fit her friend's present state of mind; it was too apparent that she and Belle were "not parallel cases." Yet Belle was her most intimate friend.

I am sorry to give you such a view of this young disciple's discouragments; and yet, perhaps it is just as well for young people to look squarely in the face the fact that there will be discouragements to meet their hopes and apathetic croakers to meet their enthusiasms, to the end of time. The main thing, and the central pivot on which the main thing will turn is, to make sure of being able to say bravely to your inmost soul: "The Lord is with us, fear them not."

All that evening Chrissy felt discouraged; but, bright little active member that she was, with the next morning's sunshine she had resolved to rise above her fears and try again. Still, I will admit that to meet with apathy or worse in the very heart of one's own home is trying to the bravest disposition.

It was not that Mrs. Hollister did not try to be sympathetic in a degree. She felt herself that she was being very patient with the child's whims.

"It is a pleasant fancy, dear," she said gently, after she had been given report of Dr. Dullard's views, so far as Chrissy cared to report them. "But it is evidently unpractical in a town like this. It is as Louise and Harmon say—societies that will do very well for little summer places like Western are not at all appropriate to city life. You must remember, Chrissy, dear, that you are still very young; your brother and sister understand society much better than you do, and they think you should give this matter up. Harmon is quite distressed about it; brothers are so careful of the reputations of their sisters, you know. He fears if you try to lead in a thing of this kind, you will be thought peculiar; and if there is any one word that brothers dread to have attached to their sisters' names, it is that word *peculiar*."

"Ye are a chosen generation, a peculiar people." The words rose before Chrissy's mind, bringing to her eyes a mist of tears; it was the sentence on which the pastor of the dear little church at Western had built his address to the society that last evening she was with them. How earnestly he had tried to impress them all with the fact that the Lord's dear people must covet that title in the sense in which he, their leader, meant it and strive for just that sort of peculiarity.

The remembrance stayed the words which were on Chrissy's lips; she had almost said that if Harmon would bestow his anxieties in other directions she thought he would be quite as brotherly and much more sensible; but that word *peculiar,* linked as it was with her memories, saved her. She kept silence, and her mother, believing herself to be making an impression, went on in her soft, soothing voice.

"And, Chrissy, dear, while we are on the subject, I may as well say what I have been waiting for an opportunity to say: I wish you would not be so pronounced in your expression of opinions—I mean outside of our own family, of course. We are all very glad to have our little girl express herself to us as freely as she pleases, but before others it does not look well. For instance, Louise says you told Chess Gardner yesterday that you did not approve of card parties. Certainly that was unnecessary."

"It was unavoidable, Mamma. The conversation was not of my seeking and developed in a manner that I did not expect. He asked the question point-blank, speaking my name."

"But you could have evaded it, child. Nothing in polite society is more important than to learn to evade direct questions gracefully. Louise was mortified. She thought Mr. Gardner would consider you presuming. He is nearly eight years older than you, remember. By the way, if he honors you occasionally with a little special attention, as he did the other day in including you in that party for the Falls, I hope you will for my sake, if not your own, show him that you appreciate the courtesy. There is probably not another girl in town who would need such an admonition; but you have grown a little peculiar in some things, I'm afraid. Mr. Gardner is as high in the social scale, you know, as it is possible to reach. Besides, his father and yours were friends in their boyhood; I suppose it is that which inclines him to be so cordial with our family. Your father will be sensitive about the way he is treated. I am sorry you declined going with the party. You need not have danced, of course, unless you chose. I do not propose to force my child's conscience, even though I do consider it a little diseased just now" (the last clause spoken with an indulgent smile); "but I would have you as cordial and courteous as possible to the son of your father's friend, especially when he is a man whose attentions are an honor."

Chrissy's answering smile was a trifle forced. It was not that she felt any personal aversion for Chess

Gardner. During her stay in Western he had returned from a four years' absence in Europe and had seemed disposed to renew his old friendship with Dr. Hollister's family, to their evident satisfaction. He seemed surprised to discover that Chrissy had grown, during his absence, from a little girl into a young lady, but while he recognized this fact by generally remembering to say "Miss Chrissy," he was inclined to be very friendly with her. As a little girl she had always liked Chess Gardner, but today she wearily recognized this little address of her mother's as another barrier in the way of her living the life she was pledged to live.

Chess Gardner's invitations would probably be few in number and of such a general character that they might easily be declined but for her mother's wishes. These, distinctly expressed as they were, made her way difficult, for she someway felt very sure that the invitations would not match the pledge card by which she was resolved to order her life.

She brooded over these real and supposed difficulties in her path, until by afternoon her usually bright face was a good deal gloomed over, and she dressed for the calls which her mother expected her to be ready to receive, in a very apathetic way, interspersing the slow process with numerous sighs. When at last, after being twice summoned, she reached the parlor, she found Mr. Gardner about to take his leave.

"I am only waiting for a word with you," he explained. "I have just enlisted your sister and Harmon for an impromptu sleigh ride. The wise people prophesy a thaw, which will spoil our sport after today. We propose a trip to the ice fountain and return by moonlight. May we have the pleasure of your company?"

Poor Chrissy's face flushed painfully. But for her mother, the way would have been clear; as it was, she stammered her regrets that a previous engagement would oblige her to decline.

"Why, Chrissy!" interposed Mrs. Hollister, "I did not know you had an engagement. I assured Mr. Gardner you would be glad to go. It will be a delightful evening for a ride, and several of your friends are going. What is it that interferes, Daughter? Can't it be postponed?"

"Why, not very well, Mamma. This is our regular church prayer meeting evening, you remember."

Mrs. Hollister was actually dumb with surprise. She had not remembered any such thing. As for Louise, she laughed.

"What an idea!" she said. "The little mouse is asserting herself in an extraordinary manner; I had forgotten that she was grown up until she came home this winter. She has been vegetating in the country all summer, Mr. Gardner, and had developed some abnormal ideas that are attaining extraordinary growth. Why, Chrissy, there is a prayer meeting every Thursday evening, and there will probably not be good sleighing very often. Do, child, reconsider, and beg Mr. Gardner's pardon for your folly."

It was very trying, the more so, because of her mother's severe silence and the brightness of Chess Gardner's curious eyes, which were fixed upon her.

She tried to keep her voice from trembling as she said:

"Indeed, Mr. Gardner, I thank you for the invitation, but I do not feel that I ought to accept it for this evening."

Of course he expressed regrets in a courteous way then concluded his plans with Louise, left a message for Harmon, and departed. The moment he was out of hearing, Mrs. Hollister expressed her mind.

11

"THINGS DON'T FIT"

"I MUST say, Christine, that I am displeased. I should have expected a daughter of mine to heed my advice, given only this morning, better than you have done. This is the result of having spent a summer with a couple of foolish young fanatics. It is nothing but fanaticism, besides being in extremely bad taste, to set one's self up to be so much better than other people. I can assure you that such narrow views as you are adopting are well calculated to put a man like Chess Gardner out of conceit with all religion. It is said that he has adopted some foreign ideas in regard to these questions, and to be met in such a spirit as you have exhibited will help to foster any errors he may have imbibed. I am astonished that my daughter should not have better judgment, not to speak of the taste of the thing. I have all due regard for prayer meetings, as you very well know; but for a girl who has never been in the habit of attending them at all to be suddenly unable to take a little sleigh ride with her friends because it is the evening for the meeting looks a good deal, I must say, like affectation. I have always supposed you to be very sincere, and I cannot understand what influences have so changed you."

Louise was not helpful to her sister.

"I am sorry it was Chess Gardner whom you refused," she said. "He will not be likely to give you another opportunity. I know that by the way his eyes flashed. He is not in the habit of having his invitations declined. It is such a pity. He would have been a splendid friend, and he was very much inclined to be friendly. Of course he doesn't care for my society—he knows I am not to be classed with the young people much longer—but if you could have prevailed on yourself to be a little less queer, he would have befriended you all winter, and any girl might consider herself honored by his attentions."

Now I ask you, was not all this hard for Chrissy? She went to the dull prayer meeting, having managed with some difficulty to retain her outward composure under the fire of Harmon's good-humored ridicule and Louise's loud-spoken regrets. She found the prayer meeting duller than before. Even Rob Stuart had deserted the ranks, and she was herself the sole representative of the young people. This, however, was not her young sister's fault. Faye, having discovered by the way the conversation turned at the dinner table that Chrissy was going to prayer meeting, somewhat eagerly petitioned to be allowed to accompany her and was curtly refused by her mother. Moreover, Mrs. Hollister called her second daughter *Christine* whenever she had occasion to address her—a sure token that she continued to be deeply displeased. On the whole, Chrissy was having fully as uncomfortable a time as she had imagined, and her long letter to Grace, written that evening after the prayer meeting, had a strong undertone of discouragement and gloom. A day or two after the sleigh ride there was to be company at dinner. Among the invited guests were Chess Gardner and his mother.

"If I were you, I believe I should hide," Louise said to Chrissy a short time before the guests arrived.

Her tone was half railing, half sympathetic.

"Mr. Gardner knows how to be elegantly haughty as well as any person I ever met. He did not even mention your name the other night, although we had several long talks; indeed, he quite attached himself to me. If Horace had been home, I am not sure but that he might have been a trifle jealous. As for Mr. Gardner, he was even more sarcastic than usual over the extravagances of speech and action that belong to the present generation. Between us, I think he thought you were extravagantly good. Couldn't you find it in your heart to apologize, for Mamma's sake, if not for your own?"

"Apologize for what?" asked Chrissy coldly. "Because I tried to be consistent and go to the places which I had publicly pledged to sustain? I would not insult my mother by making any such concessions."

She had no sooner spoken the words than she felt that they were ill advised and would have given much to recall them. Louise was very loyal to their mother and was not herself a professing Christian. Her face had flushed over Chrissy's haughty words, and she answered quickly:

"Isn't there something in your code of morals about honoring one's mother? It seems to me I have heard something of the kind. I think you are rather young to sit in judgment on her actions."

Then Louise had gone away, leaving her sister more miserable than before.

Chrissy did not hide; but she wished that she had

been allowed to do so. She was much more silent than usual and extremely ill at ease. Conscious that her manner was increasing her mother's dissatisfaction with her, she was still unable to throw off the miserable feelings that had gotten possession of her and appear her natural self.

As soon after dinner as she could, she wandered away into the remotest corner of the back parlor, taking her station at a west window, where there was a gloomy view of a dun-colored sky. The air was full of snowflakes that had evidently set out to improve the sleighing, despite the recent prophecy of its destruction.

Chrissy had never felt more utterly desolate. The long, gray winter stretched gloomily before her; she had gotten out of harmony with all her surroundings and seemed unable to find any place where she fitted. She thought lovingly and longingly of Western.

"I had friends there," she told herself pitifully; "they did not misunderstand me and misinterpret my actions at every turn. I wish I could go back; I would go tomorrow, if I could. I would be willing to stay always in that little bit of a dull village, as they call it, and never see this hateful city again, if I could find my place and my work and do it. I can't do anything in this great, fashionable city. I can't even interest Belle, my one friend who used to like to do whatever I did."

Not enlivened by these thoughts, they came to a period with a sigh too heavy for one of her years; and at that moment her solitude was broken in upon.

"What is it all about, Miss Chrissy?" a clear voice said just at her elbow.

She started nervously and turned to meet Mr. Gardner's eyes—keen and direct, but not cold, nor entirely unsympathetic.

What she said in reply was utterly unlike what she had supposed that she would ever say to him.

"Things don't fit."

Those were the words, spoken with almost a quiver of the full lips and a drooping of eyelids that betokened their nearness to tears.

Mr. Gardner drew a chair for her within the shadow of the heavy curtains and another for himself.

"Tell me all about it, won't you?" he said genially. "Don't you remember you and I used to be excellent friends? Why wouldn't you take a sleigh ride with me the other night? Do you really like prayer meetings so much? What are the things that don't fit, and why don't they?"

She had not imagined that she would ever tell him all about it, but she did.

Quite from the beginning, she spoke about that first prayer meeting and her ridiculous mistake, though she did not begin at the beginning but was led back to it by degrees. He interrupted her occasionally with questions that sent her to the root of things.

"Let me see if I understand," he said once. "What was it about the pledge card that troubled you?"

"Why, I hardly know how to tell it," said Chrissy; "it ought not to have troubled me, and that is why it did. Do you understand?"

With a half laugh, he smiled his interest and sympathy but gently shook his head.

"Why, you see, I knew I ought to have been quite willing to sign such a card as that, if the professions I had already made meant anything; and it troubled and vexed me that I could not dare to sign it, and yet ought to have been ready to do so."

"I see," he said gravely; "at least I have a conception

of how the thing might impress a sensitive conscience. Go on. What did you do?"

Then she told about that other card, and her startled, frightened Sunday, and her decision—not as she had told the story to Grace Norton, but still with sufficient power to hold her listener's rapt attention.

"I wrote my name on both the cards," she said earnestly. "One I gave to the secretary, but the other I mean to keep always."

"On both!" he interrupted again in surprise.

"Yes; on that one which has the 'I will not,' I wrote, 'I will not live such a life as this ever for one single day; so help me God.'"

"I see," he said again with exceeding gravity. "And that is why things will not 'fit'? I begin to appreciate the situation."

Now that she was fairly launched on the subject, Chrissy found it a relief to continue. She explained with unconscious pathos her loneliness since she came home, and her long desire to have a society like the one she missed; also her effort in that direction, and her failure. She showed the pledge card she had taken to Dr. Dullard, and that was still in her pocket. This listener read it slowly, with grave, thoughtful eyes; albeit they gleamed with appreciative humor as Chrissy gave a detailed account of her interviews with her pastor and Belle Parkman. They were spending a good deal of time in the shadow of those curtains. The other guests were older than this one, and Chrissy comforted herself with the thought that they were probably not missed. But they were observed.

"Chess seems to be enjoying himself," said that gentleman's mother, giving a significant glance toward the bay window at the further end of the long room, a smile on her face all the while.

Chess's mother thought that Chrissy Hollister was an unusually sweet girl. Mrs. Hollister answered the look and smile and said not a word. But if Chrissy had seen her eyes just then, she would have discovered that all dissatisfaction with her had gone out of them. For her eighteen-year-old daughter to hold in absorbed attention such a man as Chess Gardner could be only pleasure to a woman like Mrs. Hollister.

"Chrissy," said Mr. Gardner, still holding the pledge card balancing on his finger, his voice and manner serious and thoughtful (he had forgotten the formal "Miss" with which he had recognized her young ladyhood), "suppose you and I 'endeavor' together? Can not we have a society? It would probably increase, if two such persistent persons as we should set it in motion. Like Dr. Dullard, I know something about these societies; at least, I have stood outside and watched their development with a good deal of interest. Some of the time they have not impressed me favorably, but it was because their members did not take hold of the enterprise with the energy I thought their pledge demanded. I have a fancy that a criticism of that sort would not apply to you. The truth is, this matter of practical Christianity always seemed to me to demand everything, if it meant anything. There have been times when I have assured myself that it meant nothing, but something is constantly coming up to overthrow that impression. I find it very much overthrown just now; so much so that I am willing to endeavor with all my heart if you are willing to show me the way. I haven't the 'Christian' part, you understand, at all, and of course I shall be a novice in all directions; but you will find me as teachable as possible, and if you will undertake the task, it seems to me something might be accomplished."

12

A Beginning

ASTONISHMENT as well as extreme embarrassment held Chrissy silent for several seconds. Up to this point she might have been described as thinking aloud, rather than talking. It had been so pleasant to be able to put into words, to one who would seem to listen sympathetically, some of her hopes and disappointments, that she had given herself up to the pleasure without fully realizing to whom she was speaking. Now the peculiarity of the situation flashed upon her. This young man was reported as, if not an unbeliever, at least a doubter; a somewhat cynical and sarcastic one at that. What a remarkable beginning for a Society of Christian Endeavor! Just they two, and one of them not a Christian! What could the man mean? Could it be possible that he was simply gathering from her material for ridicule? His voice had not sounded like that. But what was she to do with his proposition?

"Does the situation look too discouraging?" he asked at last with a slight laugh, as Chrissy's silence continued. "Cannot you make even an 'endeavor' out of me? I am sorry, for I had honestly hoped for results."

"You are not simply making light of the whole thing, are you?" This was Chrissy's sudden question; her great brown eyes fixed upon him with a look that said she meant to know the exact truth.

The young man answered promptly and with decision: "I never was more in earnest in my life about anything."

There came suddenly into the heart of the young disciple a great longing to enlist this soul for her Master. Why should not his splendid manhood, with all its powers and possibilities, be laid rejoicing at the feet of the man Christ Jesus? Was there anything that she could do to help bring about such a result? "And Jesus beholding him, loved him." Those old words, spoken so long ago of a young man, came vividly before her. She thought they might have been spoken of this one. Surely Jesus would love him if he were here! Nay, it was certain that Jesus loved him now, wanted him. How could she help?

"Well," she said aloud, having given swift attention to these thoughts while the questioner waited: "I don't quite know how to organize a Christian Endeavor Society on such a basis, but I think it can be done. I have heard of literary organizations starting with only two members; why cannot a Christian Endeavor Society do as much? Only—" Here she made a sudden pause.

"Only one of these is not a Christian, you mean? The situation is trying for you, I admit; but then, Miss Chrissy, I have known of literary societies in worse shape. They sometimes organize when none of them are literary in any sense of the word, while in this case—" and he, too, left his sentence unfinished.

"I was going to say, Mr. Gardner, that if I understand you, there is but one active member; or will you become at once an active member?"

"I will engage to be just as active as you are pleased to make me; I put myself under your control in this matter, to do your bidding so far as I can; but just what is involved in that term 'active member' I am afraid I do not fully comprehend. Are there not conditions that I cannot meet?"

For answer, she pushed the pledge card toward him. He read it once more, very slowly and thoughtfully, placing his finger on a clause occasionally and looking away into space while he seemed to consider it.

"You are right," he said at last; "I could not conscientiously become an active member in the light of this explanation. Because, in the first place—I expect to shock you now—only you ought to promise not to be shocked with what an honest man honestly and gravely says in this direction—I am by no means convinced that we have any right to go with our little trivialities and spread them before the great God as though they were of sufficient importance to claim his attention for an instant. Miss Chrissy, at the risk of seeming in your eyes a monster, I will own that the average public prayer to which I have listened seems to me a monstrous impertinence."

I think that Chess Gardner really shrank from having an argument with this winsome girl; that he expressed his views as guardedly as he could and was sorry that the situation seemed to demand so much; I believe he had no desire to shake her faith and honestly regretted their having reached the point where she would attempt to argue him out of his position, in which case, though he answered ever so gently, he could hardly hope to keep from shocking and confusing her. He need not have been so fearful. Her tone was very quiet and assured as she said:

"You cannot, of course, become an active member with those views. If you prayed at all, Mr. Gardner, you would know better that that, because Jesus Christ would so reveal himself to you that you would know it was not an impertinence; but as it is, I shall have to receive you as an associate member, if you will come in under that article."

It was impossible for this young man of the world to keep from bestowing a sudden glance of admiration on the fair face before him and to feel a sudden accession of interest. How simply and yet with what remarkably unanswerable logic she had answered him! How had she learned, in her brief life, to give so gracious a foil to a practiced tongue? If he had but known it, that admirable weapon, "the sword of the spirit," had furnished Chrissy with the thought which she had so simply presented; for is it not written there that "If any man will do his will, he shall know of the doctrine?" Had not Chrissy read the verse thoughtfully and pondered its meaning but the evening before? Meantime, she drew from her pocket a copy of "the model constitution" with which she had also armed herself when she went to call on her pastor, in the hope that he would think so favorably of her scheme that she could ask his advice as to the wisdom of using it for their organization. But it had kept its place in her pocket. Now she had handed it to Chess Gardner, indicating with a motion of her finger the article she wished him to read. He drew closer to the window, for twilight was gathering, and read aloud:

"All young persons of worthy character who are not at present willing to be considered decided Christians may become associate members of this society.

They shall have the special prayers and sympathy of the active members but shall be excused from taking part in the prayer meeting. It is expected that all associate members will habitually attend the prayer meetings and that they will in time become active members, and the Society will work to this end."

The slowest and most meditative tone possible was used throughout the reading of this article, and there was time for Chrissy's cheeks to grow very pink indeed. Viewed in the light of a society with two members, one of them "active," and the other "associate," there was certainly some pledging on the part of the "active member" to be considered.

"Yes," said the reader with becoming gravity, "I think I can subscribe to those terms; I am certainly willing to attend the prayer meetings, but can you, representing the 'active member,' subscribe to your share of the contract, Miss Chrissy?"

Something in his tone seemed to force her to make the reply she did.

"I am not playing at Christianity, Mr. Gardner. I do honestly and earnestly desire to form a Christian Endeavor Society. I shall put all the energy I have into the effort and secure as many members as I can. It means real, earnest business with me, and I would not want you to come into it imagining otherwise."

He laid the little book face downward on his knees and looked full into the flushed face, speaking slowly and with undoubted earnestness.

"Will you tell me, Miss Chrissy, how to convince you that I am in serious earnest—never was more so? I shall be just as honest as you evidently are. I am interested in this whole subject. I am not what the church members call orthodox, though I have found that many of them haven't an idea what they mean when they use that term. But I believe in God, and in a certain deference on the part of his creatures, which is due to him. I believe that certain forms of prayer, expressive of our reverent faith in his power and goodness, may not be distasteful to him. I am honestly desirous of studying into the whole question from the Christian standpoint; because I believe you to be honest and earnest, I am more than willing to study it with you for a leader, not in its theological bearings, but in its practical effects on human lives. If you will organize a society of this sort, I pledge it my support as fully as I can conscientiously give it; and I will do my best to live up to the regulations which affect associate members. Miss Chrissy, are you answered?"

"Yes," she said gently. "I did not mean to distrust you, but it seemed so strange that you were willing to help me, because I am not wise, you know, about any of these things and, of course, cannot help you, only so far as you will let me remind you of the Teacher who can. Yes, I can keep my share of the contract. I will certainly pray for you, and I think anyone who tries to live this life without Jesus for a leader is in need of very earnest sympathy. Mr. Gardner, I have often thought that young men, of all others, ought to be Christians, because Jesus Christ was a young man, you know, and they could be in intimate fellowship with him in a sense that none others could. It seems to me that if I were a young man, I would have ambition to choose him for a companion."

Over this thought Mr. Gardner looked simply astonished. It is safe to say that he had never in his life heard a young woman speak such words before. What answer he might have made will not be known, for at that moment occurred an interruption. Louise Hollister parted the curtains and stood before them.

"What mischief is being plotted in this far corner that you are so quiet and so exclusive? Mr. Gardner, I consider it my duty to warn you. This sister of mine has blossomed into the most intense little fanatic that the century has produced. What curious spell was woven about her in that bit of a village called Western I am sure I cannot say, but the power of the incantations, whatever they were, is still upon her in full force. Before you are aware, you will have changed into a grave and gray-haired preacher, or something of that sort."

Mr. Gardner arose to give the intruder a chair and replied to her in as gay a strain as her own, deftly ignoring, however, the reference to Chrissy.

"We have become rather exclusive, I admit," he added. "I was giving Miss Chrissy a somewhat detailed explanation of certain theories of mine and became prolix, as people are liable to do who talk about themselves. I owe your guests an apology for having kept her so long a prisoner. Shall we join the others, since you decline my offered seat?"

"There are very few to join," said Louise, as they moved down the room together. "The Boardmans had another engagement and left *adieus* and regrets, and the Marshalls are on the eve of going. Truth to tell, your mother sent me to summon you. She is making up a charming little party for your box at the theater tonight. I have accepted with thanks, and she proposes to extend her kindness to Chrissy. I told Mamma I would not venture to answer for the child since the witches at Western had transformed her; that for aught I knew there might be a prayer meeting somewhere in the city that she felt for some mysterious reason bound to attend. How is it, Chrissy, will the witches let you join us for this one evening?"

Some of you will be surprised. Some of you think

that Chrissy declined this and Mrs. Gardner's more gracious invitation given a few moments thereafter to attend one of the leading theaters in the city, but you are mistaken. Chrissy's smile was rich and sweet, and her acceptance so prompt and cordial that Mrs. Gardner was confirmed in her mental conclusion that Dr. Hollister's second daughter was certainly a very winning girl. Twenty minutes afterward, the Christian Endeavor Society of that city was on its way to the Park Street Theater.

13

━━━━◆⧓◆━━━━

A New "Active Member"

IT WAS on the way to the theater that they had arranged that day and hour for that first Christian Endeavor meeting; but Chrissy, as she thought it over in prosaic daylight, felt that there was much more to arrange. Truth to tell, the thought frightened her. A prayer meeting, with Chess Gardner and herself the only persons present; and Chess Gardner did not pray! There must certainly be others found to attend that first meeting.

Turning this trouble over in her mind, she remembered her little sisters, and the flash in Sara's eyes as she had declared that she would like to belong to a meeting where they had "committees and officers, and things of that sort."

Why not let both girls come into the organization? There was a sense in which it would be almost more embarrassing to Chrissy to have them present than to be alone; but there was also another sense in which their presence would be a relief; at least, it would not afford so good an opportunity for Louise and Horace and Harmon, the trio who, she sometimes thought, seemed to live for the express purpose of teasing her. Besides, she might be of some help to her younger sisters; at least, it would afford her an opportunity to get acquainted with them. The more she thought about it the more she resolved to include them in the membership; and to this end she went, one evening, soon after the study lamp had been lighted, to the room which had been furnished for the special use of the two girls and was called the study. A large, cheerful room, hung with maps and charts; having a good globe, a reversible blackboard, and all conveniences for home study. Dr. Hollister had done his best to make his girls comfortable and wondered occasionally that they seemed at times almost discontented.

Chrissy, as she dropped into an easy chair in front of the hearth where a glowing fire was making all things bright, remarked upon the look of cheer and comfort which prevailed.

"Yes, it is a pleasant room," Faye said, "but so dreadfully lonesome, Chrissy. There is hardly ever anybody here, only just us two, and Sara keeps still almost all the time; after I get my lessons done I never know what to do with myself."

"Why don't you come down to the sitting room at such times?" Chrissy asked, smiling indulgently on her youngest sister and thinking what a pretty girl she was when her face was lighted up.

"Oh! that is almost worse than this," declared Faye with animation. "Papa is away, you know, and you and Mamma have calls, or read, and Louise is in the parlor with Horace. We always have stupid times when we go down to the sitting room; don't we, Sara?"

The only answer that Sara gave was a monosyllabic murmur that might have meant either assent or dissent. Sara's face was flushed, and she looked interrupted by this unexpected visit, and a trifle annoyed. She was bent nearly double over her Latin grammar, but it was not a Latin grammar that she had in her hand when Chrissy entered, nor that she thrust suddenly under the table. The action disturbed Chrissy. Was it possible that Sara, young as she was, could have fallen in with books that she ought not to read?

While she was turning this thought over in her mind, wondering how she could find out about it, and what it would be best to do, a servant came to say that Dr. Hollister wanted Miss Sara to come to him in the library for a few minutes. Again that startled look flashed into Sara's face; but it might have meant, Chrissy thought, that she was unused to a summons from her father. Still, she stopped hurriedly and picked up something from under the table before she left the room.

"Do you and Sara find much time for reading?" Chrissy asked directly after the older sister closed the door.

"Sara does," answered Faye, with unsuspecting promptness. "She learns her lessons a great deal quicker than I do, and then she reads and reads. I don't see how she can. I am always so sleepy when I am through studying; but Sara is never ready to go to bed. I have to coax and coax her, and often I go off alone and leave her sitting here; and I don't know when she comes. I don't think Mamma would like to have her stay up late; do you?"

"Certainly not," said startled Chrissy. Perhaps the young daughter stayed up as late at her reading as her mother and elder sisters often did at their social gatherings.

"What is she reading, Faye?"

"Oh! I don't know; stories, I think. Sara is very fond of stories—so am I, for that matter; but I don't like to read them when I'm tired and sleepy, and I don't think I like many of the stories that she does. She reads aloud sometimes, but the people seem to me to be so silly, and so—well, sort of wild; they don't act the way real folks do. But when I tell Sara so, she says that is the beauty of them; that if there is anything she is tired of, it is real folks; that she thinks they are as stupid as possible; and the people in the books she reads are refreshing, because they do something worth doing."

"Where does Sara get her books?" asked Chrissy, a note of sharpness in her voice, which made innocent Faye open her eyes wider and look surprised.

"Oh! she borrows them; we exchange, you know, with the girls. Some of the girls have hosts of books; they get them at the library. We are going to ask Papa to let us have tickets for the public library. Mamma said last year we were too young; but Sara says she cannot think that now, for girls much younger than we get books every week. However, we don't care much, for they are all willing to lend."

Poor Chrissy was learning a great deal, and of a very innocent little girl, who did not know what she was telling. She would have liked to go further into the subject but for startling Faye. It seemed desirable to keep the little girl for the present in ignorance of there being any danger in her sister's course. One question more she resolved to ask and then leave the subject until she could determine what to do.

"Is Sara ever tempted to neglect her lessons for these books?"

"She is tempted," said Faye, speaking more cautiously and with heightened color; it was clear that she accepted this temptation as wrong. "Sometimes she gets so interested, you know, that she forgets, and reads right on after the study hour has come, and then she fails in her Latin or something. But she always feels very badly about it. I think that is what Papa wants of her now. I don't believe he likes her report this week. Sara cried because she was marked so low."

Poor Sara! In the toils of the tempter thus early, discovering that even when she "would do good, evil was present" with her. A Christian Endeavor Society in the heart of her own home was evidently much needed. Some thought of this kind led Chrissy abruptly away from the subject in hand to the one about which she had come. She determined to explain the matter to Faye and try to make clear to her the aims of the organization.

"Faye," she said, "do you remember that last week, when I was speaking to Mamma about a society, you and Sara said you would like to join it?"

Faye nodded her head, a look of keen interest on her face.

"Well, I am going to organize one next week. The first meeting is to be on Tuesday; you may come if you want to, and join the society as associate members. There are associate members and active members. I don't at this moment know of any other active member for it save myself, but we shall find others, of course."

She could not help flushing over the thought, even in the presence of this little girl. She seemed suddenly to have a realizing sense of how hard it would be to pray before those three witnesses, none of whom knew how to pray.

"Are the associate members all young persons like Sara and me?" questioned Faye.

"Yes—or, that is—oh, no! Some of the active members in Western are quite young—as young as you, Faye; but—why, they do not become active members until they are willing to take part in every prayer meeting."

Faye made little outlines of trees and faces on the paper before her, using her pencil with a good degree of skill, even while she was evidently thinking of something utterly foreign. At last, without looking up, she said:

"I think I would be willing to do that, Chrissy."

The voice was low and gentle; not suggestive of vanity, yet Chrissy could not help a smile as she thought:

"What a proud little thing it is! Wants to have one of the 'chief places' at once. I wonder what the mouse would be willing to do in order to secure it? Give a recitation, perhaps, as I myself once planned to do!"

Then aloud:

"Oh! I don't mean that that is all which is involved in active membership. It is a religious meeting, you know, and the active members are those who have become Christians and are willing to speak for Jesus at each meeting or to pray."

Chrissy's voice almost trembled as she spoke those words. She could not help wondering whether, in the meeting she was trying to organize, her one active member would always be willing to pray. Then the pencil, which was making at that moment little frizzes of hair about a pretty face, stopped, and Faye looked full into her sister's eyes, her own face gravely sweet as she said:

"I think I would be willing to do that, Chrissy. I belong to Jesus, and I mean to try to do just what he wants done."

Was ever sweeter testimony or stronger resolve offered? Astonishment held Chrissy silent for some seconds. What did this mouse of a sister mean? How had she, in the atmosphere which had surrounded her, come to such blessed knowledge as this? Suddenly she bent forward and hugged her quiet little sister tenderly.

"My darling," she said, "that is very sweet news—a beautiful surprise; I did not know that you knew Jesus at all. When did you begin to serve him, and what led you to him?"

"It is almost a year now," Faye said simply. "Janet—you remember Janet? She was our nurse when we were little, you know; Mamma sent her away because she was awkward and could not learn to wait on the table properly."

The soft eyes filled with tears, even as she spoke.

"Janet was awkward, I suppose; but she was good. I loved her very much; and that day when she slipped and spilled the soup and broke the dish, do you remember? I could not eat any dinner, and I cried about it a great deal, I felt so sorry for Janet. But if I had known Mamma would send her away, I might have felt sorry for myself. It was just that very night before that I promised her I would belong to Jesus always. I have ever since that night. Janet showed me how."

Yes, Chrissy remembered very well indeed. Remembered that her blue silk dress had been spoiled by the soup, and that she had called Janet a "stupid old dolt not fit for a respectable dining room," and had urged her mother to get rid of her before they had any more company. And here this faithful and awkward servant had been the only one who had paid the least attention to the eternal interests of her charges; the one who, even while Chrissy was grumbling about her, had led her little sister's feet into safe, sure paths.

"Poor little girlie!" she said. "I remember Janet very well, and the spilled soup, and my part in the matter. If I had known you loved her so much, or if I had known many of the things I do now, or felt about anything as I do now, I would not have coaxed Mamma to send her away. I didn't care about such things then, Faye, and I did not know that Janet was a Christian."

It was Faye's turn to question. She gave her sister a swift, curious glance, and asked:

"Why didn't you care, Chrissy? You were a member of the church then. What is it that has made you different? The reason I ask," she added hurriedly, as Chrissy hesitated and the ready color flushed her cheeks, "Sara and I were talking about it; about doing right things, you know, and what was right. Sara said I had foolish, old-fashioned notions which belonged to ignorant people; that I had gotten my notions from Janet and not from Mamma; and I wondered if Janet was mistaken."

Chrissy made a swift resolve to be a true witness for her Master, even before this child.

"Janet was probably right," she said earnestly; "at least, I am sure of this much: I was all wrong. I was a member of the church, Faye, and that was about all. I did not know Jesus, nor love him, as I do now. I did not study the Bible to find out his will, and I was much more anxious to have a good time than to please him. Now it is all different. I found out while I was in Western what it really meant to be a Christian."

A swift, glad light came into the little girl's eyes, followed almost instantly by a puzzled, even a pained look, and she studied her sister's face as if in doubt what to say next.

"What is it, dear?" Chrissy asked. "There is something that you don't understand. Can I make it plain?"

In her heart were two thoughts: "What an expressive face she had! One can understand it almost as readily as her words"; and "Oh, dear! If she asks me why Mamma, who is a church member, does not think as I do about things, what am I to tell her? I must be honest, and I must honor my mother. I wonder what is the right thing to say?"

She need not have been anxious. Faye, thus encouraged, said, hesitating to choose her words carefully:

"I was only thinking that that explained why, since you came home, you have sometimes made me think of Janet; and then I thought—" Here she stopped.

"Yes," said Chrissy encouragingly, "I understand you. You thought what?"

"Why, last night, you know. I didn't think you would; and when I found you did, I said so to Sara; and she laughed at me and said that was just one of Janet's ignorant notions and that Mamma ought to have sent her away before; that I was all full of them, and I could see now that educated ladies did not think so."

"Did not think how?" Chrissy asked, greatly bewildered. "I don't understand, dear. What was it that you and Sara meant?"

"Why," said Faye simply, "Janet, you see, thought it was wrong to go to the theater."

14

ETHICS OF A CHILD

HAD the handsome bust of Benjamin Franklin looking down on her from the mantel suddenly opened his mouth and quoted to her one of the wise sayings of Poor Richard, Chrissy could hardly have been more astonished.

What a surprising thing that this mouse of a sister should undertake a question of ethics!

She laughed good-naturedly and proceeded to enlighten the child. She was not at all embarrassed, for she believed herself to be quite equal to the subject.

"Why, Faye, dear, you did not understand Janet; or, more probably, she did not understand herself. Of course there are theaters that would be wrong for people to attend, and persons of refinement and culture do not attend them. Papa, you know, is very particular as to what play he invites us; but surely you understand that Janet had no right to condemn places which Papa and Mamma attended. I never go to a theater of which Papa disapproves."

Faye was silent; two little pink spots glowed on her cheeks. She did not look at Chrissy but worked nervously with her pencil, making a disturbed face seamed with ugly frowns. Chrissy thought she was hurt and hastened to explain in very gentle tones:

"Sister is not finding fault with you, darling; you are not in the least to blame for getting somewhat confused ideas, and you did perfectly right to come to me with them. I have not the slightest doubt that Janet was a good woman; but she was ignorant, of course, and had a wholesale way of condemning what she did not understand, I presume; such people always have. I do not suppose she knew what Papa's views were. But you are not to feel worried about it, darling; and nobody will blame her, either. People who err on that side are safe enough guides, after all."

"It isn't that, Chrissy," and now Faye's grave, earnest eyes were fixed on her sister's face while the pencil waited. "I was not troubled about what you thought of her, or of me; only I don't think you quite understand Janet. She did not say anything about Papa; she would not have done so for anything, unless she thought she ought; but she said a great deal to me about being guided by what the Lord Jesus said, instead of by any person; and she said she thought the Lord Jesus did not approve of the theater."

And now Chrissy's cheeks were growing red.

"That was a very improper thing for Janet to say," Chrissy answered with decision. "I shall begin to think that Sara is right, and that it is well Janet has gone away. She was setting up her ignorant judgment in that case, making it superior to Papa's and to that of a great many good and wise people. It need make very little difference to you what an ignorant woman thinks Jesus approves or disapproves, for you have better guides than she."

The pencil had begun to work nervously again. Yet

Chrissy, looking at the grave, resolute face, could not but feel that she had not made progress; whatever this little girl had thought on the subject, she evidently still continued to think. Presently she asked a timid question:

"Chrissy, I want to know this. Papa, you know is not a Christian; he does not pray nor read the Bible; and Janet thought that was wrong. She never said it was wrong in Papa—did not mention his name. She was too polite. She has told me often that everybody ought to study the Bible to find out how to live; and to pray to Jesus every day to help them live his way. Now, do you think Janet ought to have said those things because Papa did not live so?"

Logic! Plain, clear, briefly put; confronting her in the person of this bit of a child who gravely waited for her answer. The flush on Chrissy's face deepened, but there was only one answer to make.

"Why, no, Faye; certainly not. Every Christian believes those things. That is a very different matter."

Whereupon she could seem to see her pastor with his gold-bowed spectacles lowered so that he could look over them, gazing at her with his mild, blue eyes, as he said: "My dear young friend, that is not a parallel case." And Chrissy began to feel embarrassed.

Faye was not wise in "parallel cases," but she could ask questions.

"Well, Chrissy, I want to know another thing. Don't some people go to those bad theaters where respectable persons would not go?"

"Of course," said Chrissy somewhat shortly, feeling disturbed, though she could not tell why.

"Then, if they go to the bad theaters and you go to the good ones, could you talk to them about it and urge them not to go to their kind but to come to yours? Because, wouldn't they say: 'You like your kind best, and we like our kind best; you have a right to yours, and so have we to ours'?"

"Is that some of Janet's arguing?" It was all the reply Chrissy had ready to make; in truth, she was a good deal startled. Faye's simply put questions had roused in her keen brain an instant train of reasoning, which, like a revelation, she could see, carried out, would lead her to a different platform in regard to this matter from the one she now occupied; unless, indeed, the premises were false, and of course they were. The idea of Janet, the old Scotch nurse, being further advanced in regard to these things than were some of the leading church members of the city! There was Judge Waterman—did not she nearly always meet him at the theater? And here Chrissy, thinking very rapidly— rather, glancing through thoughts instead of studying them; carrying on both sides of the argument, accord- ing to her fashion—instantly reminded herself that she never met Judge Waterman at the weekly prayer meeting; if his example was safe to follow in the one case, was it in the other? On the whole, she was not ready to answer Faye.

It was not that she was so very fond of theater-going; but there had seemed to her quite enough questions, already for conflict. She longed for points of unity between her mother and herself, and between Louise and Horace and herself, instead of finding new subjects on which to differ. She did not like to attend the theater on Saturday evenings, and she would not attend on prayer-meeting evenings; but further than this it had not once occurred to her there would be any occasion to go. It was bewildering to be confronted with a new element of discord, presented by her little sister. It was irritating to think that the instructor of this child had been an ignorant Scotchwoman. In view of all this, the only answer she had ready was the short, sharp question given above.

"It is what Janet taught me," Faye said humbly. "Of course I cannot tell it as well as she could, and I have told you very little; she knew a great deal, Chrissy— she knew Bible verses that fitted right in. We used to study some question like this until we were quite satisfied as to what the Bible said about it. We never left it for a new one until we were sure what we thought. I could tell you a good many things she said and show you some verses we found, if you cared to have me, Chrissy."

"Thank you," said Chrissy, smiling despite her undoubted annoyance. "Someday when I have time, dear, I will talk about it with you and show you Janet's mistakes; in the meantime it will not hurt you, that I know of, to make a wholesale condemnation of theater-going, at least so far as you are concerned; for you are quite too young to attend. But you must be careful how you judge other people's actions, little girl; that is the mistake which childhood and ignorance always make!"

"Yes," said Faye, still very sweetly. "Janet used to tell me I mustn't judge; we studied that verse about 'To his own Master he standeth or falleth'; but you can't help wanting people to do what you think is right, can you?"

"No," said Chrissy, smiling again; this child was certainly very sweet, if she was too wise for her years.

To Chrissy she seemed the veriest baby; for you are to remember that the girl of eighteen cannot help feeling a great gulf of years between her and the children of twelve, who in a dozen years more will become her friends and associates.

"But, Faye, it is my turn to ask a question. Why is it

that you and Sara think so differently in regard to these matters? Janet was Sara's nurse as well as yours. How happens it that she seems not to have accepted any of the good old woman's notions?"

The perplexed look which gathered on Faye's face was a study. Her answer was preceded by a long-drawn, troubled sigh:

"I don't know, Chrissy. I've often thought about it; it is one of the things I don't understand. It is like people going to church and hearing the minister coax them all to come to Jesus; he means everyone there, and they all hear him; but some of them come, and some of them won't; and I don't know why. Could you tell me why?"

The wistfulness of her tone, and the sudden searching look, as though she would penetrate to this elder sister's soul and learn whether she could really rest the perplexed little brain that missed Janet so sorely, went to Chrissy's heart.

"I'm afraid I cannot answer that, dear," she said, rising, for Sara's voice was heard in the hall, and the clock had chimed the hour for these younger ones to retire.

"I have not answered you about anything as fully as I meant to; and there were some things I wanted to say that I haven't said; but we will have our meeting of Christian Endeavor and study these and a hundred other questions, asking the Lord Jesus to help. I am so glad to know that you belong to him. We will meet on Tuesday evening in the library if Mamma is willing. Meantime you have given sister Chrissy something to think about."

And as Chrissy went away she was conscious of feeling that there might be more classes of Christians in this world than she had supposed. Her mother and

Dr. Dullard, and a great company of persons of whom she could think, belonged to one class, while Grace Norton and Stuart Holmes and a few others seemed to belong to another class. Was it possible that Scotch Janet represented still a third?

That phrase, "if Mamma is willing," with which her interview with Faye had closed, haunted Chrissy somewhat. It seemed a formidable undertaking to acquaint her mother with the plans for organizing a society of which that lady almost disapproved. She chose an hour for presenting her request when Louise would be absent, but she could hardly tell why she also carefully selected a time when her father would be at home. Truth to tell, this young woman rather held herself back from analyzing the feeling which made her shrink less from expressing her desires on this subject to her father, who made no professions in regard to Christianity, than to the mother, who was a member of the same church with herself.

"A Christian Endeavor Society!" exclaimed that lady, looking up from the book she was reading; the exclamation was all in capitals. "And in our house! I must say, Chrissy, that you are the most persistent young person I ever had to deal with. What in the world do you mean to organize with? The servants? Emmeline is the only one who is not a Roman Catholic. Is she to be the other member?"

"I had not thought of her," said Chrissy, with deeply flushed face; "perhaps she will join us."

"Join whom, Chrissy? Have you found a single young person in your set who is willing to assume any more engagements?"

"Mamma, we are going to organize with a very few and then invite others when we have something definite to which to invite them. I have not spoken to the girls generally as yet, because I preferred to wait until we are started; but if you are willing, I would like to have Sara and Faye attend the meetings, and they want to do so."

"Sara and Faye! Really, Chrissy, I don't know what to think of you. Despite the opinions which those older and wiser than yourself have freely expressed, even including Dr. Dullard, you are so determined to carry out your own plans that you are willing to take the children for associates, if you can find no others. I do not see how you can expect me to consent to any such wild scheme as this. I should consider it discourtesy to Dr. Dullard, and very poor teaching for the children, to allow them to join an organization of which he does not approve."

"Nonsense!"

It was the firm voice of Dr. Hollister which interrupted at this moment—none too soon, either; for Chrissy's eyes were flashing, and she might else have spoken words not in keeping with her "endeavor."

"I can see no possible harm in allowing the children to spend an evening a week with their sister; on the contrary, it seems to me eminently sensible. The girls are shut up to their own society altogether too much. If Chrissy will interest herself in them, I shall be glad. Sara needs help in more than one direction. As for Dr. Dullard, what he approves or disapproves need not influence the arrangements of our family circle; and if I understand Chrissy, she has no other members."

"You don't understand her, Dr. Hollister. She is bent on having other members as rapidly as possible. Did not you hear her say that perhaps Emmeline would join them? And I have no doubt, since she is willing, and even anxious, to step down out of her own set, there will be others only too glad of her notice. You do not know what you are sustaining, Dr. Hollister."

"Nevertheless, I see nothing formidable about the undertaking. It is a religious gathering, I understand, and if Christianity means anything, it surely means that all classes and 'sets' must meet on a level there. I haven't the least objection to having Sara and Faye meet with Emmeline to study their Sunday school lessons, or something of that sort, with Chrissy to direct and assist them. And for that matter, whoever else she may get to join her, as long as the meeting is in our house, it would seem to me that we ought to be able to give it a tone of respectability. It is much less foolish than most of the schemes young ladies plan. I advise that you give full consent. I will agree to vacate the library each Tuesday evening, so long as the spell lasts."

"Oh! If you choose to father the scheme, Dr. Hollister, there is nothing more to say. I might have known that you would second whatever fancy Chrissy chose to advance—you always do. Wait until you see where this thing will grow. I know the child better than you do. Chrissy, is your father correct in saying that you have only yourself and children enlisted?"

"And one other person," said Chrissy, speaking low.

"One other person; I thought so," said Mrs. Hollister, triumphantly. "Who is that person?"

"Mr. Chess Gardner," said Chrissy.

Whereupon Dr. Hollister threw himself back in his easy chair and laughed.

15

EMMELINE AND JOE

OVER one suggestion of her mother's—made by her only in sarcasm—Chrissy pondered much.

Emmeline, the pretty table waitress, chambermaid, and generally useful person in the house—what of her?

Mrs. Hollister liked her because she was neat and graceful and good-natured, having always a pleasant smile for those who noticed her in any way.

Louise liked her because she could do lace and hem beautifully; moreover, she could make ribbons and dress shirts into graceful loops and was always ready at call.

Chrissy, on the other hand, did not like her very well because she had so many little jaunty ways, calculated always to attract attention to herself. It is fair to Emmeline to say that she kept these ways chiefly for the afternoon hours when her work was done, and she was free to array herself in summer in cheap muslin, and in winter in the prettiest, gayest garment that a little money and much skill in fashioning could devise, and, with her delicate wools or lace pattern or floss settle herself in the further end of the wide hall, ready to answer the doorbell, and smile and show her pretty teeth and her many airy little movements to any caller who was pleased to notice her.

"She even tries to fascinate Horace," Chrissy said, with a darkening frown on her face. Chrissy did not like people who tried to fascinate anybody; she thought privately that Emmeline was being almost too successful in trying to win the notice of her brother, Harmon. Louise laughed good-naturedly over these suggestions and said that Horace was able to take care of himself, and Mrs. Hollister said:

"What an idea! Of course Harmon is kind to her; he is too gentlemanly to be otherwise; and Emmeline waits on him as though he were a prince."

So Chrissy had dismissed Emmeline in a somewhat vexed way from her thoughts and had really never so much as remembered that the girl had a soul, or that she might be in the least degree responsible for it, until brought face-to-face with her duty by her mother's random remark.

Ought she to try to get Emmeline interested in the meeting? Would not such a proceeding make the whole matter look still stranger to her mother and the rest? What would Chess Gardner think of it?

But this question immediately settled her in her determination to secure Emmeline, if possible. If Mr. Gardner imagined, as her mother had almost intimated, that her main object in this thing was to secure systematic and regular attention from himself, whatever she could do to show him at once his mistake, she certainly would. Not that she believed for a moment that he thought any such thing, but it was humiliating to have the idea ever so darkly hinted.

Truth to tell, the path of this poor little endeavorer was not a very smooth one. Sara, on being interviewed, was found to have lost much of her desire to join a society of the kind.

"It is nothing but a Sunday school class, as I see," she said loftily; "and I have enough of that on Sundays. I thought it would be a large society, with officers and committees, and that you would have charade parties, and card parties, and things of that sort, as the other clubs do. If it is anything like what Faye says, I'm sure I don't want to join it. I think it would only be one more poky thing."

It is surprising when one looks back, to notice how fond the Hollister family was of that word *poky*. It seemed to describe so many and such dissimilar things. However, Sara was sure to attend, for, to Chrissy's discomfiture, her father's command was upon her to do so. He had sternly rebuked disparaging words of hers which he had overheard and assured her that it was his desire to have her attend the meetings regularly; she had given him reason of late to feel that she would be much safer in her sister Chrissy's company than she would in her own; and if it were necessary, she might consider herself ordered to be present.

This was a bad beginning; Chrissy would much rather have had her coaxed to come; under these circumstances, how could she hope to be helpful in any way to Sara?

As for Emmeline, she giggled a great deal when Chrissy tried with kindness, and at the same time with dignity, to explain what the gathering was to be, and why she would like to have her join them.

"Why, dear me, Miss Chrissy, I don't know! I never went to no place of that kind. What would I do all the evening? Study? I never was much of a hand to study"—another giggle—"Ma used to say she believed I studied with my book upside down and made

faces at the boys behind it"—giggle number three—
"but that wasn't so; I never paid much attention to the
boys; it was always the other way"—a very decided
and prolonged giggle.

"You need not study unless you choose; it is not an
evening school; we shall talk about what things are
right to do, and what are wrong, and try to learn what
the Bible says about them."

Poor Chrissy's voice was more than grave; it was
haughty. Could she hope to help her? In her secret
heart she hoped the girl would decline the invitation.

"Oh!" said Emmeline, frightened into gravity, "I
didn't know; then it's a kind of a Sunday school, ain't
it? I used to go to Sunday school, but I'm almost too
old, ain't I, for that? Still, if you want me to come, Miss
Chrissy, why, of course—did Mrs. Hollister say I was
to come?"

She broke off suddenly to ask this question with
a sense of relief; evidently if Mrs. Hollister could be
found to refuse her consent, it would be a comfort
to Emmeline.

"Mamma will not object," said Chrissy with a great
sinking of heart. It was all so very unlike what she had
thought it would be, when during that happy summer
at Western which seemed now so long past, she had
planned to organize this Society.

There floated also through her mind a wonderment as to what Emmeline would say if she had heard
the manner with which Mrs. Hollister gave her consent.

"Mamma, you reminded me of Emmeline. May I
ask her to join us in the library on Tuesday evenings?"

"I have nothing to say, my dear; I retire from all
direction or responsibility in this remarkable matter.
Your father has given orders that your will shall not

be crossed in the slightest particular. I have no doubt Emmeline will be delighted; so also will Chess Gardner. He will find himself introduced to new phases of society life. If it would help you any, I might remind you that the woman who is cleaning the attic has a daughter living on Carter Street somewhere. She might like to join you."

You're not to understand that Mrs. Hollister said these words in a hateful way, nor as if she were offended with her daughter. She even smiled as she spoke and bestowed an amused pat on the flushed cheek of the girl, who turned from her abruptly.

"A little forbearance, accompanied by good-natured raillery now and then, is all that is needed," the mother said in answer to Louise's remonstrance. "Chrissy never could be driven, but she can be ridiculed out of things, if one keeps good-natured over it. She is at the enthusiastic and fanatical age and is trying to do wildly fanatical things, but the spell will not last. I talked with Dr. Dullard about it yesterday, and he says we are wise not to interfere; that he admires her zeal, and that it is not surprising, since she is so young, that it is not according to knowledge. He was very nice about it indeed, and complimentary. Let her have Emmeline, if she wants her, child. What harm can it do? The children will be there to give the character of a Sabbath school to the whole thing. I understand what Chess Gardner is about. I don't believe he expects the chambermaid and the children. He has planned a unique sort of evening, with Chrissy to entertain him by a recital of her old-fashioned, peculiar views. Young men like novelties of that sort. But the others will be an innovation, I fancy. As for Chrissy, the child thinks she means business. She is doing it with an honest purpose to help them all along. I pretended to her that I thought it might be a scheme to secure the attentions of Mr. Gardner, but that was merely teasing, of course. She is in earnest. The only comfort is, she is also young and will learn the impracticability of her plans. Oh! if it were not for Mr. Gardner's fancy to join her, of course I should not permit the scheme to develop at all, because there is really no limit to the extravagances of these young enthusiasts when they once get started. But Chess will be a check on any very extreme measures. Emmeline belongs to the house, you know. Besides, Louise, there is really nothing else to do but submit for the present. Your father is bent on allowing Chrissy to have her way. He always was absurd about her, and as he grows busier, I believe he grows worse."

So this was what Mrs. Hollister thought. Meantime, gentle little Faye, about whom none of the family concerned themselves much in any way, was busy with her own thoughts and plans.

"Chrissy," she said, waylaying her sister in the hall on the afternoon of the eventful Tuesday, "is our society that we are going to begin tonight for anybody?"

"For anybody?" repeated Chrissy with a faint smile, as she remembered the incongruous elements of which it was to be composed. "Yes, dear, I really believe it is. Why do you ask?"

"I mean, is it for boys as well as girls? Because if it is, I think I know somebody who would like to come, and who would help us, too."

"Then by all means let us have him if we can get him, for we need help, Faye—you and I. Who is the boy?"

"I don't think you know him," said Faye gravely. Her sister's tone was only half serious, while she was very much in earnest. "It is only Joe, but he is good."

"Joe?" Chrissy said, inquiringly. "Who is Joe? Is that all the name he has?"

"I don't know his other name; he's Papa's boy."

"Papa's boy!"

Chrissy was certainly very stupid. She could only repeat words in a dazed, inquiring way.

"Why, yes, Chrissy. Don't you know what I mean? Papa's stable boy, who opens the gates and waters the horses and takes care of things. You have seen Joe often, haven't you?"

Chrissy sat down on the stairs and looked at her small sister with a feeling nearly equally divided between laughter and tears. Were not her bewilderments deepening? As if Emmeline were not enough to introduce to her father's library and to Chess Gardner, but here must come the stable boy.

"What do you know about Joe?" she asked at last, for Faye waited, and something must be said. "You cannot be much in his company, I should think; Papa would not like that, surely."

"I don't know him very well, only he helps me sometimes when I am feeding Bess; and he asked me about our Sunday school and told me about his. He goes every Sunday, and they sing lovely hymns with choruses. Joe can sing, and I think from the way he speaks that he is a real good boy. He said he promised his mother to be one, and he was trying."

Already Chrissy's mood had changed. Was this little sister of hers—a disciple whom the Lord loved—sent to her with a message this afternoon from the Lord himself about Joe, the stable boy? Why not? Did not the Lord Jesus die for Joe? Then, could not she, Chrissy Hollister, hold out a helping hand in some way? Was she greater than her Lord? Had she been fancying that she was? And was this why the elements which were to compose her first endeavor seemed to her so ill fitting?

Solemn questions these—far-reaching; questions which, in a nature like hers, once started, must be answered in a way which would satisfy her conscience. It had seemed to her that her friend Belle, and the girls with whom she associated, and the young men in their set, were the ones to reach with this effort. It had never seemed to her that Chess Gardner was one, yet he had come unsought; nor Emmeline, yet she had been thrust upon her; nor her little sisters, yet they had asked to come into the circle.

Now here was Joe, the stable boy. Was it possible that she had been planning work of her own, while her Leader stood by and waited for the time when she would be ready to follow his suggestions? She sat there so long, and was so still and grave, and Faye's face grew grave also, and anxious. What had she said or done to trouble Chrissy so much? At last she ventured her meek, little protest.

"I didn't mean to make you feel badly, Chrissy, and I never said a word to Joe, of course; only I thought, when he was asking me how many verses a day I read in the Bible, and if I ever wrote out the thoughts I had about them in a little book, that perhaps he would help us make our society. And maybe you could help him, because he said once that he thought it was hard to tell right from wrong sometimes; but if I ought not to have said anything about him, I'm really sorry."

Chrissy rose up and held out her hand, bending to kiss Faye's fair, quiet face. How very sweet her little sister was, and she had really never known it until now.

"Where is Joe?" she asked. "In the stable now, do

you think? Then we will go at once and call on him, you and I, and see whether we can help make a Christian Endeavorer out of him. I had not thought of him; I had not thought of a single one who is now on our list. I am not sure who is doing the planning, but if it is the one I begin to think it is, I want to follow."

And they went to the stable.

16

GETTING HERSELF "TALKED ABOUT"

JOE was very hard at work brushing the coat of Dandy, Dr. Hollister's favorite horse. He glanced up with a respectful bow as he saw that his little friend Faye was accompanied by one of the young ladies, then went on with his work without a thought that the visit was for him.

"My sister Chrissy has come to talk to you," explained Faye, after a moment's waiting; Chrissy, meantime, wondering how to begin the talk.

The brush which was making even passes down Dandy's glossy back came to a sudden pause, and Joe turned inquiring eyes on Chrissy. Good, honest, gray eyes they were; and she noticed that his clothes, though patched and worn, were decently clean and neat looking. She had never before paid the slightest attention to this boy; no wonder he was astonished.

"Faye thinks you would like to come to a little meeting I am planning," explained Chrissy, dashing hurriedly into the midst of her subject. "It is a meeting to be held at our house, in the library; we want to try to find out how to live right; how to live so as to please the Lord Jesus Christ."

She was choosing her words with great care to meet the probable capacity of Joe. Faye had said he was "good"; but that, in Faye's language, probably meant that he was good-natured to her and kind to the horses. The first part of her sentence had been thoughtfully worded; the last clause was a sudden dash at the center of things—born of the thought that he might be a young scorner; she had heard that so many of the ignorant street boys of the city were such; he should know at once that the central object of the meeting was to honor Jesus Christ; she would make no false pretenses. She was treated to such a sudden lighting up of the gray eyes as fairly bewildered her for a moment; then Joe said:

"I should like of all things to come to such a meeting, ma'am. There is nothing in life I want to know so much as how to please him."

There was no mistaking the reverent tone, nor the simple dignity of this avowal. Chrissy felt at once that she stood in the presence of one of the King's sons.

"You belong to him, then?" she said, half under her breath. It seemed so very strange! Someway she had forgotten that stable boys were ever "joint heirs with Christ."

"I do that, ma'am. I promised my mother to serve him as long as I lived, and I mean to. But I don't know how very well. At least, there are a great many things I would like to know. If you will let me come to a meeting that will help me to learn, I'll thank you from my heart, and so will mother."

"Where is your mother?"

It was an abrupt question accompanying the

thought that she should like to go and see her and tell her that Joe was a good boy.

"In heaven, ma'am," he said, as simply as he might have said "in the country." "She went there 'most two years ago; I reckon she'll be glad to know of this meeting. I suppose some of the angels will tell her, don't you think, ma'am?"

"I don't know, indeed," said Chrissy, taken aback; feeling that Joe was reaching into depths which she had not penetrated. But Faye nodded her head emphatically and spoke with the gravity of a prophet.

"Yes, they will, I think. They are 'ministering spirits,' you know, sent forth to minister to 'heirs of salvation.' Those are the very words, and you are an 'heir,' Joe, since you belong to Jesus; you have an angel ministering to you, it is likely; and of course he tells when he goes back to heaven what is being done to help you."

Could human logic be clearer or reach its evident conclusion by more direct steps?

Chrissy turned away suddenly to hide a smile, albeit the smile was so sweet that she need not have wanted to hide it. Life in this one little inch of time had grown larger and more wonderful to her. It was like a fairy story, only so grand and glorious because it was real. The royal family in disguise, making its way by careful steps through this world, gathering in its train what kindred it could; brushing against supposed strangers in nursery, or kitchen, or stable, and finding them sons and daughters of the house. What a revelation there would be when the journey was over, and the disguises of common clay were laid aside!

"Joe," she said, turning back with another thought, "can you pray? Aloud, I mean," in answer to his look of evident astonishment.

"I never did, ma'am, because there was no chance;

I have to be right here of evenings, till the doctor gets in with the horses, and I can't get to the weekly prayer meeting."

"Would you be willing to, in this little meeting which we are planning for this evening? There will only be five or six of us."

The dark-red blood stained the boy's brown cheek a moment, but he answered readily enough:

"I don't know how to use the proper words, and maybe I'll not do it right at all, ma'am; but if you say so, I'll do the very best I can."

"Don't you think he is good?" Faye asked as they finally made their way to the house.

"A prince in disguise," said Chrissy absently, carrying out her own train of thought; whereat Faye stared and wondered and decided that Chrissy was thinking about something else.

In truth she was, almost immediately. Her mother must be told of this new recruit, and her permission secured to have him shown to the library when he came. It was not easy work. Mrs. Hollister had resolved to be good-natured and patient, but this was really more than she seemed to think flesh and blood ought to bear.

"Dr. Hollister," she said to that gentleman in an irritable tone as he came into the back parlor after dinner for his half-hour leisure, "have you time to give a few minutes of actual thought to your family? Have you the least idea where that absurd child's freak is leading her? What do you think of her taking Joe into her train? Actually receiving him in the library and enrolling him in her precious society along with Emmeline and the children and Chess Gardner!"

"Joe who?" asked the doctor absently.

"Why, Joe, the stable boy."

"What!" exclaimed Harmon, glancing up from the novel he was reading. "Mother, you don't mean it! Has she, really? Ha ha! Ho ho! If that isn't rich! I wonder what that girl will do next! Is she going to introduce him to Chess Gardner? I declare, I admire her pluck!"

"Pluck!" repeated Mrs. Hollister with increasing irritation. "It is simply ignorance; an unaccountable and alarming lack of knowledge of the world and grows out of an absurd determination on your father's part to let her have her own way. I declare, my patience is nearly exhausted. I have no fondness for having the child's name tossed about in the mouths of various classes of gossip. I think, Dr. Hollister, your experiment has been carried far enough—too far from respectability."

"Wherein lies the harm?" asked the doctor, stretching his tired limbs out comfortably and putting his arms behind his head—an attitude he was sure to assume when both body and brain were exhausted. "Joe is a first-rate fellow; the only conscientious boy I ever had about me, I verily believe. He will do no harm to Chrissy or the children; as for Gardner, he ought to be superior to contamination from that source, I should think. If Chrissy can give the boy a lift in any direction, and is willing to do it, who is going to be injured thereby? He is a smart fellow; I can see it in his eyes."

"Oh! now, Dr. Hollister, you are not so ignorant of the world as all that would imply. I have less patience with you than I have with Chrissy; she, at least, is honest. As if you did not know that she was making herself liable to be talked about—a thing which any girl of sense avoids."

"What on earth can they say?" said the doctor with more energy than he had yet shown. "That she is an unusually sensible girl, with an original mind that refuses to be content with ruts, even though they be made of operas and full-dress parties? I shall consider it rather a compliment than otherwise to have that said."

"They will say a good deal more than that, you will find, and a great deal worse; a girl cannot step outside of the regular 'rut,' as you are pleased to call it, without getting a very unpleasant notoriety; and she drags her family into common talk along with her. Louise doesn't like it, and Horace doesn't. I am not the only one who sees the impropriety of her present course."

"I am willing to be dragged into any notoriety that Chrissy has gotten up thus far," her father said with unfailing composure; "and there is no need for Horace to be troubled. Joe might teach him some wise lessons; the boy is as steady as the sun—never plays cards, even for amusement."

"I am not talking about what Joe does or doesn't do. I am speaking of him as an associate of our daughter. Is it possible, Dr. Hollister, that you don't see the absurdity of all this?"

"I don't, that's a fact. It strikes me as eminently sensible. As I understand Chrissy, it is a religious meeting she is getting up; for Bible study, and things of that sort. If she were a teacher in Sunday school, it wouldn't do to object to Joe as a scholar in her class; and this is a weekday Sunday school, on an original sort of a scale. I presume Joe has a soul, and I can't see any reason why Chrissy, in her father's house, in the presence of others, her little sisters among them, should not help him to take care of it—if she can, and is disposed to. It is different from dancing with him, you see; though I would rather she would do that with him than with some gentlemen whom the young ladies of her set honor; because, in the first place, he is only a boy, and, in the second place, he is a decent, clean-hearted boy, I believe. You see, this is a question of souls, not society; and though I don't profess to be very well posted, I rather fancied your theory was that Joe had one, worth as much as other people's."

"Oh! souls!" said Mrs. Hollister, her cheeks aglow and speaking as though she resented the entire sub- ject of souls in general, and Joe's in particular. "It is all very well for you to continually turn the whole matter into ridicule in this way, so long as you intend to let Chrissy go on as she had been doing ever since she came home from Western; but if you don't discover before long that you have made a grave mistake, I shall be happily disappointed. For my part, I wish she had never seen Western, nor any of those fanatics there."

Chrissy, coming into the room just then, felt the atmosphere as one not healthy for her, glanced timidly at her mother, and immediately looked away; studied her father's face for a second, then went with velvet tread behind his chair and softly kissed his forehead, an almost overpowering longing coming upon her at the moment to make a Society of Christian Endeavor member out of him. But she spoke no word. The air seemed, someway, too heavy for words from her. Possessing herself of the book on the table for which she had come, she made haste away.

In the library were Sara and Faye; the one eager, the other looking sullen. Emmeline was there in all the glory of her best dress and brightest ribbons, seeming uncertain whether to giggle or be frightened. Even Joe, who had blacked his boots and brushed his clothes and put on a clean collar and looked every inch an honest, somewhat overgrown, boy of less than eighteen, was seated in one of the garden chairs, Bible in hand, when Mr. Chess Gardner was announced.

Among all the people who had been surprised from first to last by this effort of Chrissy's, it is safe to say that none was more surprised than was Chess Gardner at that moment. He was in quiet evening dress—very plain, yet, withal, very stylish—and had a lovely rose in his hand which he had meant to present to Chrissy the moment he saw her, as a memorial of their first meeting. But he had expected to see her quite alone and to spend a most unique and enjoyable hour in talking with her about questions which did honestly interest him a great deal more because a young, fresh, society girl was evidently absorbed by them. This phase of the subject he wanted to study. He wondered much what depth the plant had; whether it would grow and flourish, or dwindle in uncongenial soil. He had no doubt but that in time—in a short time, probably—others could be gathered into this organization; because what he really undertook to push, even though so strange a thing as this, he believed he could accomplish; but he was in no haste to see it done. He meant to counsel great moderation in gathering in new members. He meant to plead the importance of understanding the thing fully himself before he made an effort to canvass for it. In short, he meant, in all honesty, to be a faithful, consistent member of the society of two and to have as good a time as he could. There was an undertone belief that he might shake this young girl's faith in a dozen minor particulars, if he should try; and a firm determination not to try. He took some credit to himself for this determination. He said to himself that he was much more honorable than some men of his acquaintance; he even waxed indignant over the thought of their amused comments if he should tell them about his society; above all, if he should tell them that the little girl actually prayed before him! Would she? he wondered. Would her courage really be equal to such a tremendous strain as that? Then he said he really hoped it would. He would like to hear her; her evident sincerity and single-heartedness would rob the exercise of the offensiveness of mere form, or the taint of cant; and he repeated to himself the assurance that he would certainly never make this evening a subject of remark with the average young gentlemen and ladies of his acquaintance. Altogether he was in a very satisfied mood when he presented himself at the library door.

Behold! Here were five people, instead of one, awaiting his coming!

He forgot to present the rose and looked about him for an instant in evident embarrassment. Who were these people? The little girls he knew by sight. Well, for that matter, he certainly knew Emmeline; had she not answered his ring many times in the course of the season? And the boy—why, it was the very fellow who had held his horses for him but the day before, when he went in to speak to the doctor about the new books for the reference library! There was certainly a sense in which he knew every one of these persons, but he did not know them in their present position in Dr. Hollister's library.

"These are all members of our new organization, Mr. Gardner," said Chrissy, her tone as quiet as though she had been performing an ordinary introduction. Chrissy had had her hour of embarrassment and nervous anxiety, but it was past.

Her next sentence, following rapidly on the other, was: "It is a few minutes past the time we set for beginning. Shall we open our meeting by a few words of prayer?"

And presently Chess Gardner found himself kneeling in the attitude of prayer for the first time since he reached the age of manhood; beside him knelt Joe, Dr. Hollister's stable boy!

17

An Inquiring Mind

BUT it was not Chrissy who prayed. Certainly Mr. Gardner had never before listened to quite such a prayer as was offered now by Dr. Hollister's stable boy. He did not know how to do it, he had told Chrissy, and the phraseology was that of one accustomed to praying alone and not much accustomed to hearing others.

He had not even the reverent and usual forms of the personal pronoun, as we use them in prayer, yet nothing could have sounded more reverent than his earnest:

"I ask you, my dear Lord Jesus Christ, to come and help me now, for I don't know how to pray before folks. You know I have never done it; I never had any chance since I began to pray. You know before Mother went to heaven I never prayed at all. We want to have a meeting to find out how to live right. We want you should tell us how. There are things I need to know very much; and you know I have asked you to help me find them out; and if this is the way you are going to do it, I thank you. I thank you for telling Miss Hollister to let me come here. I ask you to help us all. I don't know what these other folks need, but you know; and I pray you to help each of them, and I know you will. Amen."

It would have been hard for Chess Gardner to have forgotten that prayer. Almost equally hard would it have been for him to have repeated a sentence in it for amusement. Original, it certainly was. It would not do to say that it was made up of stereotyped phrases, or arranged for effect, or that the sentences rolled glibly from a thoughtless tongue. All these mental criticisms he was in the habit of making, but none of them fitted here.

Joe the stable boy was evidently a character worth studying. Whatever theory he had of prayer, one thing was certain: It was not merely self-communion, nor an arrangement of sentences for the ears of other beings like himself.

The entire meeting was as different as possible from the one Chrissy had planned. She had felt all day the tremendous responsibility resting upon her, and had tried, with painstaking care, to make ready for it.

Years afterward she used to say that she believed she prepared material enough for that meeting to have carried them through three months of meetings and used none of it.

The preliminaries were conducted with due regard to form and ceremony, Chrissy being unanimously chosen as President, and Sara, much to her satisfaction, made Recording Secretary.

Beyond this, the society resolved not to go, until the number of active members was greater.

"Except a lookout committee," explained Chrissy; "I think we should have that at once. We can hardly expect to increase in numbers without it."

There being a prompt call from the secretary to

know what a lookout committee was, Chrissy turned to her manual and read:

"It shall be the duty of this committee to bring new members into the society, to introduce them to the work and to other members, and to affectionately look after and reclaim any that seem indifferent to their duties. This committee shall also, by personal investigation, satisfy themselves of the fitness of young persons to become members of this society, and shall propose their names at least one week before their election to membership."

"Of course," said Chrissy, "we cannot live up to this article entirely while our numbers are so few."

She looked carefully down at her paper as she spoke and would not allow her eyes to glance in the direction of Chess Gardner. She had heard his expressive and mischievous "ahem" over the clause "affectionately look after and reclaim," but had no intention of letting him know it.

"We can make this a sort of guide as to our duties, just as we shall have to do with some of the other articles, until such time as we can formally organize. The constitution says the officers must be chosen from the 'active' members, but as these are few in number, and as we have not yet adopted the constitution, I shall take the liberty of appointing each of you on the lookout committee and shall myself serve on it with as much energy as I can. Now, I had thought that for this first meeting, in order to make it as profitable as we could, we might take up some subject for conversation; some questions, perhaps, as to the right and wrong of a matter; or as to the wisdom or unwisdom of it. We might each tell what we thought, and find, if we can, what the Bible says about it and try to decide where we stand in regard to it."

Nobody appearing to have ready any reply to this remark, beyond the prompt one of Mr. Gardner, that he was ready to follow wherever the president led, Chrissy continued, though her cheeks were beginning to vie with the rose that Mr. Gardner still held in his hand, and she had an uncomfortable suspicion that Emmeline was giggling softly.

"Suppose each of us should propose a question to talk about? Something that we want to know. Fom them we can select one for this evening, asking our secretary to make a record of the others for future use."

Now Chrissy, with astute reasoning powers all on the alert, had said to herself:

"None of them will do it. Mr. Gardner will have nothing ready that he considers within the range of our capabilities. Little Faye will need to think about it, and Emmeline has no question except how to get the most trimming on her clothes. I shall have to propose the question myself, and I shall get ready to give an intelligent opinion in regard to it, as well as a good many Bible verses to sustain me. I want to help Sara, if I can; and I have the feeling that the sooner I do it, the better it may be for her. I mean to propose the question, 'Ought people to be very careful as to what they read?' No, that isn't a good way to put it, because somebody might answer it with a simple 'Yes,' and to unthinking persons the subject would appear to be closed. I will have it, 'Why ought people to be very careful as to what they read?' assuming that of course they ought, and we are simply after the 'why.' If I am not mistaken, that subject will reach in a number of directions. Emmeline would have more sense, I feel sure, if she could be induced to read something beside that trashy newspaper I saw her poring over last night. And who knows how many dime novels poor Joe has devoured? Though he doesn't look like that sort of boy, still they say all the boys are reading those cheap, horrid books. As for Mr. Gardner, I don't know why he should read so many skeptical authors as it is said he does, unless he really wants to develop skepticism. I do hope I can make some of the arguments fit him. I wonder if he will help or hinder me?"

Such, in general, was the train of reasoning in which she had indulged while she studied great tomes from her father's library, marking passages here and there, with a view to referring to them if necessary; but all the while with a wholesome recollection that her Society was composed of greatly differing ages and intellects, and that she must avoid questions from learned men and keep to simplicity and brevity of sentence as much as possible. None of her preparation had been with a view to the possible presentation of any other question. Mr. Gardner was prompt in his approval of the plan but added that he had so many questions he would like to propose, it would be necessary for him to take time to sift out the more important ones and formulate them, and in the meantime, they might pass on him for this evening.

Sara, who had been mollified by being chosen secretary, was writing busily but said she was not ready with questions. Emmeline said "No, ma'am," giggling both before and after the words and then looked frightened. Faye, thoughtful, opened her lips, then closed them again, her fair cheek flushing, and finally shook her head.

"Perhaps I ought not to ask about it now," she explained. "I will tell you, Chrissy, when we are alone, and see what you think."

Chrissy smiled her approval of the wise little woman, who knew better than to propose embarrassing issues unexpectedly, and turned to Joe. His face, too, grew red, but it was because of the embarrassment of expressing himself in such a presence.

"Why, I dunno whether it is the kind of things you mean," he began slowly, twisting about in his chair, thereby calling forth a slight squeak from the light wicker affair, unused to such treatment, and a very pronounced giggle from Emmeline, "but you said something that we want to know, and I do really want to know this. I've turned it over in my mind off and on for a week or two, but I don't get much clearer notions than I had before. If you could give me a lift, I'd be glad enough."

Chrissy smiled and nodded her exceeding approval. It was very nice in Joe to be ready to propose his difficulties at once.

"Let us hear it," she said encouragingly; "I am sure we will help you if we can."

"Well," said Joe, settling back in his chair with the determined air of one who had resolved to carry the subject through now anyway, "I'd like to be told why it is wrong to go to circuses and shows of that kind?"

Emmeline tossed her head with a snort of both amusement and disapproval. Sara frowned, and Chrissy looked astonished. It had not occurred to her that Joe's difficulties would be of such a character. Moreover, she was embarrassed. She recognized this as a vital question in the boy's life, but none of her carefully prepared work for this evening fitted the need. Why was it wrong to go to circuses? Was it wrong? Joe seemed to have settled that, and to be only in need of the logical steps leading to it. As for herself, she had never given the matter a thought. She did not go to the circus. None of the girls in their set ever mentioned the word. When the traveling shows came in gorgeous array to some summer resort, they had been in the habit of looking on laughingly at the crowds of country people who gathered, but it had not occurred to any of them to seek their amusement by attending. Why not? Because they were superior to the attractions offered. Such entertainments had no interest for them, but if they had for Joe, for instance, why should he not attend?

Chrissy found she had no answer ready. She looked appealingly at Mr. Gardner. Was he better posted then she? Would he help?

Should they waive the question until another meeting? But, in the meantime, Joe might have a vital present reason for pressing his query. Also, there was a fascination in it for Chrissy. She felt as though she would like to know what people said about such things.

"Mr. Gardner," she said suddenly, "can you help Joseph? Why should not people go to circuses and shows? Or, rather, why is it wrong? Was that the question, Joe?"

"Is it wrong?" asked Mr. Gardner, smiling, his eyes fixed on Joe, whom he evidently expected to answer.

"Well," said Joe reflexively—he had that slow, thoughtful way of speaking which, with people in his position, is indicated by the frequent use of the opening word *well*—"folks seem to think so—some of 'em. I remember in the town where I used to live, lots of fun was made of a minister once because he went; and, if it isn't a bad place to go, why shouldn't he have gone as well as anybody?"

Chrissy looked startled, and Mr. Gardner's interest evidently deepened; this boy was something of a thinker in his line. How should he answer him? It is true he might say that the people probably "made fun" of the minister because he did not live up to his own straightlaced opinions, but Joe would not be likely to know what "straightlaced" meant, and besides, he might be keen enough to ask what made the minister have such opinions in the first place; which would indicate that in his answer he had only begged the question. It was a new line of work for him, but why should he not undertake to carefully explain the position of certain persons on this subject and discover how it would affect Joe? Here was certainly a study in human nature, which, to say the least, would have the charm of novelty. Suddenly, he sat erect and applied himself to the task.

"Let me see it I can throw any light on the problem, Joseph," he said kindly. "It is argued by those who do not approve of the circus that it is a business conducted by bad men, as a rule; men of coarse natures and coarse vices, profane persons and intemperate persons. There may be some exceptions, but there seems to be that in human nature which inclines it to sink lower, because of its associations with this sort of employment. Such have been the conclusions of thoughtful men who have studied the subject. Now, it is said that people who frequent such places encourage the business—by their money and their influence. See?"

Joe nodded gravely. He was looking the speaker steadily in the face and evidently following with great care each word that was said.

"Very well; then you have one argument, as it is advanced, not by myself, you understand, but by others.

"Now for a second one: It is said that there are at these places exhibitions more or less offensive to good taste and good manners; women who dress in a manner not agreeable to refined people, and who ride in a way that would not be pleasant to us if they were our sisters, for instance. This being the case, the latter part of the other statement applies, that to attend, and to pay money for doing so, helps to sustain such entertainments.

"Again, it is said that to witness such exhibitions as one commonly sees at traveling shows has a coarsening effect on the audience; that you, for instance, could not look at a rope dance, we will say, performed in the manner that it sometimes is, without being a little more used to a coarse scene than you were before, and that you would, therefore, not be disposed to be so good a boy afterward as you were before. These are some among many reasons which are sometimes advanced why some people think that the circus should not be patronized. Are they satisfactory?"

"Y-e-s, sir," said Joe, in a hesitating, thoughtful way; "only some of 'em, I should think, applied to some other things as well as to circuses. Well," after a moment's thoughtful pause, "then, if they do, the other things would have to go too, I suppose; that is all there could be said about that."

"If one believed the reasoning," said Mr. Gardner, greatly interested in the boy's evident ability to reach conclusions.

"Well, sir, isn't it true? Don't you believe it?"

Mr. Gardner settled back in his chair with a slight laugh.

"As to that, I do not know that I am prepared with a wholesale answer," he said; "some of the conclusions reached are undoubtedly correct; there is no denying them. But whether it follows that the circus must, because of them, on all occasions be eschewed, is not so sure, perhaps."

By this time he was looking curiously at Emmeline.

18

STUDIES IN HUMAN NATURE

THAT young person had not giggled for some time. She was sitting bolt upright in her chair, her gaze fixed on Mr. Gardner, a dark and ever-increasing scowl on her face, and her eyes flashing utter disapprobation as well as defiance. This exhibition at once interested the student of human nature.

"Evidently you do not approve," he said inquiringly. "Will you explain to Joseph why you consider my conclusions wrong?"

"There ain't no call to say that all the folks that has to do with circuses is bad. Some of 'em is as good as the people who feel above 'em any day."

She jerked the words out angrily with defiant tosses of her carefully frizzed head, her face burning the while, and her whole manner indicative of personal insult. There was no mistaking the conclusion that Emmeline's life touched the traveling circus closer than any of her listeners had supposed. Mr. Gardner, always a gentleman, and generally a sympathetic one, answered her with instant appreciation of a possible personality.

"I said there were exceptions, Emmeline; I have no doubt there are notable ones; I was only giving the rule which is supposed to generally apply, and which I am afraid has not too many exceptions. Indeed, I am so sure of this, that had I a young friend who was connected with the circus, I should earnestly urge him to choose some other way of earning his living."

"That's easier said than done," said Emmeline with another toss of her head. "Those who have their living without earning it are always talking about finding other ways; but I don't see but one way is as good as another for poor folks; and it's just as Joe says, anyway; if what you said about circuses is true, it's true of lots of other things. I've been to theaters many a time when the women and dance girls and all of them acted worse, enough sight, than they did in the circus."

Chrissy turned her half-frightened eyes from Emmeline's flushed face to the composed one of Mr. Gardner. Whereunto was this talk leading? What would Emmeline say next? Who would have supposed that the frivolous girl had such depths of passionate indignation in her nature? It was useless to try to reprove her for rudeness. She was too intensely in earnest, as well as too ignorant, to understand that her manner was rude. Mr. Gardner's voice was reassuring; she had evidently not disturbed him.

"That is true, Emmeline," he said in a tone which one would use to any angry child; "some of the arguments certainly apply to some theaters. But there are theaters, you remember, where refined people do not go. The theater has its educating, elevating side, and those who seek elevating things choose that side, having nothing to do with the other. Do you see the difference?"

No, she did not. She tossed her head in evident disgust, saying haughtily:

"Some of 'em do, and some of 'em don't. I've known them that you call 'gentlemen' to go to the kinds that you wouldn't call very high up and laugh with the rest of 'em. They all choose the places where they want to go; and some choose one kind, and some choose the other, and that's just the way it is about the circus, I think; one has not as good a right to choose as the other."

No one in the Hollister household had imagined that Emmeline could talk so fast. As for little Faye, who was giving all the while the most careful attention, at this point bestowed a startled glance, full of significance, upon Chrissy. Behold! Here they were, confronted by the very argument which Janet had said could be used by people who went to the objectionable places, instead of the refined and elevated ones.

Chess Gardner seemed to think the discussion had been carried far enough. He turned from the flushed-face Emmeline and addressed Chrissy:

"I am monopolizing the work this evening, I think, much to my own astonishment. It is quite time our president was heard from."

Before Chrissy could make any response, Joe, who had evidently been lost in his own train of thought, suddenly thrust another question upon them, looking full at Mr. Gardner.

"Are there any verses about these things?"

"Verses!" repeated the perplexed gentleman.

"Yes, sir; Bible verses, you know; about the things you have been saying. Does the Bible say so, anywhere?"

Mr. Gardner settled back in his chair again with an amused laugh.

"That is a question for our president," he said; "I am not posted, my boy, as to whether the Bible expresses itself in regard to circuses or not. My impression is that it is silent on the subject, but I may be utterly mistaken."

Little Faye regarded him with wide-open eyes of astonishment. It was quite evident that she thought he was.

"I know one verse," Joe said thoughtfully. "If what you said about bad men is true—and I guess it is—they swear, that I know, some of them; and drink, all of 'em, I guess."

He did not see the angry glance that Emmeline darted at him but continued his thoughtful musings:

"It says: 'Enter not into the path of the wicked, and go not in the way of evil men.' That fits, I s'pose; and there may be others. Well, for the matter of that, one verse is as good as a hundred, if it says the thing. Dr. Hollister was telling me only yesterday that he always discharged a boy who had to be told the same thing three times over. Once ought to be enough, if a boy means to obey; and if it is enough for just a man to give, why, then—"

Joe was not so much talking as thinking aloud. He did not seem to think it necessary to finish his sentence, the conclusion was so obvious.

"Janet found a rule in the Bible that I should think would fit; it fits ever so many things."

Mr. Gardner turned bright, curious eyes on little Faye, as her soft, clear voice made this statement. There was certainly a great deal of human nature in the room to study this evening, and a little of what seemed beyond and higher than human nature reached.

"'Know ye not that your bodies are the temples of the Holy Ghost?' Those are the words. Janet said we ought not to take our bodies anywhere that we did not suppose would be pleasant to the Lord Jesus, because the Holy Ghost, who had come here to take care of us, was just like Jesus, and would like the things that he liked."

It would have been an interesting study for the curious to note the different ways in which this statement was received by the group of listeners. To Emmeline it was Greek. She was not personally acquainted with the Lord Jesus, nor with his representative on the earth. To Sara it was baby talk. She felt only vexed with Faye for dragging into this presence the prattle of an ignorant nurse for the others to smile over when they were gone. It was humiliating to think that the handsome Mr. Gardner, who looked like the gentleman she read of in the last book she borrowed, would suppose that she was equally absurd and childish. Mr. Gardner, on his part, regarded Faye with increasing interest, saying to himself that her face was very sweet and pure; that an artist would like to idealize it for the picture of an angel; that it was a pity the child reached so high—to themes above the strength of her small body. She was probably a frail little thing and would die young. Chrissy, whom this entire conversation was helping to reach conclusions which would have startled some of the listeners, resolved to have another talk with Faye, and that speedily. The little girl was perhaps better taught than herself in these new paths where she was trying to walk. As for Joe, he was an out-and-out literalist.

He did not understand much about the Holy Spirit, nor did he see how his body could be a temple. But Jesus Christ he knew; and if this verse meant that our bodies belonged to him, as of course they did, why then, nothing was more reasonable than that he should care what we did with them. He nodded his head decisively after a moment's thought and spoke his mind:

"Yes, that sounds sensible enough. Well, I don't believe Jesus Christ would go to a circus if he were here; I don't, honest."

It was impossible for Mr. Gardner not to laugh. The whole thing impressed him as so novel. He was really enjoying this evening very much. Finding himself in a new role and helping to carry it out was exhilarating.

I hardly know how to describe to you Chrissy's state of mind. The meeting—if meeting it could be called—was certainly unlike anything which she had planned. In point of fact, Chess Gardner had really been the leader, and he had taught Joe some very important lessons, she thought. If in doing so he had unwittingly taught her some also, and of a different character from what he imagined, she had only to be glad that she had heard. The circus had not, since early childhood, at least, had any attraction for her; but it was a startling fact that some of the arguments for which Mr. Gardner had been the mouthpiece applied to the theater as fully as they did to the circus. If his logic was correct, and she saw no flaw in it, then Janet had been right, and this was yet another subject about which she and Mamma were destined to differ. More than that, and over this second consideration Chrissy could not help drawing a little sigh, Papa would also differ from her. He was fond of taking her to hear some of his favorite plays. It was almost his only recreation, and she had enjoyed the evenings thus spent better than any with which society life had to do. Was it probable that she must give them up? And could she hope to have her reasons for doing so satisfy her father?

Truth to tell, Chrissy was going off on a train of thought exclusively her own, while Joe and Mr. Gardner had some talk that she did not heed.

She was recalled to the present by the mantel clock striking the hour. It was very strange that an hour could go so soon. She had been afraid that she had not material enough to fill up the time, and now, with almost none of it used, the time was gone! But her father had been very emphatic that the little girls should not be detained beyond the hour, and Joe also had duties calling him; so, with a kindly word to him to the effect that she hoped he had received some help on his question, and a promise that he should be told in due time what question they would take up next, he was dismissed, with a cordial bow from Mr. Gardner.

The others promptly dismissed themselves—Emmeline giving the door a little bang—and Mr. Gardner and Chrissy were alone. Their first act was to look at one another and laugh, Chrissy in a nervous way, as though highly wrought sensibilities had been suddenly relaxed.

"We are to be congratulated," said Mr. Gardner. "We have had a Christian Endeavor meeting, without doubt; at least, I trust it was Christian; I know there has been a tremendous amount of 'endeavor' on my part. What an ethical-theological race that boy led me! Where did you pick him up, Miss Chrissy? He is rather an interesting fellow. On the whole, I'm disposed to like my new character—mentor, father confessor, or something of that sort. What should be my proper title in these new relations?"

The tone was merry but not disagreeable; he was

evidently trying, with honest purpose, to help her regain her usual poise; giving her time to rally before he obliged her to talk at all. Suddenly he changed the subject to that of Emmeline and her evident distress, not to say anger, over the criticism of the circus. There was undoubtedly some personality about it, he said; probably the girl had a friend in the business; was perhaps pledged in some way to one of the men so engaged. If so, he should be exceedingly sorry, for she seemed a good-hearted, simple-minded girl, easily led, and with capabilities for suffering; and the men who travel about with these shows were, as a general thing, a terrible set. It would seem a pity to have an innocent young woman like Emmeline sacrificed to one of them. Perhaps Chrissy could win Emmeline's confidence, by degrees, and help her to save herself from a life of misery. That would be an "endeavor" that she would like, would she not?

Altogether, Chess Gardner was so kind, so sympathetic, so interested to help, so entirely in accord with this strange development which was not of her planning that Chrissy felt that she had never liked him so well as at that moment. If he were only a Christian man, what an influence he might have! This was the direction of her thought, when, after a moment's silence, he spoke again:

"Do you know, Miss Chrissy, I was a little, just a little, disappointed in this evening?"

Yes, Chrissy knew it; or, at least, had supposed it. There was certainly not much vanity in supposing that he would have preferred the evening to be spent alone with her, instead of with the additions of Emmeline, Joe, and the children. She looked up, smiling:

"I knew the company would surprise you, and

perhaps the quality of it would disappoint you; but you know we pledged together to secure members to our society as rapidly as we could, and of course I was very glad to find some at once."

"It was not that," he said, his voice grave, almost tremulous; "I grant you that it would have been pleasanter alone, but I told you I was in earnest in this matter, and I welcome members. What disappointed me was, I had hoped to hear you—pray."

An absolute hush fell upon them. Chrissy's face flushed crimson at the words, and her eyes drooped. He could not know, and did not dream, that she was accusing herself of having in a cowardly manner shirked this responsibility. Why he spoke of it he could hardly have told, save that he was still curious to know to what extent she was different from other young ladies of his acquaintance. The answer he presently received was one that astonished him more than any event of his life had yet done. It was low toned, but resolute:

"Mr. Gardner, I will pray now, if you will kneel down with me."

Mr. Gardner had never heard his mother's voice in prayer, nor, for the matter of that, his father's. There were no tender associations to stir within him and help him with hallowed covenant influence. Neither had he ever in his life heard a young woman pray. This one prayed as she talked, with a simple direct-ness of speech and an assurance of being heard, as complete as though she were addressing a personal Presence.

As this man, once more on his knees, listened and heard himself prayed for—simply, briefly, and with direct and solemn earnestness—for the moment his study of human nature was forgotten; his curious desire to analyze this unique character faded into the background, and he felt, perhaps for the first time in his life—carefully trained man of the world that he was—as though there were present One to whom it was entirely fitting that all knees should bow.

19

━━◆━━

A Religious Whirl

AND now an unexpected and surprising thing happened to this branch of the Christian Endeavor Society.

It became popular. There were reasons for this; chief
among them, perhaps, being the fact that Chess Gardner was a popular man in the city. Whatever he chose
to interest himself in was more or less a subject of
conversation among the more cultured and less frivolous young people of the circle in which he moved.
And he chose to become decidedly interested in this
organization, even after its new departure. In order
that you may fully understand him, his motives need
analyzing. They were several sided.

In the first place, there was his promise to "stand by
the effort"; true, it was not such an effort as he had
planned it to be, but it was evidently such a one as the
original "active member" desired, and he felt himself
pledged to stand by her. In the second place, the
meeting had, as I have intimated, interested him.

He had been for years, in a general and somewhat
purposeless way, interested in what he had been
pleased to term "the lower classes," meaning, as a rule,

the better class of rather low-down, laboring people. Dr. Hollister's stable boy, for instance, might do very well as a type. Emmeline, with her pretty face and rather pretty ways and her ability to make herself look somewhat "stylish" with very limited resources had possibly been a notch above the type and had not interested him so much; but if she had to do with circuses and immoralities of that sort, she had become a trifle more interesting. He had thought a hundred times that something was different from what had been ought to be done for these classes, but it had never seriously entered into his mind to set about doing it, until he found himself actually engaged in the work while seated in Dr. Hollister's library. And the work had fascinated him. It had pleased him afterward to meet Joe in the street and see his face brighten and feel himself singled out from other gentlemen by this intelligent-looking boy as an object of special interest.

"There ought to be others of that class interested in something besides lounging, and smoking, and reading trash, or doing something worse," he said to himself once more; and this time he made a decisive addition to that remark: "I believe I'll work out my pledge in that direction."

On the other hand, it interested him to gather a company of young people from entirely the other class about him and test their intelligence by explaining to them somewhat in detail this new interest of which he had heard; it gave him a pleasant surprise to see that some of them were immediately and unfeignedly interested, even in Joe; they asked questions with an eagerness and a discrimination that did credit at least to their thirst for some new thing. It may not be necessary to say that Mr. Gardner did not make the religious side of the society very prominent; though he was careful to explain that there was some emphatic obligations involved, among which was regular attendance at a religious meeting once a week. Their undoubted interest in Joe awakened his curiosity. Was there not, after all, so great a gulf between circles in society? he asked himself. Could people be brought together on a social plane and made to become wholesomely interested in one another, even though their homes were as wide apart as Beech Avenue, where Dr. Hollister lived, and Ann Street, where Joe the stable boy boarded?

Another feature of it made him curious. The wide-awake, semi-earnest girls were evidently much more interested in Joe than they were in Emmeline. Why was that? Emmeline was a young woman of nearly the same age with themselves and supposed to have, in a degree, like aspirations and impulses. Why should she not awaken their instant sympathy, instead of a boy about whose temptations and aims they could, in the nature of things, know but little?

Besides, I would not be just to him did I fail to explain that Mr. Gardner had been deeply touched in the higher part of his nature by that earnest, simple prayer to which he had listened on his knees. To hear one's self prayed for definitely is always more or less impressive to a soul not utterly callous. On Mr. Gardner it had a strange, almost startling, effect. In thinking of the matter beforehand, wondering, as I told you he did, whether Chrissy would pray before him, realizing, as he did, how easily such a scene could be turned into ridicule, he had resolved, you will remember, never to speak of it before those who could treat it lightly and had taken some credit to himself for so doing, feeling something of the "I thank thee that I am not as other men" spirit about it.

Thinking of it afterwards, he had told himself that he would be an impious scoundrel ever to mention it, or to think of it, save as a sacred scene, a privilege for which, if it were true that there was to be a Judgment Day and trial, he should undoubtedly have to give account.

Taking all these things into consideration, Chess Gardner resolved to push the Christian Endeavor Society with vigor and to see whereunto the thing would grow.

Moreover, Chrissy Hollister herself was a born leader and had an influence over the young people which she did not understand and had always underestimated. They might differ from her, they might fret to and at her; some of them might even sneer; but the chances were growing every day more probable that they would, in a sense, follow her lead.

So, before many weeks had passed, it had become apparent to certain lookers-on that the new society was quite the thing and had come to stay. Dr. Dullard looked up over his gold glasses and beamed on the row of new faces which presented themselves at the Thursday evening meetings—for, as may well be supposed, Chrissy aimed all her energies from the first at getting this heavy midweek meeting reinforced—beamed on them approvingly, publicly congratulated himself and them on their presence, and took occasion afterward to shake hands with Chrissy, call her his "dear young friend," and assure her that nothing could give him greater pleasure than to have her succeed in the way she was doing; that when he had mildly questioned the prudence of the effort, he had not taken into consideration her force as a leader; and that he should take early occasion to say to certain of his brethren in the ministry that it made all the difference in the world who stood at the helm. Dr. Dullard always did do things handsomely.

As for Mrs. Hollister, she was a much mollified woman. Since the Maxwells, and the Brainerds, and a few others of her world had chosen to take hold of the affair, and above all, since Chess Gardner boldly advocated it on all occasions, it had become quite another matter. She still smiled, it is true, at many of the persons who became members; but she smiled instead of frowned, and that was a great point gained. She by no means allowed herself to understand that it was because of the Maxwells, and the others, that she had somewhat changed her base; she assured herself that she had not understood the scheme; how should she, when it was so new, and Chrissy was so young to lead? Now that she understood it, it was eminently proper for a member of the church to interest himself in others, even though they were entirely outside of her set; that it was work which was being taken up in all the large cities now by the very best people. Had not that charming Mrs. Max Garretson, whom she met last summer, just written her about being thoroughly absorbed in an evening school which had been started in their neighborhood for the lower classes? If Mrs. Max Garretson, with her millions and her elegance, could be so absorbed, why not her Chrissy, since the Maxwells and Chess Gardner were willing? In short, Mrs. Hollister began, in a certain sense, to approve of "the masses" and "the lower classes" and talk about them; too much for Chrissy's peace of mind, inasmuch as they were terms never heard in the Christian Endeavor Society.

That young woman may be described about this

time as living in a whirl of engagements and excitements. She had always lived in a whirl of some sort, ever since she had screamed for an hour after a brightly lighted lamp, and kicked her box of playthings over, and thrown away her dolly because she could not have it. This was simply an exchange of whirls.

The society had fairly blossomed into order. "The Lookout Committee," the "Social Committee," the "Flower Committee," and every other committee under the sun had been duly appointed and were flying hither and thither. Constitutions and bylaws and schedules and programs had swarmed about her, clamoring for attention; committees on music and committees on entertainment had sought her advice and assistance until almost every hour of the busy day was taken up with plans and programs.

"It is just a fever," said Mrs. Hollister, smiling indulgently when Louise complained that no one ever saw Chrissy nowadays; she was always copying something or outlining something for some committee. "It will reach its height presently and begin to decline; young people cannot do things moderately. Chrissy, especially, always was wholesale, you know, and she has a faculty, someway, for leading others in her train."

Mrs. Hollister's tone was patience itself; she could afford to be patient; for had not Estelle Brainerd almost as high a fever as Chrissy? Was she not at this moment closeted in the library with her, arranging the literary part of the next meeting? And had not Chess Gardner rung the bell three times within the last two hours to confer with the young ladies a moment, or to ask a question which he had previously forgotten? There were alleviating circumstances connected with fevers.

Meantime, some things disturbed Chrissy, when she had time to think of them; she seemed to have very little time. Even her morning Bible reading had to be cut short sometimes, there was so much to do. She had had no idea it was such a busy world. She wondered, with a feeling of secret triumph, what the members in Western would think if they could look in upon this Society. It was so large, compared with theirs, and there was so much more to do; they had to shape their programs to meet so many more needs.

Occasionally, as I said, came the disturbing thoughts. Sara seemed a good deal interested in the meetings—at least, in writing out the reports, and she certainly made a very skillful secretary for one so young. But she took no part in the general exercises other than those assigned to her on the literary program, and she still read her favorite books. Chrissy was afraid, though she had not had time to look into the matter very closely. Neither had there been time to say anything to Papa about it, as she had fancied perhaps she ought. On the few occasions when he was at leisure Chrissy had been particularly engaged. Then, too, Joe had not seemed to be so interested and so much helped as she had thought he would be. He came to the prayer meetings and always took part, which, being an "active member," he was pledged to do, but it was often only to repeat a Bible verse—and sometimes the selections were so strange. If they had not been from the Bible, Chrissy would almost have thought they had been chosen with a view to fault-finding; they seemed so sharp. To the literary gatherings Joe did not come at all. Chrissy decided, however, that she ought not to wonder at that. Doubtless, they were beyond his grasp. They could not, of course, hope to meet all intellects always.

As for Emmeline, she came quite regularly to all the meetings. But she invariably selected for herself a seat quite far removed from the leader's table, securing in her train a choice spirit in the shape of one of the boys whom the Lookout Committee had tolled in, and the two whispered and giggled contentedly through the hour. Emmeline had not been roused to any exhibition, either of irritation or special interest of any kind since that very first meeting, which, by the way, was the only one held in Dr. Hollister's library. The number of persons pledged to attend before a week from the following Friday, the evening selected of regular meetings, had grown so large that it had been deemed wise to move at once to a hall which Chess Gardner had secured for the gathering.

Among the things for which Chrissy had not had time was that of trying to win Emmeline's confidence, as Mr. Gardner had suggested. Truth to tell, Chrissy did not like her well enough to feel a strong desire for her confidence and was too much absorbed in her "whirl" to feel her conscience pressing in that direction. She had almost forgotten the episode of the circus. Emmeline might be going to join a traveling troupe the very next week, for aught she knew to the contrary. What she did know was that there were three committee meetings that week which she must attend, besides planning the cards for the Lookout Committee to distribute in the hotels and at the railroad houses, and drilling little Fanny Browning to recite "The Fairy Dance," which was really an exquisite thing, and the child danced her part almost as a fairy might.

You are all ready to moralize, or you would be, if you knew that this was a veritable history. You would say that it was no more than you expected; that these fever heights in religion were no better than they were in any other phase of life; that had Chrissy been content to walk before she tried to run, and to walk with much painful stumbling at that, she would not have so soon lost her interest in these themes. That, in short, you consider it always unfortunate when young persons are stimulated to try for heights which they cannot in reason attain.

There are some things in which you are mistaken. Prominent among them is the notion that this "young person" had lost her interest in these matters. On the contrary, if there was one thing in which she was absorbed, and which she was pursuing to the utmost of her strength, it was this matter of practical Christianity. I admit that she was simply disappointed in present results, but she did not lay the blame on the efforts made. On the contrary, she redoubled them; tried to be at all stations along the line at once; tried, in fact, to accomplish the impossible and to shut her eyes to failures. If ever Satan had transformed himself into an "angel of light," surely he did it in this case and was driving this young soul with an earnestness that betokened how fully he knew her worth. Meantime, there was one subject which she resolved to study fully as soon as she had time, and with this thought in view, wrote the following letter to Grace Norton:

Dear Grace,

I want to visit with you, but I haven't time. You have no idea how crowded I am. I thought we were busy in Western, but it was no comparison. The field is so large here, you know, and there are so few to help—really help, I mean; there are a great many to keep watch of and plan for. I have three committee meetings today. We are going to try to get hold of the railroad men in some way; I hardly know how; not to hold meetings—that was what I wanted, but there were none willing to undertake it. They say we must interest them in us first, and afterward we can hope to reach them. So we are planning an entertainment that we think will please them. The songs and recitations—everything, in fact, have something about railroading in them. The songs are lovely, and there is a great deal of work about it all. Well, I did not intend to tell you all this; I know I hadn't time. What I am writing for just now is to ask you why you don't attend the theater. I know you don't, and I presume you think it is wrong, although I never heard you say so, and I don't know why I think it, except on general principles. We have had a little talk about it lately, and I find I don't know what I think, nor why I think it. Can you help me?

Yours in great haste,
Chrissy

P.S.—I cannot conceive of Stuart Holmes as attending the theater, and yet, to save my life, I cannot tell why.

20

A Day to Be Remembered

THERE came a day, late in the spring, which, because of the many and varied things that happened to disturb and bewilder her, stood out vividly long afterwards in Chrissy's memory.

If I may be justified in the expression, I might almost say the disturbing day began the evening before.

It was Friday evening, and there was of course the regular meeting of the society. It was largely attended; there was much singing; and many Bible verses; two young men from the theological seminary, having been called on beforehand and earnestly invited to do so, offered prayer. The secretary's report was lengthy, and a somewhat lively discussion arose in regard to certain points in it. All these exercises consumed the hour, which was immediately followed by a rehearsal in preparation for the very unique entertainment which was to "get hold of" the railroad men. The program included tableaux, in which Emmeline posed exceedingly well; but when Joe was kindly offered a part he shook his head, declaring that he "had no head for such thinking" and slipped away as soon as the regular meeting was concluded. The rehearsal held the managers to a late hour and sent Chrissy home dispirited. This was in part owing to an episode which occurred earlier in the evening. Her father, who had been unusually busy during the mild and sickly winter, found himself on that particular evening with a leisure hour at his disposal and much in need of mental rest and recreation.

He claimed Chrissy as his companion to witness a favorite play in the leading theater of the city.

Now Chrissy had by no means settled that question to her satisfaction; she continually told herself that she hadn't time to look into it; yet she was sufficiently unsettled to feel an utter distaste for the amusement and to have resolved not to indulge in it until she "felt differently."

Yet the very cloudiness of her objections served to give her an irritable sensation when the question presented itself; for these reasons, and also because body and nerves were overtired, she answered her father almost petulantly: "Why, Papa, I can't. Don't you know it is our meeting evening?"

"But your meeting doesn't last all night, Daughter. I do not want you until nine o'clock."

"I can't go at nine o'clock any better than I can at seven. We have a very important rehearsal tonight, and if I am not there to manage it, there will be nothing but confusion."

"It seems to me," said the father, annoyed more at the words and manner than at the refusal itself, "that you have extremely little time these days for anything but rehearsals and committees. I think it would be well for that society of yours to 'endeavor' to practice some home duties."

Now Mrs. Hollister, although she had long since ceased her opposition to the society, and, when she saw the elegant preparations which were being made for the coming entertainment, and the number of "first people" who were getting interested in it, was only pleased, belonged to that class of persons who never omit an opportunity for saying "I told you so." This was, therefore, her hour of triumph.

"I told you, Dr. Hollister, you would learn in time some things which you did not understand, when you let Chrissy go into this. I am sure you have only yourself to thank for her increasing absorption in the society. You encouraged the effort from the very first and took it from under my control."

It will be remembered that fathers have nerves, as well as the children, and perhaps an utterly worn-out physician may be pardoned, if anyone may, for exhibiting them on occasion. Dr. Hollister very rarely spoke as he did at this time, but then, he was very rarely spoken to as his daughter Chrissy had just addressed him.

"It was a misnomer," he said testily, "I suppose that was why it led me astray. They called it a Christian endeavor, and I foolishly supposed it would have a Christianity about it that would shine at home as well as elsewhere. However, I don't understand these matters, nor the meaning of that word, it seems. Don't let me detain you, my daughter; I may find some wicked worldling to help me pass my leisure hour."

Is it to be wondered that the president of the society was exceedingly distraught that evening? Or that one of the girls whom it was her duty to drill, said of her afterwards: "Chrissy Hollister was as cross as two sticks tonight. She needn't think she is going to order us girls around in that way; I don't mean to endure it."

It was this accumulation of weariness which awoke with her on the morning of that day, bringing in their train a dull, nervous headache; not alleviated by the fact that there was a raw east wind and a drizzling rain and that she must go out in them to plan the decorations for the "palace car" which was to form one of the attractions in a tableau.

She dressed for walking; but the rain grew fiercer, and, wet and dispirited, she finally signaled a car and found herself, presently, seated beside Minnie Powell, a young woman whose father, so far as money is concerned, was much richer than her own, whose dress was also correspondingly richer; but who was, nevertheless, not at all of Chrissy's world. A few months ago, the utmost that would have passed between them, meeting on the streetcar, would have been a civil "Good morning," with perhaps a passing sentence or two about the weather or some equally general and long-suffering topic. But Minnie was one of the prominent associate members of the Christian Endeavor Society; she greeted Chrissy with effusion, changing her seat at once in order to be beside her, and began a conversation in a tone much too loud for the street, according to Chrissy's ideas of propriety.

"Didn't we have a large meeting last night? Did you see I had Fred Walker with me? I had the greatest time getting him to come. I had to coax and coax. He kept saying he knew it would be dull, but I told him we had the jolliest kind of times at the rehearsals after the meeting was over. Don't you think our meetings are rather long? Now that we are so busy, it seems to me we might shorten them a little; we do need so much time to get ready for those tableaux."

"The meeting lasted an hour," said Chrissy.

"Oh! I suppose so; but then an hour is a good while for a meeting of that kind, don't you think? Goodness! It seemed endless to me last night. I suppose I was worried about Fred, and that made it seem longer. That is why I think we ought to shorten them, so we can get those young men coaxed into coming."

"Coming for what?" Chrissy thought but did not say. Fred Walker had been one of the young men who had especially tried her the evening before; he not having had even self-respect enough to keep from whispering during prayer. How could she help wondering what special advantage there had been in his attending that particular meeting?

"But then, of course, it is good to get them to come," thought poor puzzled Chrissy. "It is what we are working for, and the hymns were good—some of them. There were a great many Bible verses repeated, too. How can we tell what he may have heard?"

This was all true, but it did not give her the encouragement which she thought it ought, and the poor tired worker did not know why.

Her companion, seeing that she was not to be answered and feeling that she had perhaps been too pronounced on that point, essayed to smooth it over.

"Of course *I* did not mind the length of the meeting. I'm used to meetings; it did not compare with the way in which things are drawn out on Sundays. Don't you think Dr. Dullard preaches just horridly long sermons? But then, some of the boys don't go to church at all, you know, and haven't learned how to endure. I am fond of the meetings. You would have thought so if you could have heard me last night. Our nurse girl is sick and Mother wanted me to stay with Callie while she rested. Callie is sick, too, and Mother has to be up with her some nights, so she proposed that I stay at home. 'Goodness!' I said, 'I can't do any such thing. I promised to go to those meetings, and I mean to do it. Besides, they depend on me, and nothing short of positive necessity shall keep me away.' So I called Jane—that's the nurse girl—and told her if She *was* sick, she would have to amuse Callie for a while and let Mother rest; that I was obliged to go, because it was a meeting of importance that I had promised to attend."

Utter disheartenment held Chrissy silent now. How sure she was that the earnest pledge to be present at the meeting "unless hindered by some reason which could be conscientiously given to Jesus Christ," did not bind this girl on the occasion she had explained. Why did not Minnie see this for herself? Was she actually being injured instead of helped by her pledge?

"It is different from my experience," thought poor Chrissy. "If Papa had asked me to read to him or to do anything that I felt I could do—" yet here, she paused abruptly, feeling that this was not strictly true; the manner of her refusal to her father had been such as to make it impossible to salve it over with a conscientious scruple. Was she then, in any sense, like this girl? Meantime, the busy tongue was at work on a new theme.

"Isn't that tableau of angels hard to get up? Don't you think Lou West makes a perfectly horrid angel? So fleshy, you know, and awkward. Angels ought to be light, graceful creatures. Fred Walker and I fairly exploded with laughter when you were trying to make her wings lie down as they should. 'It can't be done,' Fred said, 'She isn't made of the stuff that etherealizes.' What has that tableau to do with the entertainment, anyway? I think it is out of place. Who proposed it? There is nothing about railroad men in it. I am sure they have nothing to do with angels and never will have, I imagine."

The sentence closed with a light, careless laugh; but Chrissy shivered and drew her wraps closer about her as though an east wind had struck her. It seemed to her that her very flesh was sore with this jarring of sensibilities. It was she who had proposed that tableau, and planned it, and rehearsed it, and sat up nights to fashion the wings of the angels; her chief object in bringing it into the program being to dignify the whole thing with something that would be high toned and spiritual in its conception. She hoped, poor child, with this one tableau to make an impression even upon some of those railroad men, which would help them to wish to see and hear the angels. How could she endure it to have her special creation over which she had worked so much, and even prayed a little, held up to such gross criticism?

What a relief it was to have Minnie catch sight of Mannings and exclaim: "Oh! I've got to stop here to see about my slippers. I hope it won't be as muddy as this the night I have to wear them—don't you? Good-bye."

The conductor was smiling in a supercilious way while he waited for the loud-voiced young lady to finish her sentence, and Chrissy was frowning heavily. "Disagreeable creature!" she muttered to her inner self. "The idea of her setting up for a critic as to what is appropriate when she cannot conduct herself on a streetcar in a way to avoid remark." This "Christian Endeavor" woman's face took an even gloomier shade than before. As she rattled along over the rough pavement, she was conscious that her head ached, and her eyes ached, and she thought societies and tableaux and angels very weariful affairs.

The rain and wind grew fiercer, and the car filled rapidly. Two young men of the stamp Chrissy was in the habit of mentally setting down as "fast" presently gave up their seats and hung on the straps quite near to her, continuing their desultory conversation, meantime.

"Have you seem Harm lately?" questioned one.

"Harm Hollister? No, what about him?"

"He's in a bad way, they say."

"What, sick?"

"Yes, running down. Oh! He's out every day and doesn't call himself sick, I believe; but he looks wretched and coughs in a way to scare one—especially nights; he stayed with me last night after the frolic. It was so horribly rainy and slushy and everything mean when we broke up that I prevailed on him to go with me. I half repented it before morning. He coughed fearfully. I should not be surprised if the fellow did not live through the summer. I heard that Dr. Douglass had a poor opinion of him."

Had the speaker glanced behind him, he might have been shocked at the effect of his words on one weary-looking girl.

She had given the most eager, strained attention from the moment she heard her brother's name; and with the last sentence, her face assumed almost an ashy pallor. For the famous Dr. Douglass to pronounce an unfavorable opinion was almost to seal one's death warrant. The talk went on, as careless talk will, without a thought of whom it stabs.

"Why, Harm's father is a physician, isn't he?"

"Yes, a very skillful one—quite celebrated, indeed; but you know doctors are proverbial for paying very little attention to their own families. I don't know what Harm's immediate friends think, but I shouldn't be surprised to hear of him as down at any time; of course, the sort of life he is leading helps tow disease along."

Chrissy pulled the strap with such violence that the bell gave a sharp clang; and the two young men, who lifted their hats and stepped aside to let her pass, looked a second time, then exchanged glances of pity for the white, distressed face of the girl who brushed by them.

How Chrissy lived though that rehearsal was a question which was afterwards a bewilderment to her. That she listened to the song of the angels, watched the dance of the fairies, answered the endless questions which were poured upon her, got away from them all, and went with rapid strides homeward through the rain—too nervous even to wait at the corner for a streetcar—became apparent from the fact that, at last, after what seemed to her almost a lifetime, she was applying the latchkey at her father's door. That sickness and suffering and death with which, because of her father's profession, her life had been so familiar should come into other homes was to be expected, of course; but that they should enter their family circle was someway a thing which had never seemed within the possible.

"Where is Papa?" she asked, dashing into her mother's room without ceremony. "Oh, Mamma! Do you know where Papa is, or when he will be at home?"

"No, I don't," said Mrs. Hollister, looking up from her reading and speaking with utmost composure. "I haven't the least idea where he is, nor when he will return. Why? Have you seen a ghost?"

21

DID I DO RIGHT?

"I HAVE seen someone else," continued Mrs. Hollister, still in that composed tone, as Chrissy was turning away without explanation of her excitement. "A gentleman, from Boston, I think he said; a friend of yours. He met you somewhere; Emmeline thinks he said at Western, but I do not know; I have an impression that people of this stamp rarely find their way to Western. He is very fine looking; even more so than Chess Gardner and reminds one slightly of him. He was greatly disappointed at not seeing you, as with the discouraging statement that I had not the least idea when you would return, or indeed if you would get here at all today. He left his card, however, and in the forlorn hope of your getting through with the numerous committees which I told him you had in charge in time to see him before he left the city, he is going to call again this afternoon."

"Where is the card?" interrupted Chrissy, a touch of eagerness in her voice. Somebody from Western, or who had breathed the atmosphere of Western, it seemed to her, would be a relief just now.

Mrs. Hollister did not know; she presumed it was in its proper place. Emmeline had it in charge.

Chrissy went in search of Emmeline, stopping at Louise's door to ask if she had happened to hear Papa say where he was going, and whether he might be expected for his regular office hours. Louise was a trifle more curious than her mother had been.

"I haven't seen Papa today; I was up late, you know, last night, and was therefore up late this morning"; with a little laugh over her own mild pun. "What is the matter, Chrissy? Have any of your performers been taken suddenly ill, that Papa is so much needed? I declare, I am afraid you will be the first victim. How wretched you look! You are working too hard. If I were Papa I would oblige you to take a prescription of freedom from committees and all such worries for a long while. What makes you do it all, Chrissy? It won't pay in the end. Everybody will criticize and grumble and tell how they would have had it, and some of the performers will blunder, and some of them will quarrel and refuse to perform at the last minute. I know all about it; I've been through the war, you see. I tried to manage the world when I was a schoolgirl, and I found I couldn't, and that it wasn't worth managing, anyway. Why don't you ask the butler about Papa?"

"He doesn't know," said Chrissy, dropping into a chair, realizing for the first time how weary she was. "He says Papa sent him to the drugstore on an errand and went away while he was gone. He must have had a hasty summons, for he left no message with anybody, so far as I can find. I don't suppose I could see him if he were here; the reception room is crowded with people, waiting their turn, and it is nearly his office hour."

"What do you want of him, Chrissy? Oh! Chris, somebody has been wanting you—a very stylish-looking gentleman. If he is a specimen of the society at Western, I don't wonder you were fascinated. I shall hint to Chess Gardner to look well to his interests."

"Louise, I wish you wouldn't!" said Chrissy, flushing angrily. "Mr. Gardner is a good friend of mine, and I like him; but I do hate to have such silly things said to me when there is no foundation for them whatever, either in Western, or elsewhere. Who was it that called?"

"How do I know? A very elegant gentleman, who looked 'dreadful disappointed,' Emmeline said, when he found you were not in. He left his card, but I don't know what Emmeline did with it."

Neither did Emmeline, it appeared. She was on her way to place it in Miss Chrissy's own receiver when she heard Miss Faye scream and, running to her, found that she had cut her hand; and she was that flustered at the sight of blood, and Dr. Hollister not being in, and the child feeling faint, and there was so much to do for her, that really, Emmeline was very sorry, but she could not think what she had done with that card. But the gentleman was coming again; he was very particular to say he would call in the afternoon.

Before this long-worded explanation was concluded, Chrissy was on her way to Faye's room.

It took some time to hear the story of the accident, discover the extent of the injury, and caress and comfort Faye, who was lying limp and pale on the school-room lounge.

"I don't think it is a very deep cut, darling," said Chrissy, kissing the troubled little face, mouth, eyes, and even nose. "I am sure Mamma has bound it up quite like a surgeon, and when Papa comes, he will put something on it to relieve the pain. Does it hurt so badly?" noticing the drawn look about the mouth.

"N-o—or, that is, it hurts, of course; but that is not the worst of it, Chrissy. I got hurt by not doing just exactly as Papa said. You see, I was cut by that great big knife of his that he told me never to touch."

"And did you forget the direction, darling?"

"Oh, no! I only thought I knew better about it than Papa did," with the faintest little shadow of a smile on her face at the words. "It was lying on the table in the hall, exactly where the postman tosses down Papa's mail; and I thought, 'What if he should cover it, and Papa should take up his mail and not see the knife blade and get hurt?' He never leaves it around, you know. So I took it up very carefully, I thought, and was going to carry it to the office. The wind blew the door back against me, and the handle of the knife turned in some way—I don't know how—but I almost dropped it, and I got hurt."

Chrissy could not help bestowing several more kisses. "I wouldn't worry about that, dear," she said, "Papa will not be hard on you when he understands the motive."

Now a pair of very large eyes were fixed on her face, and the slow, grave voice of Faye made answer: "I am not in the least afraid of Papa; he is never hard on anybody, I think. But the trouble is, did I do right to try to plan for myself, instead of doing just exactly as he said?"

"She's a little goosie!" said Sara, looking up from her book and speaking contemptuously. "I cannot understand how a girl twelve years old can be such a goose. What Papa meant was that she was not to play with the knife, of course. As if we didn't always have to use our judgment about things."

Chrissy, as she went down the hall afterwards, studied over these two types of character. There were different theories about obedience, it seemed. How tender little Faye's conscience was! Chrissy wondered if she been as careful about her heavenly Father's directions as Faye's standard required? Or had she, like Sara, judged that he meant, sometimes, thus and so, instead of what he said? In all this busy whirl which she was leading, was she conscious of doing, as Faye put it, "just exactly as he said?"

At that moment she heard her father's voice and ran down to him. He was in the midst of office work—bowing one caller out with a last cheery word or two while Porter was opening the door for another to enter the private office.

"Papa," said Chrissy, flying down the stairs, "Oh, Papa! May I see you just for one minute? I want to ask you something."

Her father paused with his hand on the door. "I haven't half a minute just now, Daughter. Is your business so urgent?"

"Oh, Papa! It seems as though I must ask you one question; I have been waiting so long."

"Very well," he said, "let me see in how few words you can put it." His tone was not encouraging; he had a dim idea that she was going to ask whether he thought she ought to have waived her engagements and gone with him the evening before. He had no desire to trammel her life, nor to have her society because she ought to give it; but it hurt him to think that she could be willing to cut herself so entirely from companionship with him, or to put any interest in his place. The busy father had appreciated this young daughter's evident relish for his company; had missed it of late, more than he liked to own; but he disliked under the necessity of having to petition for it and to almost apologize for having been so inconsiderate as to have done so.

He was not prepared for the question: "Papa, is Harmon seriously sick—in danger, I mean?"

An instant flash of anxiety swept over her father's face. "Why do you ask?" he said hurriedly.

"Papa, I overheard some young men talking on the cars; they did not know me, and they spoke freely. They said Harmon was in a bad way, that they had heard it was Dr. Douglass's opinion that he was in danger. It isn't true, is it, Papa?"

The doctor removed his hand from the knob of the door, behind which his next patient was waiting, and took a few disturbed steps down the hall. Harmon was his eldest born, and his only son.

"I do not know just how to answer you, Chrissy," he said at last, stopping before her. "Harmon is far from well; I have been anxious about him all winter, some of the time extremely anxious. I would have had him go away somewhere for a change of climate, if I had dared to send him; but he is careless—excessively careless; he has brought the trouble upon himself in the first place by the most reckless imprudence, and he continues, despite my frequent and very plain cautions, to be recklessly indifferent. I have not thought him so alarmingly ill as the words you overheard would seem to imply, and I cannot think that Dr. Douglass has expressed such an opinion; he would have been likely in such a case to have said something to me. However, as I say, I am in deep anxiety. I will look into it with greater care immediately. Meantime, Chrissy, if you were not so engaged with other matters, it seems to me you might do something for your brother. These miserable evenings in early spring, with a raw east wind a great deal of the time, are disastrous for one like Harmon to be out in, yet he is out every evening. When I remonstrate, he assures me that it is very dull at home for a young fellow, and I cannot but see that it is. How is it, Daughter, that with such extreme interest in humanity as you have shown of late, you have none to spare for your brother? Isn't there something in your Bible about people working 'over against' their own houses? If you could get such an influence over Harmon as would induce him to give up late hours, late suppers, and cigars, I might be more hopeful than I am. As it is—"

His hand was on the doorknob again; this time it turned, and Chrissy heard an eager, tremulous voice say: "Oh, Doctor!"

He had left his daughter utterly crushed. She had looked to hear from her father a prompt and emphatic denial of her fears; she had pictured to herself how he would laugh at the thought of Dr. Douglass, the specialist, making such a statement about his son. Instead of this, it seemed that he had been living a life of daily anxiety for a long time on this account and that he felt there were things she might have done to have saved her brother. What a terrible thought it was!

What could she do? Harmon had alternately petted and teased her, in the short intervals when they had been at home together, since both were considered grown-up, but she felt that she really was not acquainted with Harmon and did not know how to set about getting acquainted.

It was absurd to think of getting him interested in the Christian Endeavor Society. He was, someway, not of the stamp which she could hope to influence by it. He was—Chrissy hated the word and had never, certainly, applied it to her brother—but when she stopped to analyze it, did he not belong more especially to the set which people were liable to describe by that word *fast?* Not vulgarly so, of course; Harmon Hollister was a gentleman; his mother thought him as perfect a young gentleman as could be found in society. If she meant his bow, his graceful carriage, his immaculate toilet, and his skill in dancing, he certainly was. But Chrissy had realized a wide space between him and men like Chess Gardner, for instance. Harmon was not a reader, except of certain kinds of literature, which he admitted he read to "kill time." He was not intellectual in his tastes and pursuits; in short, he was not anything that belonged to Chrissy's world. How was she to help him? Yet he was her brother, and of course she loved him. Loved him so much that the thought of his possible physical danger struck a cold chill to her heart. But had the fruits of this love in her life been just exactly what her Father in heaven had intended when he set her and Harmon together in this family relation?

Her thoughts went back to little Faye and her grave query: "Did I do right when I tried to plan for myself, instead of doing just exactly as he said?" Had she been trying to plan for herself, leaving the work "over against" her own house to run to waste? Was there something she might have done? Could she have interested Harmon in the Christian Endeavor Society if she had really tried? But even had she succeeded in this, what good would have come of it? There was time for his late hours, his late suppers, and his cigars after the society meetings were over. Was there any influence going out from those meetings which would make it impossible for a young man to carry on the two interests? If not, was that in any sense doing what she had planned?

These later thoughts brought back the entire perplexed question again which haunted more or less her leisure hours. She had met her father in the hall which connected with the office. People were constantly coming and going through this hall, and as soon as her father left her, she had passed from it into the one connected with their own street door and had dropped into one of the hospitable easy chairs to try to recover from the stunned feeling she had and, if possible, to think what was to be done.

She closed the review of her immediate past with a troubled sigh and felt as though, someway, she had heavy weights too hard for her young shoulders to carry. The bell rang just as she arose, and she lingered on the stair to learn what was wanted a moment, while Emmeline unlocked the door and a familiar voice sounded in her ears, then she went with swift steps forward, and there was unmistakable pleasure in the voice that said:

"Mr. Holmes! I am very glad indeed that it is you."

22

PERPLEXING QUESTIONS

"SO AM I," said Stuart Holmes, with a cordial smile over Chrissy's frank greeting. "Does that mean you were uncertain as to the identity and are relieved that it is no one worse than I, or does it mean that you are glad I am myself?"

"It means," said Chrissy, breaking into one of her merry little laughs, "that I could not discover whether you were yourself or somebody else." Whereupon, the story of the lost card was told him; after this, they hurried from one topic to another, after the manner of people who have been separated for some time and have several interests in common. It was not until that first fifteen minutes of his time was gone, that Mr. Holmes said, quite abruptly, "And now, what of yourself?"

"Why," said Chrissy, smiling, "I am here myself; that answers your question. Why don't you ask about our Christian Endeavor Society? I thought that would be one of your first questions."

"I am more interested just now in a bit of personality. Is it the same Chrissy we had in Western?"

"Why, yes," said Chrissy, still laughing; albeit she blushed under a certain penetrativeness to the question, "the same, only perhaps a little more so. Of course we do not stand still for five months. Does it seem possible that it is five months since I left Western?"

"It seems longer than that since I left there; yet it is barely three months."

"How very much they miss you! Have you left there permanently, Mr. Holmes?"

"Oh, no! I hope to return each summer, perhaps, for a few weeks. That is as nearly as I can be said to have been a permanent resident since my early boyhood. Only this fall I stayed late—quite into the winter, indeed. I was in a sort of transition state—plans all immature, but I am quite settled now."

"In New York?"

"In New York. A bank clerk, so far as the matter of breadwinning is concerned; a Christian worker in places where work is sorely needed the rest of the time. It was one of the fascinations which the business always had for me, that it gave me the most of my evenings for real work. How is it, Miss Chrissy? Has there been progress this winter?"

It was of no use to try to waive the personal question; he knew a great many roads back to it.

Up to this half hour Chrissy had not known that she wanted to waive it; now she felt puzzled and constrained.

"Why," speaking hesitatingly, and with most evident embarrassment, "I hope I have. We have a very large Christian Endeavor Society here, Mr. Holmes."

"So I have heard. What are you doing?"

What made Stuart Holmes's questions always so hard to answer?

"Doing? Why, the usual things," with an attempt at a smile.

"How many active members have joined you from the associate list?"

"Not one," said Chrissy, low toned and grave.

"Well," with a pathetic smile, "that is not always so discouraging as it looks; the break may come suddenly and bring you in a harvest. If your two or three active members are doing aggressive work, with wisdom and patience, watching in prayer, the harvest is sure some time. Does it satisfy you, Miss Chrissy?"

"Does what satisfy me?" Chrissy had always a habit of repeating questions in a half-dazed way when she was perplexed as to how to answer.

"The Society. Is it doing and are you doing in it with all your soul what you meant when it was organized? Are you finding in it the spiritual help which it should give and which you expected?"

"Does anything ever do that, Mr. Holmes? I mean, do things ever reach one's ideal, accomplish what a person may have meant, who started them?"

"If the person who started them is the Lord Jesus Christ, I should say yes."

A sudden silence on Chrissy's part; after a moment's waiting, another question from her caller:

"Miss Chrissy, will you not begin at the beginning and tell me all about it? What you are trying to do, and how?"

What was there to tell him? That they had seventy members—seventeen of them "active members," so called; that their activity consisted for the most part in reciting a Bible verse, or a verse of a hymn at the regular meetings, or in suggesting the number of a hymn to sing. A gain, certainly, on what used to be; but a gain which was reached with the first meeting, since which time there had been no advance. On the other hand, when the devotional part of the meeting was over, the entire seventy, with few exceptions, had been very active indeed in planning songs, recitations, charades, and whatnot, for their own entertainment. Should she tell him this? Well, why not? Were not songs, recitations, and all those things entirely legitimate means to certain ends?

Did they not use them in Western as stepping-stones? Yes; but what higher step, because of these, were the young people of this Society, which everybody called hers, preparing to take?

They were planning, it is true, with all their energies, a most unique entertainment for the benefit of the railroad men; the costumes had cost them all the money raised in the Society for current expenses, and there would be endless other expenses which would have to be met from private purses.

Mr. Gardner was just as generous as he could be and had himself offered to pay for the use of the large hall they were to have and to provide carriages for the fairies and angels to ride home in after their arduous work was done, lest the thin clothing and kid slippers which angels are supposed to wear might give these young human angels severe colds. They had already spent almost endless hours on the rehearsals and were expecting to have the largest and most successful entertainment that their little city had ever given under the auspices of any religious organization.

All this Chrissy knew and felt that she could have told it off volubly to many of her old acquaintances—even to Grace Norton she could have described the whole with animation. Why was it so hard to talk about it to Stuart Holmes?

While she waited, uncertain how to commence, or

where, and suddenly conscious that she disliked the idea of some of the tableaux very much—actually hated that one in which she posed as "the exhausted traveler" with Chess Gardner as brakeman, struggling to raise her car window, another question was suddenly thrust at her.

"May I ask you, Miss Chrissy, have you really a Christian Endeavor Society, or only an endeavor after one?" And while she looked utterly perplexed, he continued: "Because there is a difference. I have watched these organizations with deep interest, as you may imagine. I feel sure that in some few instances, there has been commenced what I might call a frantic endeavor after the real thing, with a sort of photograph of it to start on; and I have seen them degenerate into almost burlesques of the original idea; insomuch that loyal members of that great Society might have wept for shame over the thought that caricatures of them were flitting about, using their title. Does that seem severe? I do not mean to be unjust. I want to be honest. I ask you, Chrissy, in all earnestness, do you feel that you are banded together as aggressive Christian workers, whose object is, as our constitution has it, 'to promote an earnest Christian life among the members and make them more useful in the service of God?' Or are you simply a society which means to have religious principles for its basis and has been snared by that specious form of reasoning which plans to get hold of people, win them, draw them in by entertaining them to the best of their abilities, and which has no actual defined place to which to draw them, and no paramount Object to Whom to win them?"

"Mr. Holmes, why do you ask me these questions?"

She was looking steadily at him now, and her cheeks were red.

"Because," he said, promptly and frankly, "I met, a few days ago in New York, Nellie Tudor—you remember her? She had been visiting Grace Norton, and Grace had just received a letter from you, parts of which she read to Nellie, and parts of which Nellie quoted to me, naturally supposing me to be interested in this work wherever organized. From nothing which either Grace or Nellie said, but simply from your own narrations of your work, as quoted to me, arose the feeling which prompted the question to which I am still awaiting an answer."

"I don't know what we are doing," said Chrissy, her eyes dropping suddenly, her voice almost irritable. "We haven't the material here that was to be found in Western; not in our church, at least. We did the best we could. Our Thursday evening prayer meeting is better attended—at least, it was for the first few weeks—than ever before, and our members are interested in something which has the name of the church on it, at least. We are not doing what I hoped and planned, Mr. Holmes, I may as well own to that; but I thought it was better if we could not accomplish what we wanted, to accomplish what we could."

"Always provided that the accomplishing is in the line of what we are after, and not something obstructing the track," said her guest. Then, "Chrissy, I wonder if you remember the words we studied so carefully from our 'Model Constitution?' They help me frequently when I get on doubtful ground. I am in the habit of quoting them to myself: 'Do not lower the standard or cater to the worldly laxness of the average Christian by making the way in easy. Make sure that everyone who joins fully understands his duties and obligations and is willing, in Christ's strength, to undertake them.'"

"But people must be won before they are ready to join a society of that kind," said poor Chrissy.

"Won to *what*, my dear friend? If I should create a theater and make it free to a large company of people in whom I was interested, do you think I would thereby succeed in winning them to Christ? If such are the true ways of winning souls, ought not our churches to take them up?"

"Do you estimate the work we are doing here on that basis?" Chrissy was looking at him again, and her eyes were blazing.

He returned the look thoughtfully in silence for a moment; not as if he were thinking of her at all, but as though he might be considering the wisdom of some step, which consideration was apparent in his next sentence.

"Miss Chrissy, at the risk of hurting you, which you may know I would not willingly do, I have determined to quote to you some things I have heard this morning. I do you the honor to believe that you will surely understand my motive; the quotations, while they prove nothing, are worthy of thoughtful consideration, perhaps, as determining the wisdom of the next step. I have been waiting in town for several hours in the hope of seeing you, and I strolled about aimlessly, to dispose of time.

"Among other adventures, I heard a gentleman, who was just leaving his carriage, addressed as Dr. Hollister. I at once decided that he was your father and wondered if the boy holding the horses was the Joe about whom you once wrote to Grace Norton.

"Having nothing else to do, I entered into conversation with the boy, found him to be the veritable Joe, and a most interesting character. Him I questioned about the Christian Endeavor Society. He expressed enthusiasm for the first meeting; said he got 'lots of help' there which would last him all his life. The other meetings he confessed he had not liked so well; he said the reason was, he supposed, they had got way up above him, somehow. The verses were good, and he liked some of the singing first rate; but the prayers mostly had a good many words in them that he could not get hold of. He admitted that he did not pray himself, verbally, because he did not know any such words as they used, and moreover, he had a kind of a notion that you might not like to have him, lest he should make mistakes."

At this point, Chrissy felt that her cheeks must surely be the color of the crimson rug on which her feet were resting.

How had Joe been able to discover that she often trembled lest he should, by one of his peculiar prayers, convulse the Society beyond all pretense of decorum?

"At last I questioned him about the entertainment of which Nellie had told me," continued Mr. Holmes, politely oblivious of the blazing cheeks.

"He said he had nothing to do with it, did not stay to the rehearsals, did not mean to go to the entertainment. When I pressed for the reason, he gave me this remarkable reply, which I have decided you ought to hear: 'Well, I dunno as I ought to say it, but the fact is, I used to go to circuses a good deal; and I never thought there was much harm to 'em except the wasting of money until I got to reading Bible verses and praying, and then it began about the circus. I used to go twice a year regular when I was up in the country, and liked it first rate; but at that first meeting I told you about, the gentleman, he made plain work of it, and I know before I got out of the room that Joe Trueman couldn't go to any more circuses—ever. But I never thought a thing about theaters, and them I used to go to whenever I got a ticket for doing an odd job; and I liked 'em better than the circus, a good deal. But one night it come over me, after I had been to one of 'em and was at home reading my verses for the night, that the talk about circuses fitted 'em just as if it had been made for 'em! There was nothing to do but to say I mustn't go; and it was tough work—worse than the circus, enough sight—because that, you know, was only once or twice a year, and this was every night if you could get a ticket. Well, sir, I gave 'em up, of course. There was nothing else to do. But it was a real tough job. I kind of hankered after 'em, nights, you know, when I hadn't anywhere to go. But I began to forget 'em and be interested in other kinds of things, till these rehearsals begun at our society. Well, sir, if you'll believe it, they made me think of the theaters. There I'd seen fairies, you know, and angels, and folks making themselves into pictures, and all them things; and it made me want to go again as bad as ever! And one other thing, I dunno why it is'—here Joe's eyes looked away into space, and his mind evidently philosophized over the question: 'I dunno why it is, they are ladies and gentlemen, and they are better acting and nicer in every way than the theater folks I was used to; but they can't do that kind of work as well as the theater folks can—by a long sight, they can't. And I found that watching 'em made me just hanker after the theater the worst kind. I'm making a long story, sir,' said Joe, 'but the long and short of it is, I had to stop staying to their rehearsals. After the praying and the verses and the singing is done, I bolt, every time: It's the only safe way.'"

After this remarkable recital, Mr. Holmes paused only a moment and then hurried on, conscious that Chrissy did not want to speak. "From Joe, I went to your reading rooms. There, seated near a group of young men, I heard your Christian Endeavor Society freely discussed. I gathered from the talk that three of the young men were nominal Christians, the fourth an outsider. He argued heartily in favor of the organization; said it was a 'jolly thing.' I shall have to ask your pardon for the adjective—I am quoting, remember. The other three were more or less rude, perhaps positively coarse in their criticisms. Had I not full confidence in you, knowing as I do, that you will appreciate my motive, I could hardly quote their words. The Society was characterized as a 'young theater,' a 'religious frolic,' and the like. One of them took exception to the name; he said there was nothing religious about the thing; that the initials *CE* did not mean 'Christian Endeavor,' but 'Chrissy Endeavor,' while the fourth young man declared emphatically that you were the best actress among them and could make your fortune if you could be induced to go on the boards!"

23

"CHRIS, I WOULDN'T"

WHILE repeating that last sentence gravely, as one who disliked to repeat it but felt the necessity, Mr. Holmes had looked at his watch and had risen at once.

"I have stayed to the extreme limit of my time," he said, "and must make all haste. My train leaves in twenty minutes."

Chrissy held out her hand for good-bye, struggling for self-control enough to speak.

"Do you expect me to thank you?" she said at last, trying to offer the ghost of a smile while her lips quivered.

"Yes," he said, giving the small, cold hand a cordial pressure, "I do; not now, perhaps, when you are surprised and pained and cruelly disappointed; but afterwards, when you have rallied from what I know is a shock and have had time to gather up your energies and try again, you will thank me for being straightforward and plain; for believing in you so thoroughly that I could use a powerful remedy to antidote the evil."

When he was fairly on the steps, he turned back to offer that last word: "By the way, do you know that

Nellie Tudor is in your city? She is at 14 Meridian Street. Miss Chrissy, I think you would find that Nellie could help. She has been growing. She will be here until summer."

Then he lifted his hat and was gone.

Even in her bitterness of soul, Chrissy could have smiled at herself for her folly in realizing that the bitterest drop in this cup was contained in that last sentence! To think that she, Chrissy Hollister, a "born leader" as she had heard herself called ever since she was a bit of a child, was actually expected to get help from Nellie Tudor! "A girl without brains," as she had thought of her contemptuously at first, excusingly afterwards, when the girl's warm heart had stolen some of her own.

She had certainly learned to like but not to admire her. "She will never be anything but a bright, good-natured, loving, little goose!" said poor Chrissy as she closed the street door with a slight bang. "And to think that I am expected to consult her and secure help! When I do, Stuart Holmes will be likely to hear of it! He is likely to hear of everything if it is bad; he gives one almost the feeling that he is omniscient. Nellie Tudor, indeed! I wonder if that last suggestion was only 'by the way,' or whether he came for the express purpose of offering me Nellie Tudor's wisdom and grace for any assistance? I didn't think it would be she who would interest him. I thought he had brains enough to prefer Grace Norton. He calls himself straightforward, and he is—more so than he thinks."

This was only surface; deep in her heart, Chrissy knew she was wounded too much even for thoughts just now. How sharp a thrust it was that Joe, whom she had honestly set out to try to help, should have been actually hindered in his progress Christward by her influence!

Very little was seen of Chrissy by her family during the remainder of that day. When she met them at the six o'clock dinner table, both mother and elder sister exclaimed over her jaded appearance, and her father bestowed on her a searching look, half disapprobation, half sympathy. He, too, looked jaded and troubled. As for Harmon, it was impossible for Chrissy's newly opened eyes not to see that he ate very little and was constantly annoyed by a slight dry cough, so slight as to be almost unnoticed by those not listening for it; but Chrissy observed that her father glanced frequently in the direction from which it came, and that the wrinkles on his forehead deepened.

As they were about to leave the dining room, and Harmon moved toward the hall, his father turned to him:

"You are surely not going out tonight, Harmon? It is a wretched evening, and the east wind is very penetrating."

Harmon made an impatient movement and muttered something about not being a baby to be shielded from every rough wind that blew.

"It is only ordinary prudence, my son, for a person, who can as well as not, to protect himself from such nights as these." Dr. Hollister's voice was controlled; he was evidently, Chrissy thought, trying to suppress his anxiety, in order not to alarm his son, but there was almost a pleading note in the voice, which the young man seemed to recognize. He paused irresolutely; his mother, always anxious that he should have his own way, if possible, essayed to help him. "Why, it isn't such a terrible night, is it? Chrissy expects to go out to one of her endless rehearsals. I should think Harmon might venture out if she could. Is there something special going on tonight, my son?"

Dr. Hollister darted an angry glance halfway divided between his wife and Chrissy, as he said sharply to the former: "You don't know what you are talking about."

Harmon laughed somewhat drearily and replied to his mother: "There is nothing in life going on, except the same stupid things. I am tired of them all, but a fellow has to kill time in some way."

"Go with me to Mrs. Emerson's. It is a quiet little company, but Mrs. Emerson will be delighted to see you; you are one of her favorites, you know. I am going in a closed carriage; you won't need to breathe the air of which your father has suddenly become so much afraid."

The young man shrugged his shoulders.

"My dear mother, I hate closed carriages; and if it would be gallant, would say I detested Mrs. Emerson. As it is, I will content myself with saying I detest one of her 'evenings.' They are infinitely duller than solitude at home."

Then Chrissy, eager, coaxing, irresistible: "Harmon, stay with me, that's a dear boy. I'm not going out of the house tonight, and I shall be all alone."

"You!" The monosyllable came at the same second from both mother and brother.

Then, the former: "I thought you had another ponderous rehearsal?"

"I am not going, Mamma; Harm, can I depend on you for company? To be honest, I want more than company. I am in need of a few cards written in your best style."

"Oh! I am to be pressed into service at last, am I?" in a half-sarcastic, half-pleased tone. Harmon was an excellent penman; it might, perhaps, have been called his one talent. "Why, I suppose I could, if it would accommodate you. But you are not supposed to be afraid of east winds. Why are you not going out?"

"Because I am staying in," spoken with great apparent glee. Chrissy was not too much absorbed, however, to lose the gleam of pleasure in her father's eyes, nor his smile and very slight nod of approval as he made ready to answer an imperative summons out into the darkness and sleet.

Looking back over this period of her life, Chrissy always singled this out as one of her hard evenings. She was not, as she pathetically phrased it herself, "acquainted with" her brother; they had no assured tastes in common for her to fall back upon. She was by no means at her best; there was a dead weight of anxiety and disappointment tugging at her heart, there were endless questions knocking at the door of her mind, clamoring to be taken up and thought about; there was, beside all this, a sort of undertone of nameless heartache, which she did not even care to define but which added its share to the general gloom. All these must be put down with resolute hand, and her brother, Harmon, interested and amused, if possible.

She bent her energies to the task. Whatever was to be done tomorrow, this she would accomplish tonight or learn that she could not do it.

The cards were written with many a graceful flourish and admired. Bits of city items were read from the evening paper, Harmon volunteering the information that he rarely read even so much nowadays because his eyes ached so confoundedly; he didn't see why a young fellow like himself, with nothing in the world the matter with his eyes except a wretched cold now and then, should need to have so much trouble with them. Then Chrissy chattered about a dozen nothings which she thought might amuse him. She detailed with happy mimicry certain conversations she had heard that day, though never a word of that one which had sent her home with such a blanched face and throbbing heart. She described with animation she was far from feeling some of the costumes planned for the coming entertainment; with rigid determination to carry the thing though at all cost to herself, she gave a minute description of the tableau which she hated and remembered for years the thrill of actual pain, mingled with unbounded surprise, when she was interrupted by his sudden, "If I were you, Chris, I wouldn't."

"Wouldn't what?"

"Oh! go into that sort of thing. It is well enough for other fellows' sisters, but not for mine. That's unselfish, isn't it?" with a slight laugh. Then, in answer to her stare of astonishment and dismay: "I can't define the feeling. I suppose it is all folly, anyway. There's no harm, of course; I don't mean that. It doesn't begin with the things one sits and stares at nightly at the theater and admires and applauds. That's all right, no one objects to it because, you see, it is somebody else's sister, or nobody's sister; nobody that one cares for, you know, or ever expects to. But when it comes to setting one's own sister up to be stared at, and commented on, and talked up the next night when they get to their clubs—why, it goes against the grain. You won't understand it; you are not expected to understand; fact is, you don't know how some fellows talk, and it's just as well you shouldn't. I know it is quite the style, done in the name of the church, and for the cause of benevolence, and missions, and all that; and I know perfectly well, Chris, the motive, as far at least as some of you are concerned, is all right, but I have often thought if your girls could be present at some of the clubrooms afterwards and not be visible, you wouldn't like it. Of course you can say that people talk about everybody, and so they do; but they can't make so much out of an evening party, for instance—unless you dance a good deal—as they can out of private theatricals. That is what they call them, Chris. You may name them 'entertainments,' or 'tableaux,' or any other pretty name that suites you, but what the fellows say when they get together is 'theatricals.' I didn't mean to say a word of all this. I've thought it, and I've wished young ladies—especially you, somehow—wouldn't go into such things; but it didn't seem worthwhile to say it—not for a fellow like me. I can't make it plain to you, you know; it is only a feeling, and I meant to keep still. I don't know how I happened to go on like this. You can forget all about it if you like and go on with your story. It is a pretty thing, anyway, and must take oceans of work. There's one thing you may understand, Chris, of course no fellow will say anything rude about you before me without getting knocked over for it. You see it is such a confounded mean world; nobody can do anything without wishing he hadn't."

Harmon did not seem to know how or where to stop. He had plunged into this subject unawares and was embarrassed by Chrissy's blazing cheeks and utter dismay. He was stopped at last by a more violent attack of coughing than Chrissy had ever known him to have. An attack which he characterized, when he could speak again, as a "regular old midnight spree, come ahead of time."

He looked at her anxiously as he spoke, wishing within himself that he had been deaf and dumb before he upset her bright, pretty talk by any of his notions. Why couldn't he have held his tongue? Of course she would go on with it—why shouldn't she? The young ladies all did. Now she would go and be offended with him; and he hadn't meant to offend her.

Meantime, Chrissy, holding back with resolute will the outburst of passionate tears which longed to have their way, holding back with equal firmness the sharp sense of failure and humiliation, refusing to think of the young men who had talked about her that day, who had dared to say that she might distinguish herself if she would go on the boards, putting aside even her bewildered astonishment over the thought that in their separate worlds, with their two entirely opposite planes of life to start from, Stuart Holmes and her brother had seemed to reach the same conclusion, bent over Harmon when the cough was at last subdued, wiping with her own fine bit of cambric the moisture from his forehead and said gently, soothingly: "I did not know you felt like this, Harmon. I would not have done anything of which you disapproved, if I had dreamed of such a thing. I wish you had told me before. But now you must not talk anymore tonight; it is that which has made you cough. I'm going to play for you some of your favorite music while you rest. Then I'm going to send you to bed. You didn't know it was after ten o'clock?"

He assured her he did not. It was a remarkably short evening. She needn't be worried about the cough; it was no harder than he coughed every night since this last miserable addition to his cold. He thought of doing himself up in pink cotton and lying by on some upper shelf until June. What did she think of the plan? And he smiled and leaned back, white and worn against the pale green of the chair cushions and closed his eyes. While Chrissy played brilliant waltzes—his favorite style of music—he said to himself that she was a brick, anyway; most girls would have gone and sulked if they had been pitched into that way, and it was very nice of her to say that she wouldn't have done anything of which he disapproved, if she had known it.

A languid wish that he were the sort of brother whose approval would be a safe guide in all things floated in his mind, along with a half-formed resolve to cultivate her Society and be different in some things for her sake. Chrissy did not know it; she might have felt less utterly cast down if she had. As it was, she kept that rigid pressure of control on herself until the evening was quite over and she was shut into her own room, with the blessed consciousness that Louise, who shared it with her, would not be in for an hour or more. Then the weight on heart and nerves found vent in a burst of the bitterest tears she had ever shed in her life.

24

A LOST ANGEL

THE RESULT of that day's experience was not simply tears. Out of the chaos of disappointment and bewilderment into which she was plunged stood boldly one resolve: She would not take part in that horrible entertainment which was, so much of it, of her own planning. Not all; there were features about it that had seemed, to say the least, disagreeable to her; but she found, like many another worker, that she had evolved something which she could not control; there were other tastes than hers to be consulted. And since she had, in a sense, opened the gates and let in the world, all unawares, it is true, but no less certainly on that account, the world had her in possession to a degree. She did not see her way out of its grasp. She saw endless misunderstandings and loud-voiced debates confronting her; she was by no means certain what she would, or could, say. She was certain of but one thing: She was not going to take part in the entertainment so near at hand.

If not the loudest voice in objection to this resolution, certainly the most voluble tongue was her mother's. Her remarks were the most trying to Chrissy, as well as the hardest to meet. "I did not approve of the affair in the first place, as you very well know, but to make the commotion about it that you have, to work yourself and your friends into a perfect furor, to insist on carrying out your scheme in the face of very important opposition, and then to desert them when they have worked hard to please you and are on the eve of success is a most unheard-of proceeding, unworthy of a daughter of mine. In fact, there is no use in talking about it, Chrissy, I shall not consent to it. I was weak enough to yield before, but this time you will find that I shall be firm. You have begun, and you will have to carry the matter through; to do any other way would be disgraceful. I wonder you can be so silly. One who did not know you well would actually suppose that you wanted to make your name prominent in the gossip of the town."

Whereat Chrissy winced. What would her mother say if she knew that her daughter's name was already prominent in the gossip of the town? Why had her mother not known it and warned her? Was she as ignorant of these ways of the world as Chrissy herself had been?

I, the writer, answering for her, want to say for the benefit of other Chrissys, and in defense of some mothers, that in all honesty I think she was. It would be well for mothers, and for busy fathers, too, to stop and consider this fact in society, of which I believe many of them remain ignorant. That a good deal of loose and disagreeable, not to say coarse, talk, which they know nothing about, is floating through the village, or town, or city in which they live, having in it the names of their own treasured sons and daughters and concerning which their young gentlemen acquaintances, very often their own young sons, could enlighten them, were they so disposed. Such a state of things will account for Mrs. Hollister's blind adherence to her decision that what was begun must be carried through. You will observe that in her talk she confused the entertainment and the Christian Endeavor Society as though they were one and the same. In reality she had never objected to the former but had been genial toward it from the first, and Chrissy was not talking about deserting the Society, only the entertainment. But you may have noticed that a certain class of talkers always mix things in this bewildering way, thereby making themselves harder to talk with than any other beings under the sun.

Chrissy was dumb before her mother. She felt that she did not stand on sufficiently assured ground to carry on an argument. She was sure of but one thing, that she would not "pose" at the hall for the benefit of the class of talkers who had complimented her talent in that direction. If it came to that, she must tell her mother of the prominence she had already attained, but she shrank from doing it with a dismay which was pitiful, when one considers that one is talking about mother and daughter.

While she was miserably considering what step to take, how to meet the next rehearsal which was due on Tuesday evening, circumstances came to her aid, so far as the present emergency was concerned; or was it rather, a watchful Providence?

Harmon Hollister added just a feather's weight to the cold under which he had been struggling all winter and was seized with an illness so sharp, and of a character so alarming, that all thought of rehearsals and entertainments was put aside by the entire family. On the Tuesday evening which had troubled her,

Chrissy was hovering between her own room and that of her brother's, conscious from the look on her father's face and from her mother's constant weeping that a battle for life, which it was terribly feared would result in failure, was being fought in that room.

And when, on Wednesday morning, her father, who had not left his son's bedside during the night, went out in haste and returned presently with the specialist, Dr. Douglass, Chrissy's heart sank within her. She had forgotten all about the entertainment—about the Society, indeed; there was nothing in it for her tortured soul to lean upon. She could only on her knees make this importunate cry: "Oh, my Father in heaven! spare him to us, if only for a little while; he is not ready to die." As the need grew sorer, she caught little Faye's hand as they were passing each other in the hall with a murmured: "Oh, darling! Pray for him all the time."

"I do," said Faye, bursting into low sobbing. "Chrissy, I have this long time, but I've been afraid to ask him to love Jesus. Did you ever?"

One more effort she made for human help. She fled to the stables, the only place about the grounds where work was going on in the usual way and said without introduction or explanation: "Joe, I have come to ask you if you will pray for my brother."

"Yes'm," said Joe, with grave sympathy in voice and manner. "I am praying for him; I begun a good while ago. Little Miss Faye asked me to, ma'am."

Chrissy turned away with a curious mixture of relief and pain. It seemed that little Faye had been faithful, if she had not.

It was not until Thursday evening that her father met Chrissy's eager, questioning look with a weary smile.

"We have conquered this time, my daughter," he said. "I think he is out of danger from this attack; that is, if we can keep him from taking more cold; but it was a terrible drain on his system. Two hours more of such a fever as that would have burned his life out."

Chrissy could not trust herself to speak; she had shed no tears since that first hour when the hurrying of feet, and the quick opening and closing of doors, had roused her to know that there was trouble in the house, and she had dressed hastily and gone to Harmon's room.

Now, with the sense of relief came the feeling that she must cry with all her might, or she should die.

"I should think now was the time to laugh," Louise said curiously, but not unkindly, as she watched Chrissy throw herself on the bed and cry as though her heart would break. Louise had suffered with the rest; her white face and haggard eyes told of sleepless hours and heavy anxiety, but the strain was gone from her now. Her nature was different from Chrissy's.

As for Mrs. Hollister, all the mother in her—and you are to understand that there was a good deal—was roused. She had been indefatigable in her care, unfailing in her tenderness and watchfulness. She had forgotten all other interests and fully appreciated the fact that the other members of the family had done the same. She seemed even to have forgotten the last talk with Chrissy before the alarm came; so when that young woman approached her with fear and trembling on the afternoon before the final rehearsal for the entertainment, beginning with: "Mamma, they have their last rehearsal this afternoon, but I do not feel that I can go," she received an instant response. "I should not think you would, poor child. Harmon's sickness has told on you almost as much as it has on him. I do not wonder, I am sure. No, of course you cannot be expected to think of such things now; you are too tired. I don't believe your father would consent; and Harmon seems to like to have you with him, especially in the evening. They must do without you. Poor things, I am sorry of them; it will be a heavy disappointment, no doubt, but of course they will appreciate the situation."

Chrissy turned away with a sense of relief so decided that she could almost smile. It was not by any means in the way she had asked for help, but assuredly help had come to her.

On her way to write her note to the committee, Faye claimed her for a few minutes' talk, her face looking full of anxiety.

"What is it?" said Chrissy tenderly, dropping into an easy chair and drawing the child to her with a caressing movement. "You look as though a little world of responsibility rested on your small shoulders; you must not take life hard so early, little girl, or you will wear out before you die. There are a good many hard places in a girl's life, Faye," with a sigh.

"Yes," said Faye simply; quite as if she realized it, though with barely twelve years of life to look back on. "Chrissy, I want to speak to you about Emmeline. Do you know she means to be married in the summer? And it is to a man who plays the clown in a circus. She says he is going to teach her to ride on a pony without any saddle or bridle, and to jump through rings, and over poles, and do a great many other dreadful things, only she doesn't think they are dreadful; she says she wants to learn, and she thinks she can do them better than any of the ladies who are with the company now."

Chrissy listened with dismay to this alarming bit of news—alarming in more senses than one. What stories of this phase of life might not have been poured into the ears of her young sisters? Not that Faye would be injured thereby, but there was Sara.

"How came she to tell you these things?" she asked with a gravity that was almost sternness.

Faye's fair face flushed. "Why, Chrissy, I was talking with her. I wanted her so much to be a Christian. That time when you thought to invite her to the Society, I began to pray for her. I took her, with Papa, and Harmon, and Sara to be prayed for, every day. Then, of course, I began to think about her a great deal and want her to know Jesus. But she never would say much about it, only to laugh and call me a 'queer little chicken,' and all such names, until that night when Harmon was so sick. She said she was 'scared to death' for fear he would die; she thought it would be dreadful to be in the house where there was a death. When I tried to tell her how easy it could be made to die, how it was only like going on a little bit of a journey to a beautiful palace if you had Jesus to go with you, she said she couldn't do that; that she was going to be a circus woman, and they never prayed, nor talked about such things; that folks would laugh at them if they did.

"She said when she got to be an old woman, all wrinkled and ugly, and couldn't ride the ponies anymore, nor jump, she would think about these things and remember all I had said to her; but she couldn't do it before, because circus people never did. And when I asked her how she would tell whether she would live to be old, she said she guessed she would; that her folks all lived a long while, and she wasn't sickly, nor consumptive, like Harmon; and at any rate she would have to stand her chance, because she couldn't think about such things and live the way I wanted her to. Chrissy, isn't that a perfectly dreadful way to talk? Joe says he has seen the man she is going to marry, and he is a bad man—one of the worst of the set, Joe said, and they were all bad enough. He says he had a wife once, and he struck her and hurt her so that she died, and she wasn't old and wrinkled, either. Isn't it terrible to think he may strike Emmeline? Joe told me to coax her not to have anything to do with circus people, to tell her they were all wrong; but when I tried to, she got quite angry and said that I needn't talk so, that I did things just as bad in their way as the circus folks did; that it was the same thing as our entertainment, only we did the things that pleased us, and they did the things that pleased them."

Poor Chrissy's comment was almost a groan; it was enough for Joe the stable boy to become unwittingly her accuser, but here was Emmeline.

"She did say just that, Chrissy, and a great deal more; when I tried to tell her how different it was, she said it was only different because we were rich people and did not have to earn our living; that we would do it every night if we had to, just as circuses did; and that we picked out the things we liked to do, and could do, and did them, and so did they. That we couldn't ride on ponies and jump through rings, if we tried, because it took a long while to learn, and was dangerous, too, sometimes; so we had to be fairies and angels and such things. She said there were some ways they had that she did not like herself, and that when she got to be one of the company she was going to have them different. She was going to put in some of the pretty things she had learned at our rehearsals, and dress some children up as we were, and have things more refined."

Emmeline among the reformers; and of all places to begin, the traveling circus! Chrissy could have laughed if it had not seemed so much more appropriate to cry.

But Faye's tale of troubles was not yet told.

"And, Chrissy, the worst of it is, when Emmeline said that about there not being any real difference, Sara was in the room, and she said she thought so, too; that it was all nonsense what people said about such places, she believed. That Emmeline could be a lady in a circus just as much as you could be a lady in a tableau. She said suppose some of the people were wicked and used bad words and all that; so did some of the people who belonged to our entertainment; that she had heard Harmon tell how Fred Walker, who was one of the conductors in our tableau, was taken home by four men one night because he was intoxicated and could not walk; and that being a clown in a circus did not make a man bad, any more than being a conductor in a play made a man bad, unless he was bad anyway. I can't tell you all the things she said, Chrissy; there was a good deal more. Talk that Emmeline liked and that helped her to think she was not doing wrong, and I couldn't answer her. I knew Sara was wrong, but she talked so fast and quoted things she had read in books and kept mixing up things that were right with things which were not right, that I did not know what to say. But, Chrissy, isn't there something we can do to help Emmeline?"

"I don't know," said Chrissy with a sigh that had a hopeless sound. This was the young woman for whom Chess Gardner had actually bespoken her influence; had suggested that she use her winning power to save the girl from exactly the life for which she was planning! Chess Gardner, himself not a Christian, pleading for another; and she, the young Christian worker, so engaged otherwise that she had not even remembered the plea! Chrissy remembered once to have heard a sermon, the text of which had impressed her deeply and lingered in her memory. It came to her now: "While thy servant was busy, here and there, he was gone."

25

PROBLEMS

"I DON'T know," said Chrissy again, seeing that Faye still wistfully lingered. "I am afraid we are too late to do anything for Emmeline except to pray. God sometimes does things to stop people, Faye, when they cannot be stopped in any other way."

"Chrissy," said Faye, hesitating, her cheeks taking a deeper hue and looking down in evident embarrassment, "I don't know what you will think of what I want to say; but, though I know that Emmeline and Sara are not right, and that there is a great difference, still, since they think so, at least Emmeline does—sometimes I think Sara only talks things because she likes to, but if Emmeline feels that way, maybe we—maybe I, I mean, ought not to—"

She broke off in inextricable confusion. She had not been in the habit of expressing these inmost thoughts save to Janet; but Chrissy, curious as to what might be coming, would not help her, other than with a gentle, "Well, dear," waited until she began again, abruptly:

"I mean, Chrissy, if I could be excused from being

an angel, I would be so glad." Another moment, in which Chrissy could have laughed, had not tears seemed the wiser expression.

"I know there is a difference, Chrissy," was repeated with touching earnestness, "but then, she truly cannot seem to see it, and so—"

"And so, 'shall the weak sister perish for whom Christ dies?'" Chrissy did not repeat the words; but they seemed to be repeated to her with startling clearness.

"You shall not be an angel unless you choose," she said soothingly, accompanying the words with tender kisses. "Not now, at least," she added, with a sudden thrill at her heart over the knowledge that Faye was very frail looking. What if she should be intended for the society of the real angels before long? Those night rehearsals and heated rooms had not been physically healthful to her, at least.

The committee was, on the whole, as considerate, I think, as could have been expected. In a sense they "appreciated the situation," as Mrs. Hollister said they would. It is true they pleaded for Chrissy to come just a little while, for one of her parts, the one hardest to fill; but when she was resolute, they said: "Well, you do look jaded out, that is a fact. We'll have to get along without you, somehow; but it doesn't seem as though we could."

There was a loud wail over the lost angel. Really they must have Faye—the very sweetest and most natural angel in the group; couldn't she come for just a little while? They would take excellent care of her and send her home in a carriage as soon as her part was over. Or, couldn't Chrissy come and look on, to see how they managed without her, just for that little time, then she could take Faye home with her?

But Chrissy was emphatic, almost sharp in her refusal; Faye must certainly be excused. They had all been through a very heavy strain, and Faye had borne all her strength would admit.

When they were fairly out on the street again, they talked it over, and on the whole, as Mrs. Hollister and I said, were considerate.

"I think they might have let Faye come, at least," said one and added immediately: "But she is a very frail-looking child, and I suppose they feel especially nervous just now."

"I thought Chrissy would certainly come and look on a while, after all the trouble she has had," said another; and a third was ready with the response: "Oh! I don't know; that would be almost as hard as performing, when she has had so much to do with it. I suppose her nerves are all unstrung, poor thing; she looks as though she had had a fit of sickness herself."

Then the second speaker again:

"They almost idolize Harmon. He is the only son, you know, and he is nice, real good-hearted, and accommodating. I always liked Harm Hollister. They say he looks dreadful; I don't suppose he is really out of danger yet, and I heard that his own father said it was only a question of time with him."

As if it were any other than a "question of time" with all of us!

It was on the evening of that day that Dr. Hollister sought a confidential interview with his second daughter.

There was a small, pretty room opening from Harmon's, a sort of second-best guest chamber, to be used on occasion. It was very neatly fitted up with a single bedstead and all the usual comforts. Said Dr. Hollister:

"Daughter, what would you think of occupying the

room next to Harmon's for a few nights and keeping a little oversight of him? Are you too worn out for that?"

"Oh! no indeed, Papa. I should like to do it."

"You see," said Dr. Hollister, sitting down with an air of relief, as having found one whose nerves were sufficiently quiet to let him talk rationally about the sick one, "it is this way: Harmon is out of present danger, I hope, but I am very anxious about that cough and I would like to know just how much he coughs during the night. I would like to stay with him myself, but he is nervous and would get the impression at once that I thought him in danger, which in his present weak state would be bad for him. Your mother is nervous, too, and I have to keep down her fears as much as possible. I had thought of getting one of the medical students to stay nights and care for Harmon's comfort, but I can see that he dislikes the idea very much, which would make it unwise. On the contrary, he seemed quite pleased with the thought of your being near him, so if you do not feel that it will keep you awake too much, we might try it. Most of the nights you can sleep, probably."

She hastened to assure him how ready she was and how careful she would be; he looked relieved and pleased but still waited, as though he might have more to say, taking a meditative walk meanwhile up and down the room.

Then, "Chrissy, you asked me just before this illness, about Harmon's state. I do not wish him nor your mother to know it, at least at present, but he is in a very critical condition. His lungs, if not permanently diseased, are in imminent danger, and his habits of life in almost every direction are utterly against him. If he were like a very few young men whom I have known—I am sorry to say they are a very few—we might make a brave fight through the next few years, with some hope of success; but as it is—" He drew a heavy sigh and after a moment added: "As it is, we must do the best we can and be ready for failure. That was not what I intended to say to you; I hardly know how to word what I want to say; perhaps I do not now what it is I want, only you give me the impression sometimes that you are different from most young ladies—have different aims and hopes. I am on ground that I do not understand very well, but I felt like saying to you that if you could do something in some way for your brother, to help him, I would be glad. The fact is, Daughter," his voice growing husky, "in my thirty years' practice I have had occasion to stand looking on at a great many deathbeds, and there is a difference in them, a great difference. There is no gainsaying that— every physician knows it. I would not have my boy come to such a deathbed as I have seen for anything this world contains; and yet, the life he lives—"

He broke off abruptly again. Chrissy's face was wet with tears, and her voice was tremulous.

"Oh, Papa! I know what you mean. Harmon needs the Lord Jesus Christ. He needs to be shown the way to him and to accept his friendship for life, or . . . Papa, I will try the very best I can to help him. I haven't done it; I have been cruelly thoughtless. I don't know as he will listen to me, but I mean to try. Dear Papa, if you were only a servant of Christ, you could help Harmon so much better than I, or than anyone else could."

He smiled on her—a very grave, sad smile.

"I do not know," he said; "sisters can do a great deal for their brothers, if they will; at least some sisters can. But, Chrissy, you will need to be very prudent indeed.

Harmon is extremely weak; this attack has taken his strength fearfully. It will not do for him to be excited or disturbed in any way."

And then they were interrupted; it had already been a longer interview than the suffering world often gave the busy doctor time for with his family. Chrissy's personal appeal remained unanswered; forgotten, she thought, in the father's anxiety for his son.

She moved into the little room at once, Harmon seeming pleased at the idea. He murmured that he was going to be as peevish and exacting as a sick child and that she would have a horrid time, but he smiled in saying it and looked as though the prospect rather comforted him.

Then began days, and especially nights, that were to be long remembered. It was not that Harmon grew worse; instead, he rallied steadily, and his father grew daily more cheerful about him, assuring Chrissy that she was a famous nurse, and that he would recommend her heartily whenever she grew tired of running societies and wanted to take up the business. Still there was a good deal of coughing, enough to get Chrissy wide awake by midnight and require her patient ministrations, sometimes for an hour or more—often less, as the days passed, and the disease yielded by degrees. But when the paroxysm was over for the night, and Harmon had fallen into quiet sleep, and Chrissy had carefully darkened the night lamp again and tiptoed back to her room, there came hours of wakefulness, when absorbing topics of thought came and stood before her, utterly refusing to be put aside until daylight and sternly insisting on being gone over then and there. They were not wasted hours. Although it seemed almost impossible to reach any conclusions in regard to some of the subjects, others were carefully gone over, step by step, and decisions made from which Chrissy felt in her soul she should not waver. Nevertheless, the way looked perplexing to her.

Chief among her questions of absorbing interest was how to redeem her pledge to her father and "help" Harmon. There were ways in which it seemed hard to help him, although she felt as the days passed that they were becoming very well acquainted indeed. Harmon was evidently well pleased with his nurse. He was uniformly gracious to her, though there were gloomy hours when he had only gruff words for others, even his father, and almost silence for her; yet, after ever so short an absence she was greeted with a glad smile, and in various nameless yet distinctly felt ways he made known that her presence was very agreeable indeed. That was not to be wondered at, for she exhorted herself in every possible way to please him, anticipating not only his wants but his whims and consulted his tastes in the smallest particular.

"You will spoil him even more than he was," Mrs. Hollister said one day, watching her ministrations with a smile, well pleased that he should receive the petting. "He always was a spoiled boy." A fond smile for the "boy" accompanied the words. To her eldest daughter Mrs. Hollister said: "It is strange how many specialties that child has. She is a born nurse, and I should never have imagined it in the world. She does a dozen little things for Harmon's comfort that I should never think of. I do hope that circumstances, or fate, or something, will not succeed in spoiling Chrissy. She would make a splendid woman." The sentence closed with a sigh, whereat Louise laughed.

"Why, Mamma, you seem to feel lugubrious about her. I don't see any occasion; she is very far from being spoiled. As for the streak of fanaticism that troubled you, I think Chess Gardner is fully equal to managing it and any other whim which attacks her. I'm sure he has succeeded very well thus far; look with what admirable skill he has manipulated that Christian Endeavor Society, until from being a cause of annoyance, it has become quite a pleasant resort. Horace and I are talking about joining it."

"I don't know," said the anxious mother, speaking doubtfully. "Chrissy is the sort of girl one can never tell anything about. She wouldn't have anything to do with that entertainment at last, you know; though to be sure, one didn't wonder at that, but she hasn't attended a meeting since. It doesn't suit her, for some reason. I knew that before Harmon was taken sick."

"Oh, Mamma! You are borrowing trouble about Chrissy. She will do you credit at last in every way. I know what is the matter with her—she was dreadfully frightened over Harm, as we all were, and being at a most impressionable age, it takes her longer to rally than it does older people. She feels as though she must never leave him again for fear something will happen. She will recover from that and all her other whims in due time. I'm so glad she had Chess Gardner to manage her. He is eminently prudent and, at the same time, skillful."

"Do you think he is really seriously interested in her, Louise?"

"Why, bless your heart, Mamma, one would suppose you had forgotten your young days. I know he is; I have been through the experience too recently to be mistaken."

A happy little laugh following these words showed that Louise Hollister believed her "experience" to have been in every sense a joyous one.

"Well, then, do you think she understands it and feels kindly disposed toward him in that sense?"

"As to her understanding it, I can't be sure. Chrissy is peculiar in some things, I will admit; but as to approving it, when she does come to understand herself and him—why, Mamma, what possible reason could there be for her doing otherwise? It is Chess Gardner, you know."

"She seems very young," said Mrs. Hollister with a sigh. Not a deep sigh; she felt a shadow of loneliness creeping over her at the thought of so soon giving up her second daughter; but then, as Louise had said, it was Chess Gardner, and his name covered every mental, moral, and society requirement that a sane woman could wish for. So she answered only with a smile Louise's final sentence.

"Young! Why, she will be nineteen in another summer; girls are often married at that age; and Chess is rich enough to wait several years if he pleases—it is a frightfully expensive business. Look at this pin, set in diamonds, that Horace bought me yesterday for my birthday. He wouldn't give it to me on the day, because it was when Harm was so sick; but he never forgets special occasions; that is why I say it is so expensive. They all seem to forget after they have been married awhile."

26

"FIDDLESTICKS!"

AT LAST Harmon was downstairs again, was riding out on pleasant days, was beginning to talk of going out to his club once more, thereby making his father say decisively: "Not until the weather is better and you are stronger than you are now"; and Chrissy was still wondering how she could "help" him, wondering if her present efforts were something like the attempts of the Society to "win" the railroad men. The entertainment, by the way, passed off in almost satisfactory manner and was pronounced a brilliant success; the morning papers complimenting some of the performers by name, and in language so fulsomely flattering as to make Chrissy shudder and throw down the paper in utter repulsion. The railroad men had attended in large numbers and had been "won" into passing resolutions of thanks at their next club meeting. It was also told as a joke that one was overheard to say it wasn't every evening that a fellow could get invited to a first-class theater and nothing to pay!

Chrissy had not yet attended one of the meetings. There was an ostensible reason for this. A slight cold, contracted when Harmon was at his worst, had given her sufficient excuse to play the invalid, so far as going out evenings was concerned. But Chrissy's constitution was not delicate, and no one ever worried about her colds; besides, it was quite gone now, and calls for her were growing louder and more frequent.

Sara, in particular, was very frank to express what she had heard. "The girls say they think you are a pretty president! They say they excuse you as long as Harmon was at all sick, but now that he is able to be out again, they think you ought to be in your place, and I think so, too. Yes; they had the regular meeting, of course; only you might have called it rather irregular. The treasurer made a full report. They made quite a little money at the entertainment, Chrissy, for all the expenses were so heavy. They had a discussion as to what should be done with it. Some of them want to spend it in getting a few costumes for tableaux and charades, you know, that shall belong to the Society. Just a few yards of black-and-white, and silver-and-gold paper, and such common things as these which are used for almost everything. Some of them did not like the idea, however; I think it is an excellent one. They want to get up a cantata next—a perfectly lovely one, Estelle Brainerd says. She says she knows you will like it, because there is a queen in it who has some exquisite singing to do that you could do beautifully; but Belle Parkman said she didn't think you were tall enough for a queen and that the music ran too high for your voice. She wants to be queen herself, I guess. Mr. Gardner said you were the only one of the entire company who could possibly personate a queen; but he didn't say that before Belle. The girls say, of course he would think so. Well, Chrissy, you needn't frown at me—all the girls say so; they say he thinks whatever you do is a little nicer than anybody else can do. Still, he seems to get along with all of them very well, and they all like him ever so much. I don't. I think he is too dictatorial. I hope you won't marry him, Chrissy, ever; he tries to manage too much; he even tries to manage me now," with a marked emphasis on the *now*. "He asked me about the book I was reading the other evening and said it was too old a book for me to read. The idea! He showed his ignorance there! The chief character in it is a girl not quite two years older than I."

One might as well try to stop a brook from flowing downhill as to stop Sara's tongue when she was well underway. Chrissy opened her lips to ask the name of the book, then closed them again, feeling that this was not the time, nor was she in the right spirit to speak wisely. It was as much as she could do to get her few questions about the meeting answered.

"Why, of course they had singing—enough of it, too; some of the hymns they sang were real silly, I think. After the first part of the meeting was over, the glee club sang once, a lovely selection. What did you say? Prayers? Oh! They didn't have any praying this time. No, I said they didn't. They couldn't help it; you needn't look so vexed—there was nobody to pray. The theological students are gone home; it is vacation, you know. I told Belle Parkman that our Joe knew how, but she giggled so loud I was ashamed of her. Why, they chanted the Lord's Prayer for the opening. Why wouldn't that do just as well, Chrissy, every time? Or why need they open all the meetings with prayer? They don't at the other clubs."

And this was Chrissy's dear Christian Endeavor Society, patterned after the one at Western! Perhaps nothing opened that young lady's eyes more effectually to the state of things than to realize suddenly that the caricature of "Bingen on the Rhine," which would have been such a terrible mistake at Western, would not be glaringly inappropriate at any of these meetings of hers, at any time after the first fifteen minutes!

Meantime, Grace had responded to her letter and question by sending her a small gray book containing less than a hundred pages, all told, with this hurried note accompanying:

> *Dear Chrissy,*
>
> *I am, like yourself, very busy, though in a different way. I am teaching, you know, and have been made president of our Society; we are having precious meetings. Several of the girls made the great decision only last night and signed our active membership pledge.*
>
> *Stuart Holmes is not with us, you know; we miss him sadly, of course; but there are some splendid boys growing into young men here, getting ready to take his place. I never spent a winter at Western before. It is almost as pleasant, in a different way, of course, as it is in the summer.*
>
> *Chrissy, dear, I do hope you can come back here next summer. You will enjoy hearing so many new voices. The interest is extending to the school; two of the girls in my geometry class are growing interested in more important problems than they find there. As to your question, I send an answer fuller and much more satisfactory than any I can give: Plain Talks about the Theater, by that grand man, Dr. Herrick Johnson. Stuart Holmes gave the book to me once when I asked him how to answer one of my Sabbath school boys on that question. I think every young*

Christian ought to read it in order to help them in being "thoroughly furnished."

I cannot say you will like the book, because the revelations in it are too solemnly terrible for one to apply that word, but I can say that the book will help you to a distinct and intelligent conclusion on the subject in question; and that, I am sure, is what the writer of it wanted to accomplish. My school bell is ringing.

Good-bye, dear. May our Father keep you in his love.

Grace

This very plain book Chrissy studied until brain and heart were fairly on fire with the thought of the terrible mistake which was being made by the intelligent Christian world, of which even her own mother was a member.

Why did not people inform themselves in regard to these questions? Why had it been left to Scotch Janet, the nurse, to try to build her little wall of protection around the children?

While these questions were being painfully revolved in her mind, there came an evening when she had opportunity to ask some of them. Chess Gardner dropped in, as he had done frequently during Harmon's illness; and finding that young man comfortably established in the back parlor with his mother, as well as Chrissy, for company, boldly presented his appeal.

"Miss Chrissy, you are growing pale. You have too much indoor life for your good, I imagine. Let me break in on your seclusion and carry you captive to the Duane Street Theater this evening. One of your favorite Shakespearean plays is to be presented."

Chrissy's refusal was so prompt and decided that even Mrs. Hollister hesitated, but the flush of annoyance on Mr. Gardner's face emboldened her.

"Why, Chrissy, I see no reason for your insisting on remaining at home every evening now. Harmon has been a bit of a tyrant, I know, but he can manage to tolerate his mother's company this evening, I fancy. Your father was speaking of the play just after dinner and said he would like to attend, if he possibly could."

"Go, by all means, Chris," interrupted Harmon. "I wouldn't keep you at home on such a splendid evening as this for the world; I'd even accompany you, if my father had not grown positively bearish and babyish about me."

Then, Mrs. Hollister: "Go, child, and get ready. Your dress will do very well if you brighten it with a ribbon or two."

"Mamma, I do not wish to go. Mr. Gardner, I found that piece of music for which you were inquiring last week; if you will come to the music room, I will sing it for you now."

As he followed Chrissy down the long room to the alcove partly cut off from the main room by heavy curtains and called the music room, there was still that shade of annoyance on his face. Chrissy found the music in quick silence and sang the verses, saying as she finished: "You see, Mr. Gardner, I was right; the third line is an almost exact reproduction of the strain from that old opera we were discussing, and the accompaniment suggests two others; but I did not ask you here to discuss this music. I wanted to define my position in regard to my refusal of your invitation. I am not going to attend the theater anymore."

"No?" he said lightly, elevating his eyebrows but speaking as one who was resolved to be prepared for anything which might come. "This surprised me; I thought the theater had a special fascination for you; I am not myself particularly anxious to see this play; it was your pleasure of which I was thinking. What has become the matter with theaters?"

"It is nothing new, I fancy, so far as they are concerned. It is rather that I have been ignorant of their true nature and have had no opinion about them, simply because I accepted them without thought. Your own talk with Joe about the circus was almost my first enlightenment, Mr. Gardner, since which time I have studied the subject carefully."

"But surely, Miss Chrissy, you do not class the theaters to which I invite you with the traveling circus?"

"I do not class them at all. I merely say that some of the arguments you advanced apply to the one as well as the other and were unanswerable arguments; they convinced Joe, and they have me. At least, they set me to thinking and to studying. I am not going to try to argue with you. I am only stating my position. I have discovered what I might have known before, that there are no theaters but have their nights in which they cater to the appetites of the low and immoral; my eyes have been opened to the fact that even some of the most popular plays which it is the fashion to admire, educate the morals downward. It is like the gilded saloon preparing its first-class victims to graduate into the low-down grogeries. I will lend you the book I have been studying, if you wish it, Mr. Gardner, and are interested enough to read it carefully; but for myself, I feel that the question is decided. I settled it on my knees, and I have no doubt that it would be wrong for me to attend the theater. For other people I do not presume to judge."

"Very well," he said after just a moment's pause,

"then we will consider the question settled so far as you are concerned; neither do I presume to judge, nor to dictate. I will read your book with pleasure, Miss Chrissy. Not that I feel the need of argument in this matter, but because I want to hold myself always open to conviction. Moreover, I confess to being very desirous of understanding *you*."

There was a marked emphasis on the pronoun which Chrissy did not notice. She was occupied in thinking how entirely his face had cleared from its dissatisfaction and in wondering over and admiring, as she had a hundred times before, the readiness with which this man, not a Christian, accommodated himself to the wishes and plans of others, yielding his own preferences with a grace and heartiness that seemed unusual even among Christian people.

They returned to the back parlor, where Mr. Gardner devoted himself to making the evening pass pleasantly to the invalid with such success that Harmon said of him, the moment he was out of hearing, "He's the best fellow in the world. Always ready to give up his way for the sake of others and to do it with a good grace, too."

"It is more than can be said of some young people of my acquaintance," Mrs. Hollister said.

Chrissy's face flushed, and Harmon laughed.

"That is true," he said good-naturedly. "Chris, it was my gain, and I'm immensely obliged; therefore I can afford to speak plainly. Most fellows would have gone off to sulk if they had been treated to so cold a refusal as Chess Gardner received tonight."

"It was childish," said Mrs. Hollister coldly. "It could be called nothing else; he probably took that into consideration and was patient; though I should suppose he might consider your sister old enough to be governed somewhat by courtesy, instead of whims."

"Mamma," with a little accession of dignity, "it was not a whim which governed me tonight, it was principle."

"It was fiddlesticks!" said her mother irritably. "I haven't much patience left, I know that; and I don't understand how his can hold out much longer. I tell you plainly you are very silly to annoy him in this way. He would almost be justified in leaving you to your peculiar 'principles.' Even Chess Gardner will not bear everything."

"Mamma!" in a great fever of wounded feeling and indignation, "I do not understand you in the least. Mr. Gardner is not obliged to bear with me in anything. My principles are my own; so is my time, so far as he is concerned. I do not know why you speak in this way to me."

"Then you are an unmitigated simpleton; that is all I have to say."

"He plays a good game," said Harmon musingly, evidently not considering this little family hurricane worth noticing. "I was surprised at that. I really think he would beat any of the fellows readily, and yet he never takes a hand at the club."

27

"WISE AS SERPENTS"

OVER this last sentence of Harmon's, together with a conversation which followed hard after, Chrissy pondered anxiously.

Dr. Hollister had come in before any response could be made to Mrs. Hollister's emphatic opinion of her daughter, if indeed Chrissy had had any to make. Not feeling equal to meeting her father at that moment, Chrissy had retired to the alcove which was called the music room, ostensibly to gather up the music and close the piano. Harmon, meantime, had risen and waited only to say good night to his father and mother. Left alone, Mrs. Hollister began to tell her husband how kind Chess Gardner had been. Calling with an entirely different plan for the evening, he had graciously put aside his own preferences and exerted himself to make the evening pass pleasantly to Harmon. "Played cards with him all evening," said the admiring mother, "though I heard him say once that they were an actual bore to him."

Chrissy, about to enter the room, could see the perplexed frown with which she was growing acquainted gather on her father's face and could distinctly hear his reply:

"I could wish that his benevolence had taken some other form. Harmon, unfortunately, does not consider cards a bore; he plays altogether too often for his good."

"Nonsense! Dr. Hollister, what a croaker you are getting to be. As if there could be any harm in his joining in a social game of cards here in our own parlor. I should think you would much prefer it to his being at the club. You must be taking lessons of Chrissy. If you progress at this rate, we shall have two fanatics in the house instead of one. She has utterly exhausted my patience for this evening. What do you think she has done now?"

Whereupon Chrissy fled in haste and noiselessly. But over the card episode she thought anxiously, as I have said.

If you are accustomed to doing careful thinking along these lines; that is, if, as a young person, you have been brought up in the atmosphere of an advanced Christian home, you will doubtless be surprised that a girl like Christine Hollister could have reached the age of eighteen without having pronounced views on all these points.

It may be well for you to know her thoroughly, to help you to be charitable to those in her position.

It simply had not occurred to Chrissy but that to play cards occasionally, or frequently, for social amusement was the legitimate thing for young people in society. Just as it had not occurred to her until very recently that there were some Christians who set their faces like a flint against all theaters. Of course, to gamble was low and vile, and of course there were plays to which people of refinement would not listen.

But neither of these facts had, until a few weeks ago, affected the classic drama and the parlor card table.

Suddenly and solemnly the former question had been settled "on her knees," as she told Mr. Gardner. Not a doubt remained in her mind; but no sooner was it disposed of, than behold! here came another, which her father's tone and her own enlightened conscience, coupled with her logical mind, helped her to see might very possibly be relegated to the same world to which the theater evidently belonged. It sent Chrissy to bed that night with a painful sense of having been defrauded in some way of her rights as an intelligent Christian in not having been thoroughly trained, logically, on these and kindred questions, until at least she should have known what she believed, and why she believed. "My father is a believer in a certain school of medicine," she said to herself as she tossed uneasily from side to side, turning her pillow often to find a cool place for her cheek; "and ever since I was a little child, I have been trained to talk understandingly about it; to know in what general lines he differed from the other schools, and why, and to give a reason for my adoption or rejection of certain views; and I am not expected to practice medicine, either. But here is my mother, a believer in a certain line of ethics as laid down in the Bible, I suppose, and I am expected to practice in just the same line all my life. Yet, what do I know about the position which I ought to take on any moral question beyond the plain laws which govern the civilized world? When I confront my own mind squarely, I find that I do not know why I believe or do not believe anything which relates to Christian ethics. Even Janet and Joe know more than I do about these things. I wonder why Mamma—"

Here the questioning came to an abrupt pause. One law she knew, at least. The One who had said amid the thunders of Sinai, "Honor thy father and mother" was listening now and must not hear this disciple of his arraign her mother for unfaithfulness.

"To his own Master he standeth or falleth" was another familiar verse which floated through her mind. Also, this thought: "Perhaps poor Mamma was brought up as I have been, and nobody ever said things to make her stop and think. If there were only more people to help others think out things!" She tossed to the other side of the bed, changed pillows entirely, and drew a long, tired sigh. It was of no use to go over her list of friends. "What is the matter with my friends?" said poor Chrissy. "Grace is a long way off; and besides, Grace is different from me in another direction from the rest. I have taken it for granted that things are right, as a matter of course, and she has taken it for granted that they are wrong, and neither of us knows why." It was evident, even on the very slight examination which she gave it, that Chess Gardner was the most intimate friend she had, and he was certainly not to be leaned upon—was not even a Christian at all. "He would be positive enough," said Chrissy, trying to analyze his position, "but he does not start out on the same platform. It is not for him an all-important argument that Jesus Christ would or would not have done thus and so. But since it is with me, why have I not known? Gambling holes! That is what Papa calls them. I have been taught to look upon them with horror. And the very same kind of cards are used in them which were used in our parlor this evening; even the very same games played, sometimes; and Papa evidently sees that Harmon is being led into danger by cards. It is Janet's old rule: They choose their style of game, and we choose ours, and they cannot understand the difference, and we have not brains enough to see that the one fosters a taste for the other. I wonder how many more things there are!"

I am sure you are glad to know that, unable to answer this question, she went to sleep.

And the next day was Sunday. A dull, dreary, rainy day; a day which tried Harmon's soul to the utmost. He had planned to go out in the evening to a choral service in one of the uptown churches. He was very fond of music and was very tired of staying in the house, and he gloomed and growled until his mother, pitying him, petitioned his father to know if they called a closed carriage for Harmon, and he wrapped up well, whether it could hurt him. And the father, tried by what seemed to him the childishness of his son in the face of a great physical risk and the ignorance of his mother, declared angrily that he had no patience with any of them; that a five-year-old child would know better than to go out on such an evening after barely getting up from such an illness as Harmon had had; and that if he went out tonight, he needn't expect him to try to bring him through.

All folly, of course; and the father knew it. So did the son—knew that should he go out and get wet to the skin and come home ill, no one would hang over him with more persistent, skillful care than his father; yet with the strange perversity of the human heart, it vexed him to hear himself spoken of in this way. "One would think that I was a child of ten," he said to his mother, "bound to obey Father's every whim. I don't expect to get sick again for him to take care of; he needn't worry. I'm going to take every precaution; and I don't believe in such nonsense as that it would hurt me to step from the door into a carriage if it does rain. I'm tired of moping at home. Sunday evenings are worse than any other."

"Oh! but," said the alarmed mother, "you know you must not go after your father has said what he had."

Chrissy, listening, could not but feel that this, to a young man like Harmon, was the very worst thing she could have said, and resolved to make a bold dash into the midst. Fortunately for her, she was not supposed to have heard a word of what had preceded. For all that appeared, as she stepped in from the hall, she might just have descended the stairs. She went over to Harmon, standing moodily by the window, laid her head caressingly on his shoulder and said: "Could you find it in your heart to pet me tonight? I'm not a choral service, it is true; but I'm a piece of one. I'm learning a most difficult part from an oratorio, and if you would let me sing it to you this evening after the others have scattered, I'd like it ever so much."

He looked down on her doubtfully, the scowl on his face letting up a little. She was so pretty, and her head rested so comfortably on his shoulder.

"I thought you wanted to hear Dr. Dullard's guest preach tonight?" he said.

"I did; but it rains, and little Faye cannot go out; and Emmeline has a great desire to go, for some reason, and I thought I would pet Faye for a while, until eight o'clock, provided you would pet me afterwards."

"Very well," he said, smiling, "but I was going out myself this evening, you know."

"I remember, but being a person gifted with the ordinary amount of common sense, of course you would not risk such a rain as this while a vestige of the cough lasted; I took that for granted."

This seemed to the young man, somehow, a very different way of putting the thing from what there had been before; and in a half hour from that time it would have been hard to have persuaded him that he had entertained a serious thought of going out.

No one tried. Dr. Hollister went away well pleased, more than ever convinced that sisters could do a great deal for their brothers, if they would.

As for Chrissy, it was more than an oratorio that she wanted to present that evening. Not that her statement was not strictly true; she sang the difficult part several times, indeed, surprised by her brother's correct taste and discriminating criticism; and was unsparing in her thanks for his help. In the very midst of one of the solemn, majestic strains, when her voice was rolling out high and pure, she came to a sudden stop, whirled herself from the music stool to a little hassock at Harmon's side, laid her head on his lap and said in a voice throbbing with earnestness:

"Oh, Harmon! I wish you and I could be quite one on this subject. I do so want a friend!"

He placed his hand caressingly on the brown head and looked down on her with a smile as he said:

"What a queer little puss it is! How did you jump so suddenly to so different a theme?"

"It isn't different, Harmon; it is the same theme. Didn't you hear that line, 'In the Lord put I my trust'? That is my confession of faith; so do I—utterly, entirely, forever. Could I help wishing that I might say to you: 'Isn't is glorious, Harmon, that we, you and I, have such a trust—a tower of strength that will never fail us, come what may?' It would be so pleasant to talk it over with you, to live it with you."

She had raised her head to look at him as she spoke, but it drooped again as soon as the sentence was concluded. It was a most sincere sentence; she felt utterly desolate and friendless. Friends enough, but none of them satisfying. None of them sympathetic, so far as this question of questions was concerned. A little more sore on this account her heart was, because of a conversation which she had had with Chess Gardner since the entertainment.

In a gentle, guarded sort of way she had taken him to task for his share in the embarrassment in which she found herself; taken him to task without his discovering it; weighed him, indeed, and in some respects found him wanting.

What had he thought of her for not taking her part in the tableaux, and charades, and all the rest? Why, he had thought her eminently excusable. Did she suppose he would have liked to have that weight put upon her after her long strain of sleepless watching and anxiety?

But what would he think if she should tell him she should not have kept the engagement even had Harmon not been taken sick? What would he say to the fact that she had grown more than surfeited with the whole thing; had come to believe that it was putting her in a position of most unpleasant notoriety?

Well—with a little laugh—they would not quarrel on that subject, he imagined. It was, perhaps, being unnecessarily particular, but now that she asked him, he would confess that he liked quite as well to see her in her own dress and character, as posing in a representation, however beautiful it might be. That was being overfastidious, he had no doubt, and he certainly should not have pushed his opinions had she chosen to gratify the committee, but as it had turned out, he was eminently satisfied.

But did he think that people—well, to put it

plainly—that street loafers, if she might use the term, were in the habit of talking over such entertainments when they were gotten up among the young people in an exclusive way, as theirs had been, and managed in the interests of a church society? Did he believe it was necessarily a conspicuous place to occupy?

As to that, street loafers talked, he must confess, about anything which came to hand and showed very little respect for church or position. Nothing very dreadful could be said, of course; yet it was presumable that their entertainment had suffered at the hands of this class, in common with other doings of the day. That was to be expected. It was not pleasant, and he could but be glad, as he had said, that her name was not at the last included.

Chrissy asked no more questions; she turned away looking grave. He saw the gravity, mistook its cause, and exerted himself to draw her thoughts away from the unpleasant topic; to convince her by his manner that nothing certainly which she had done had changed his estimate of her in the least.

But what Chrissy was thinking was somewhat after this fashion:

"He has felt this all the time and been silent; allowed me to plunge heart and energies into that which, to say the least, has, it seems, its questionable side. He says he is outspoken, that he admires frankness, treats his friends to it, and asks it at their hands in return. Has he been frank with me in this thing, does he think? Did he suppose, I wonder, that I understood the talking world as well as he did and accepted their talk as one of the evils which must be endured? Stuart Holmes did not so judge me, and that is not his idea of frankness."

These thoughts were not what I may call formulated. They simply floated in a sort of chaotic state through Chrissy's mind, increasing her unrest, and making her feel more than ever, as she waited for Harmon's answer, that it would be blessed to have a brother to whom she could speak freely, sure of being understood.

28

"Suppose I Should?"

HIS answer, if answer it may be called, was not such as she could have wished.

"How is it, Chris, that you seem to be so different from other girls of your set? So different from yourself, I may say? I don't remember you as such an earnest little thing in this direction. You were intense enough, I know, and original, for that matter; but there was certainly a difference. What happened to you in that little dried-up village where you spent the summer? Is that what did it?"

"I found it there, Harmon."

Then, after a moment of intense thought, and a little breath of prayer for guidance, she began in a low, sweet voice to tell him the story of her Western experience. Not as she had told it to Grace Norton in its first flush of beauty. Not as she had told it to Chess Gardner behind the curtains that December day but with a simple, tender pathos, born of experience and some regrets. Told it more in detail than she had meant at first, for Harmon was listening impressively, as one who was held by an influence outside of himself.

Very simple and plain she tried to make the story of her final self-surrender, of her solemn signing of the pledge which made her by her own act not her own, having freely, fully, and forever accepted the terms on which she had been "bought with a price."

Once he interrupted her, "But you were a member of our church, Chris, long before that. I remember as well as if it happened yesterday, the Sunday you stood up there before the altar and bowed your little brown head in assent to all that reading, very little of which I understood."

"Neither did I, Harmon. I thought I did. I was sincere enough. I think now that if I had been taught what it all meant and how I should live, I would have been different; but I don't know"—with a little sigh—"it is very easy to get astray, even when you think you are on the safe road. I know this, Harmon. I never deliberately felt what it was to give myself utterly to Christ until that evening when I signed the Christian Endeavor pledge. I have never for a moment regretted that promise, nor desired to be free from it. But it is easier to live right in Western that it is here."

Whereupon she launched into a description of the Christian Endeavor Society at Western, and of the young people who centered about it and radiated from it in all directions, and made it glow with life and power. Being just then all but heartsick for a ray from its shining, she told her story well; so well, that when at last she paused, Harmon said:

"And that was the sort of society you wanted to start here out of Louise, and Horace, and Belle Parkman, and Chess Gardner, and me! Poor little Chris!"

"Yes," said Chrissy humbly, "and the thing I have

started, named for it, isn't it at all; and I cannot help it, nor get rid of it; and everybody calls it mine. It needs making over, Harmon, just as people do. I was reading in the Bible today about the valley of dry bones, and I could not help thinking that that was precisely what our Society needed. We have the bones, and they are all standing about in regular order—officers, and committees, and subcommittees, if we could only be breathed upon!"

She spoke with an intensity that was almost startling, having for the moment forgotten her audience; being engaged only in voicing the cry of her soul.

Her brother did not laugh; he did not even look amused, but regarded her with an intent, half-curious gaze, his face presently glooming over until it might have been discovered by one watching that he had gone into the depths of some thought which troubled him. Chrissy was not looking at him. Presently her thoughts came back to him, and without raising her head she murmured: "If I could only have you, Harmon, to help me, to be in sympathy with me!"

There was no reply. A silence fell between them for several minutes. Then, in a low, almost sullen tone, Harmon spoke:

"I ought to think about these things, I suppose. In fact, I know well enough that I ought. Father thinks he has hoodwinked me; made me believe I was getting as well as I was before. I hoodwink myself— pretend, you know, that there is no sense in coddling me and that I hate to be babied; yet all the while I know it is the coddling and babying which keeps me here at all. And I know, as well as Father does, and as I overheard Dr. Douglass say, for all they kept it from me so carefully, that it is 'only a question of time'; and a very short time at that, I dare say. A fellow as well posted as that, who knows he isn't in the least ready to die, ought to set to work at once and get ready, of course; but the fact is, I can't. Can't even want to. I haven't had a remarkably good time in this world, somehow, for all I've tried hard enough to, and I don't know but I may as well go in now and get as much pleasure out of it as I can and let the rest go."

His sister was looking at him now, all her soul in her eyes; she interrupted him eagerly:

"I don't want you to get ready to die, Harmon. It was not of that I was thinking at all; I thought of it when you were sick, but tonight, all my thought was, how splendid it would be for you to get ready to live. To be the kind of man that I know you could make. Outspoken for true and right and noble things. Can you possible imagine what a joy, for instance, it would be to me to say: 'My brother does not think such and such things are right,' and to have your position such before the world that the thoughtful ones would turn away with a doubt in their minds to be argued over, with a feeling that said, 'If such a man as Harmon Hollister speaks against it, there is reason to hesitate.' Don't you know what I mean, Harmon?"

Yes; he knew very well indeed. She had gauged her brother with a good deal of skill. It would be a pleasant thing to him to be looked up to, to be depended upon as a man of consequence, to have his opinions carry weight with them. He knew very well that he was not now such a man, except, indeed, in certain lines. It was true that none of the fellows at the club cared to make a purchase of a horse until Harm Hollister had tried him; it was also true that he was often shouted at by some of his friends to know what he thought of a certain brand of cigars, but these, he knew, were not the questions Chrissy meant. Neither did he mean them. He had had other ambitions. He went back in memory to a certain day in his early youth, when a man whom he admired, whom all the boys admired, was a guest of one of the professors, and interested himself in them all, and did more for them during the five days of his visit than any man had ever done for them before. He remembered how the boys had said, one and another of them in moments of confidence: "I'd like to be such a man as he is." He remembered how the professor one morning at prayers had said: "Young gentlemen, if you should make it your ambition to fill such a place in the world as my friend who has just left us, and should succeed, the world would have reason to honor and bless you." In his secret soul Harmon had told himself then that he meant to be just such a man. "And there isn't a trace of him in me; I've made a failure of it!" thought this poor, pale youth of twenty-four, skilled in selecting horses and cigars and in arranging and presenting bouquets of expensive flowers and weakened mentally and physically by late hours, rich suppers, and choice wines.

But his sister must be answered.

"To tell you the truth, Chris," trying to throw off the sense of gloom and speak lightly, "I've never been such an admirer of the Christians with whom I have had to do, as a rule, as to care to imitate them; they have seemed to me amazingly like the rest of us."

She did not try to tell him how weak and maudlin such an excuse as this was; how unworthy the breath of a person of brains. If she had, he would have argued with her, and without making a single logical deduction would have been able to point to so many brilliant failures as to apparently strengthen his position and weaken hers. Chrissy felt too humbled to argue.

"I do not wonder at that," she said simply. "I felt in exactly the same way, and said it, too, although I knew it amounted to very little as an argument; yet it served me well as an excuse. It is an unanswerable fact that there are many exceedingly weak imitations of the real thing. But I'll tell you another fact, Harmon Hollister: There is such a person as Jesus Christ, and he will bear just as ardent admiration and as close scrutiny as you can give. He isn't a bit like the rest of us, but people can and do grow like him in a degree if they really want to."

It wasn't in the least the sort of answer he had expected. He had expected her to argue. He had heard a great many semi-witty surface arguments concerning Christianity based on the shortcomings of its professed disciples. He had felt as though a little tilt with this bright young sister would be interesting; he needed enlivening. But he was not prepared to argue as to the consistency of Jesus Christ.

It came to him suddenly, with overpowering force, what a thing it would be to grow like Christ.

He was not ignorant in regard to what this thought meant, nor could he in the least plead ignorance as to the way to begin this growth. In his early boyhood he had been blessed with an earnest and faithful Sabbath school teacher; he had been well taught; he had, several times in the years past, almost reached decisions. But those times seemed to him long past. He had not imagined that such "fancies" would ever possess him again.

Suppose he were one of "this sort of men"; how little he should care then for the coughs, and fevers, and wasting flesh, and weakening limbs of which he was at times so painfully conscious! Suppose he could look the grim monster whom he hated squarely in the face and say: "Yes, I am on my way to my inheritance. You are welcome, for you have come to hasten my journey. I expect to settle on my estate before long."

A man of title! His mother thought a great deal of titles; she had an ambition for him to go abroad to complete his education. She had had a hope that he might possibly meet some of the nobility. What if her own son should become heir apparent to the throne!

Does the motive seem to you a low one—an unworthy one? Was it not for the purpose of rousing our ambition that the terms *heirs of God, joint heirs with Christ,* were repeated to us?

At all events the thoughts thrilled through and through the sluggish soul of this young man, moving him as he had never in his life been moved before. There came to him then and there an intense desire to make the acquaintance of the man Christ Jesus—to become intimate with him.

There came more than a desire; creeping through his veins, quickening every pulse in his being, came that mysterious, solemn, all-potent "I will," the only thing for which the Lord waits before he can save a soul.

Chrissy did not know it. The young man did not even know it himself. Did not realize, I mean, that with the determination came the solemn power of Omnipotence to seal the bond. He only knew that he trembled as though in a chill and felt the perspiration starting on his forehead and yet felt strangely jubilant, as if, perhaps, he might almost give a shout if he were alone.

What he did was to bend forward and kiss a little brown curl which was straying over Chrissy's forehead and murmur:

"You are a grand little sister, and I won't forget it."

It was not the answer which she had desired, but I cannot say that she was disappointed. She was sowing seed as well as she knew how and praying for a harvest; but like many another laborer, she did not really expect a harvest; not now, at least. Had some swift angel on his way to give the news in heaven paused and whispered to her:

"In another moment all the choirs of the celestial city will burst forth in hallelujahs over a soul new born," she would have inquired with eager interest but with utmost ignorance, "Who is it?"

Among the first things that Chrissy Hollister did next morning was to make her way to 14 Meridian Street to call on Nellie Tudor.

Nellie, who had come to spend the season with an aunt and take charge of her little cousin's studies, had been thoughtful and patient during these weeks of waiting for opportunity to renew her acquaintance with Chrissy.

While Harmon was still seriously ill, she had called twice to leave bouquets of exquisite flowers, with her love and sympathy for "Miss Chrissy." Once Chrissy was sleeping, after a long night of watching, and could not be disturbed. At another time, she was with Harmon and made it an excuse for being excused. After that, Nellie had waited for her, wondering a little, it is true, as the days passed but making excuses which Chrissy did not deserve for her nonappearance.

The truth is, perhaps one of the hardest things that Chrissy ever did in her life was to go to Nellie Tudor for "help" out of her present difficulties.

Once there, it seemed as though she would never get away. The story was long, had many windings and turnings, and there were bypaths which did not seem to belong to it at all that yet had to be gone over before the main track could be clearly seen. Through it all, Nellie was eager, sympathetic, tender, and humble. Moreover, she was helpful. She had "grown"— that was evident. Taking long strides forward, indeed, during the months that poor Chrissy could but feel that she herself had gone backward.

The keen insight which this girl, who had been supposed to be so frivolous, had into subtle difficulties and embarrassments, and the straightforward way she had of taking it for granted that a thing once proven to be right was to be done, however difficult, both surprised and humbled Chrissy. She had been hesitant for some time over certain things which she knew to be right because they were difficult.

Moreover, Nellie had an inexpressibly soothing way of saying "we," as though she included herself in the work to be done and meant to stand shoulder to shoulder with her friend. In fact, Chrissy found to her grave bewilderment, that she actually was, before this interview was over, leaning on Nellie Tudor.

"I'll tell you one thing, Chrissy, dear, if we could get Stuart Holmes to address them, it would be worth ever so much. You don't know how earnest he is. You—yes, you do—know all about him, don't you? But he has grown, Chrissy. Oh! he is just absorbed. It really seems as though the Lord had raised him up for just this work and as though no young people could hear him without being helped."

"She is very sweet," said Chrissy to herself as at last she bade Nellie good-bye and hurried homeward. "Very sweet, indeed. I do not wonder that he finds in her all he does. Yes, she had grown very much." And then Chrissy sighed.

The evening mail carried the following short letter to New York:

> Mr. Holmes,
>
> Dear friend, I thank you. Our regular meeting of the Christian Endeavor Society is to be held on Friday evening. New York is but two hours from us, and the spring arrangement of trains now gives us one each hour after three o'clock. Could you find it in your heart to come and help us? We want to reorganize on a different basis. We need help sorely. If you can, I am sure you will, for the sake of Jesus Christ.
>
> Your Friend,
>
> Christine Gordon Hollister

29

RECONSTRUCTION

STUART Holmes had one other paper in his possession signed with the same name. He put this away
with it in a private drawer in his secretary and took
the four o'clock train on Friday, for the little city "two
hours away" from the great one.

It had been a busy week for Chrissy, and, in many
respects, a sad one. In order to be ready for Friday
evening, a good deal of her preparation was of necessity retrospective. Yet, after all, it was a better week than
any she had had for some time. The feeling of unrest,
of painful indecision, was gone; she knew just what
she meant to do and moved with straightforward step
toward its accomplishment. One little drop of exceeding sweetness came into her life on Friday morning.
She was coming uptown in a streetcar. A plainly
dressed girl of about her own age with a good earnest
face sat opposite her, watching her with an intentness
that was only excusable because of the absorbed and
almost tender light in the girl's eyes, which lifted her
act far above the commonplace stare. At last, seeming

to have gathered courage for a resolve, she arose and took a vacant seat beside Chrissy.

"I beg your pardon," she said in low, well-bred tones, "may I speak to you? I am a stranger, but I see that we are kindred." Touching as she spoke the tiny silver badge she wore, bearing the magic letters *CE* and glancing significantly at the corresponding one of gold, which fastened Chrissy's linen collar.

There was an instant clasping of hands and an exchange of cordial smiles.

"I thought I might venture," the stranger said. "I was especially anxious because I was in this city. Do you live here? Then let me tell you a little bit of a story. I am one of the clerks at Hearn's, in New York, you know. I had never heard of the Christian Endeavor Society, and I had never done much thinking of any sort; only to think how I could have as good a time in the world as possible. But one of our girls came here in December, to spend her vacation, and she went to one of the first meetings of your society, in Gardner Hall; is that yours? Well, and she heard the constitution read, and the pledge, and all that; and she liked it so much that she came home and told about it and did not rest until she had started a society out of our class in Sunday school. I joined as an associate member, because I was ready to do whatever the others did, but I got acquainted in that society with Jesus Christ. I signed the pledge and gave myself to him forever; and I've had a good winter. We do enjoy our society so much; and it has always seemed to me that this one here ought to know about ours, because it is the mother of us, you see. We've been having lovely meetings; several of the girls in my class have signed the full pledge this winter. Excuse me for speaking to you; I couldn't help it, someway. Perhaps you will like to tell your president. Callie said she was a sweet-faced girl. Good-bye! I get off here."

Almost before Chrissy could murmur a tremulous "Oh, thank you!" she had received a cordial nod and smile, and the stranger was gone.

"Tell the president!" Yes, indeed, she would; tell it over to her own heart, tell it to Jesus on her knees in the humblest strain of thanksgiving her soul ever knew. Unfaithful, unreliable in every way, yet he had used her in the harvest field!

Without having an engagement with her to do so, Chrissy had hoped and believed that Nellie Tudor would call for her on Friday, but she did not. Chrissy, coming down at last to join Emmeline and Sara, found that there was other company. Louise and Horace were in the hall, dressed to go out, and waiting for her.

"We are going with you," Louise said. "Horace has been talking about it for several weeks; he has quite caught the fever. Are the exercises to be interesting tonight, Chrissy?"

"I do not know," said Chrissy, her face growing a shade paler. At that moment Harmon came from his room.

"I've escaped," he said, smiling, as he buttoned his overcoat. "Even Father thinks the night is so fine that there can be no possible risk in my going out."

"Whither?" said Mrs. Hollister, lingering in the hall to see the party off and returning the smile of her son.

"Going with Chrissy, if she will let me."

"Really!" the mother said, well pleased, turning now to smile on her second daughter. "You are becoming the most popular young woman in society; almost the entire family in your train! If I had not to keep Faye's cough in charge, I might be tempted to

ISABELLA ALDEN

join you, just to learn the source of the bewitchment. There! you are all superseded now, I fancy."

This last in a lower tone, called forth by the sound of the bell and Chess Gardner's voice.

"Is Miss Chrissy—" he began to Emmeline, then with a smile for Chrissy, "Yes, I see you are. May I take care of you?"

The entirely well-pleased mother looked after them all with admiring eyes. What a mistake it would have been to have checked her daughter's ambitions with regard to this organization! How exceedingly well she was managing the whole thing. Or rather, "how well he is managing her through it," was the amused mental comment.

As for Nellie Tudor, she reached the hall a few minutes late, and Stuart Holmes was with her. While the opening hymn was being sung, a pencilled note from Nellie told Chrissy the story:

> The train was twenty minutes late; I waited to show Stuart the way so there might be no unnecessary delays. He will speak directly after the opening, if you wish. I told him I thought you would want him to pray at the opening. Is that so?

Chrissy crushed the note in her hand, inclined her head toward Nellie for answer, and joined with steady voice in the verse that was being sung:

> My mistakes His free grace will cover,
> My sins He will wash away,
> And the feet that shrink and falter,
> Shall walk through the gates of day.

She did want Stuart Holmes to pray; and there were those present who never in all their after lives forgot that prayer.

"Is he a minister?" was Sara's question on the way home. "Well, he prayed like six ministers all put into one."

The meeting was largely attended, and in the air seemed to be that curious sense of expectancy which close observers have sometimes noticed on the eve of a crisis of some sort. Expectancy, even on the part of those who have no reason for thinking that anything unusual is to occur. A moment, while the young president's head was still bowed on the table before her, then she lifted it, and in the hush arose and began to speak, her clear voice filling the room.

I will not undertake to tell you what she said. Not that it was not simple and direct enough, but it was one of those things hard to repeat unless one could also have repeated the atmosphere which enveloped it.

"A synopsis of failure," Chrissy was wont to call it long afterward. The story, in brief, of what the Christian Endeavor Society really was, and what she, taking its bones without its spirit, had made of it in their church. She laid the blame nowhere else than on herself; she was not bitter, even about herself; she was simply honest. She did not want them to think that she was discouraged and desired the Society to drop into oblivion. She had never in her life longed for a real, genuine Christian Endeavor Society as she did tonight. But she wanted the great Head of the organization to breathe into them the breath of life so that they might indeed become "living souls." She hoped the Society would reorganize, would profit by her mistakes and failures, and become the spiritual power that it ought to be in their church. To this end, she would, with the close of this meeting, resign her position as president of the Society in the hope and belief that there could be chosen one who would reconstruct it on more solid ground.

As her last official act, she proposed to ask Mr. Holmes of New York to give them a few words of advice.

I certainly wish, for the sake of the cause, that I could report to you that young man's words.

It was no set speech which he gave them, carefully written and memorized. It was not even what Stuart Holmes had meant to say when he reached the hall.

He knew from Nellie Tudor that the president meant to resign her office, but he had not known that her explanation of the causes which led to this step was to be so full, so humble, and so solemn.

If Sara Hollister thought that he "prayed like six ministers," she must have felt, during the twenty minutes he occupied, that he preached like the embodiment of a dozen!

Certainly the listeners felt that they had never before heard from a man of their own age so impassioned an appeal for wholehearted service.

What followed was as bewildering to Chrissy as to any person present. It appeared that Nellie Tudor, though a very recent addition to their number, had been by no means a passive one. She knew exactly what she wanted to accomplish and had taken careful steps toward accomplishing it. In less time than it takes me to write it out, the president's resignation had been accepted, Stuart Holmes had been appointed chairman, two of the theological students had expressed their desire for an organization of the very sort which Miss Hollister had described to them; then there had followed certain developments which surprised Nellie Tudor with the rest. One, and another, and another of the quiet members, who had heretofore kept very back seats and maintained strict neutrality, declared their sympathy with the ex-president's views, and their earnest hope for a genuine society which should borrow the soul as well as the name of the true organization. Moreover, certain members who had apparently been among the gayest and most absorbed workers confessed in few words their belief that they had made a mistake and that their consciences had often hinted that something better than they were doing ought to be done.

"In short," said Chrissy weeks afterwards when she was writing out the story for Grace Norton, "I believe I went to the meeting feeling that I was a sort of Elijah under a juniper tree; like him at least in that I thought I was the only one who had not entirely bowed the knee to Baal and almost ready to request that I might die. I did long for a true Society, but I did not expect it. I did hope they would organize on a different basis, but I did not believe they would. Judge, then, of my utter astonishment to find how many there were ready to sympathize with my most advanced hopes and longings; ready to much more than meet me halfway."

When the voluntary testimony was concluded, which was so much more than Nellie Tudor had planned, that young woman, with very satisfied eyes, proceeded to carry out her scheme and showed her skill as an organizer, or else the oneness of sympathy that there really was among the young people, when the entire membership arose to their feet to vote that Chrissy Hollister be elected president of the reorganized Christian Endeavor Society.

I do not know what Chrissy would have done with

this movement, had it not been for a surprise which all but took her breath away. She had been very honest with her resignation. She had been honestly distressed over the unexpected reelection. She was genuinely sure that she was not the one to lead. The election had been rushed forward with most unparliamentary haste, but she was on her feet to make earnest protest, when the society was electrified by a new voice.

"I want to say," came in clear-cut words across the hall, "that through the efforts of one of the members of your Christian Endeavor Society, I have been led to choose Christ for my Leader. I want to serve him with my whole heart. I hope someone will propose my name here tonight as an active member of this reorganized society, and I pledge you my most active efforts to sustain it in its new character."

"Harm Hollister," murmured Belle Parkman, nudging her companion and speaking in a half-hysterical whisper. "What next! I'm not going to be surprised now at anything."

Joe the stable boy put his head down suddenly on the seat before him to hide the rush of tears. Joe was not surprised; he had been expecting something of this kind—watching for it; it was just what he and little Miss Faye had been praying about ever so long, and Joe was a literalist and expected results; but he was very happy.

As for Chrissy, her distress, and her doubts, and her shrinkings from further leadership all went off in a thrill of thanksgiving so lifting her out of herself that her speech was:

"Oh! I don't know. I meant to say that I couldn't. But if you think I can, I feel now as though I was willing to try to do anything."

There were several scenes yet to live through that night.

"Such a succession of excitements!" declared Louise the moment they were at home. Chrissy was there, but Harmon had not yet come in.

"Mamma, you ought to have been there. Talk about dime novels! The sensations in the best of them are as nothing compared with what we had tonight. Mamma, what would you think of your daughter Christine as a preacher? She did preach a regular sermon, didn't she, Horace? Did it well, too; I had no idea that excitement could carry a person to such lengths. There was something intoxicating about it, though. Really, Horace, at one time I did not know but you were going to catch the spirit of the hour and follow suit."

The gentleman thus addressed was perfectly grave and answered with marked coldness: "I confess I did not see anything amusing in the gathering. I like to see people in earnest, if the thing they are talking about is worthy of it."

"There, Mamma! didn't I tell you it was a wonderful meeting? You see Horace is almost ready to become a preacher himself."

"What are you talking about, you silly child?" said the smiling mother.

"I'm talking about wonderful things, and you sit there unmoved; you ought to get up and be excited— we all are. Wait till Harm comes. What do you say to Harm speaking in a prayer meeting! That was what it was—a regular revival prayer meeting."

"Harmon!" exclaimed Dr. Hollister, throwing down the paper which he had been pretending to read and rising suddenly to his feet.

"Yes, sir; Harmon. Spoke well, too, didn't he, Horace? I never was so astonished in my life. Papa, you'll have two ministers in your family before you know it—Chrissy and Harm." Whereupon the door opened quietly, and the son of the house entered, pausing midway to take in the excitement of the moment and its cause, if he could. They were all very much excited; Louise, perhaps, most of all, though attempting to cover hers with a flow of wild words unlike her in several respects.

"Is anything wrong?" asked Harmon, looking from one to another of the family group.

Dr. Hollister was the first to respond.

"My son," in a strange, moved voice, such as Harmon never remembered to have heard from him before, "is what your sister is saying true? Have you become interested in—in religious things, Harmon?"

"Yes, sir, I have. I meant to tell you tonight. I have turned over an entirely new leaf, Father. I'm going from this time forth to serve the Lord."

"My boy," said Dr. Hollister, holding out his hand, his voice trembling as none of his children had ever heard it tremble before, "nothing that ever I heard in my life was as good as this. I haven't got it myself, but I know there is such a thing, and I have coveted it for you."

"Scene number sixteen!" said Louise, low toned, but with a half-hysterical laugh.

"Louise, don't!" said her affianced husband sharply.

30

AN UNAPPRECIATED SACRIFICE

YOU are not to suppose that life became all rose colored for Chrissy Hollister. There were many perplexities and embarrassments. As the days passed, it became increasingly apparent to her that one cannot in a single evening, however much in earnest one may be, undo the mistakes of previous weeks and months.

There was Emmeline, for instance, whom possibly she might once have influenced, even as Chess Gardner had suggested, slipped quite beyond her reach; bent on marrying herself to the fiercest and sullenest-looking clown of which any traveling circus in the land could boast and going off with him on her perilous life to trials and dangers that Chrissy, in her sheltered home, could only with bated breath imagine.

Also, there was Chess Gardner himself, a source of constant torture to poor Chrissy, though all unintentionally so far as he was concerned. To understand it, you need a bit of history relating to the days which immediately followed the evening of reconstruction. Of course Mr. Gardner accompanied Chrissy home. He had waited courteously while she said her goodbyes and earnest thanks to Mr. Holmes, who had gone back to New York on the eleven o'clock train. He had been kind and careful of his charge during the homeward ride and walk; had kept her wraps thoughtfully about her, had shielded her from draughts on the street cars, and in every way shown his thoughtful, protective care; had bidden her his usual cordial good-night at the door, and then had gone home to think.

This young woman interested him profoundly. The study of human nature which he had commenced through her had some time before narrowed into a study of her. He was interested in the problem of Christianity in a general and dignified and gracious way; he was interested in Chrissy Hollister in a profound and daily increasing way. It was becoming apparent to him that this fair, unworldly, simple-hearted girl was growing necessary to his happiness. There were things about her which he did not like, and they had to do with this very question of religion which had at first drawn him into studying her. He approved of her being a Christian woman. But a Christian woman who would not accompany him to the theater or opera, who declined to dance, even with him, who frowned on all games of cards, even for social parlor entertainment, who broke loose from the ordinary church entertainments—not because she was too exclusive for them—that idea he would have approved; but because she did not think them right—all these things, his mother said, were "religion run mad." He confessed to himself that many of them were inconvenient. Then, when she added to them that remarkable talk which she made, he was undecided and ill at ease.

He had said to himself that he could shape her acts

to suit his will. He admitted to himself that an influence greater than he possessed over her as yet was certainly shaping her acts without regard to his will.

He went home, as I said, to think. The result of his thinking was the conclusion that Chrissy Hollister, with her fanaticism—if fanaticism was the proper name for it—was more to him than all the world beside. He resolved to sacrifice his tastes so far as necessary and conform his life so far as at all convenient, to her standard, wherever she would not yield to his, and to make her happy at all events in her own way. In short, he resolved to make a sacrifice: to overlook certain things for which he was sorry, for the sake of certain other qualities which had won him.

With this in view, he came one evening, not long after the Society had taken its new lease of life, prepared to tell his story in a frank and manly way.

Mr. Gardner knew that he was superior—could not help knowing it, in fact; in one way or another he had been told so by every person with whom he came in contact all his life. He believed that he was conferring an honor upon any woman whom he asked to share his life. But he believed this in no offensive way. He was always, and in all respects, a gentleman. He also fully believed that Chrissy Hollister would confer an honor on the man whom she accepted. Had he not believed this, he would not have desired to secure her for himself. He did so desire most heartily; his entire better self was in the thought; and he did not emphatically expect to succeed. Judge, then, if you can, of his surprise and bewilderment almost equaling his dismay, when Chrissy, with a face alternately flushing and paling, not because of the excitement naturally attending such an experience but because of real distress, struggled to make plain to him what at first he seemed unable to understand: She could not accept his sacrifice.

"But, Chrissy," he had said in his bewilderment and pain, even after she had thought the interview all but closed, "let me understand this, if I can; it is so sudden, so strange. You will pardon the question; we have been close friends for so long, and my attentions have been so universally accepted that I cannot seem to realize your meaning. Am I to understand that you did not at any time mean other than ordinary friendship?"

Then Chrissy, in great distress and embarrassment, hesitated, shrank from what she felt perhaps ought to be said, and finally, with resolute will, took up the cross:

"I will be entirely frank with you, Mr. Gardner. There was a time when it seemed to me I could give you, if you should ever wish it, much more than friendship; at least, I felt that I was in danger of reaching a point when it might not be possible for me to give only that. I thought about it a good deal and prayed about it. I studied your character to learn whether it was such as I could rest in. I do not know that it would be considered womanly to think in this way before ever one was sought, but I have never quite understood why. It seemed to me that an intelligent and conscientious girl ought to be able to know whether she would be willing to put her life into the keeping of another before he was ready to ask the gift. At any rate, I thought of it and came to the conclusion that, whatever may be right for some, it would not do for me to give my choicest friendship to one who did not love and serve my Lord. I found that I needed helping in this direction almost more than in any other, and that you were not helping me. Rather, you were—never intentionally, I believe—by the force of your preoccupied mind, leading me further away from

Christ, making me every day better satisfied with the world. Then on my knees I promised my Savior that only those who served him supremely should have first places, after his, in my heart. After that, Mr. Gardner, I came to the conclusion that my fancies, which I have vaguely entertained for a time, were but fancies; that you meant only kindness and hearty, unselfish friendship such as I could return; and I gave myself up to the pleasure of it, so that this which you say to me is a revelation and a pain."

He had flushed under some of her words, although at others his face had brightened. He understood her perfectly as regarded his own manner; there had been a time when he had almost asked her to be his wife; and then he had been held back by a sudden flashing out of theories which had seemed to him fanatical and calculated to build up barriers between them, and he had gone over the question again coolly, carefully, coming slowly once more to the inevitable conclusion that, despite the drawback, there was only Chrissy Hollister for his world.

"I understand you," he said, speaking eagerly. "You think I will not be in sympathy with your life, with your aims and plans. You mistake—I admire them, I bow before them. I will accord you all sympathy and help, I will leave you as free as the human soul can and should be to follow out your higher views, and I will further them in every way in my power."

She had tried to interrupt him, only distress in her face.

"It is not that, Mr. Gardner. Do you not know that your life is not in accord with the One to whom I own allegiance; that the supreme love of your soul is not for him, and that, therefore, you cannot be in sympathy with his work and worship?"

Perhaps the poor self-absorbed human heart may be almost excused for making even a haughty reply under such circumstances. Mr. Gardner not being able to reach the plane of life where she stood, did not understand her. "Surely," he had said coldly, though evidently deeply pained, "you cannot desire a man to profess that which he does not possess, in order to please you. You would not ask me to seek to be the sort of ideal character you would see me, simply for your sake. I have offered you all there is of me. How can you ask more?"

"I ask nothing for my sake," she had said hastily and added with deep earnestness, "I could wish indeed that for you own sake you would become the character I would like to see you; a character not ideal but patterned after the man Christ Jesus; but I do not ask it for myself. You force me to add what sounds hard and perhaps hateful; that were you to become today the Christian man I long to see you, it would not alter in the slightest degree the answer I have already given you. The time when I could have had it otherwise is past."

He had been walking at intervals with restless steps up and down the library during the latter part of this interview. With this sentence he turned and stopped before her, looking at her steadily, almost incredulously:

"Is it so, Chrissy?" he said. "You do not care for me in the least?"

"Not in that way, Mr. Gardner, though I value your friendship more than you can understand."

He made a gesture almost of impatience. "Tell me this," he said. "Is there someone else who has usurped my place?"

A scarlet flush dyed Chrissy's face for a moment,

but she lifted grave, truthful eyes to his and answered steadily, "There is no one else."

"Then I will go," he said after a moment's pause. "No," in answer to her low-spoken sentence, "I have nothing to forgive; neither am I angry, of course; at least, I do not think I am. I seem to be stunned. Good-bye, Chrissy."

But if he was not angry, there was certainly one who was. Also, she was bewildered, as Chess Gardner had been; though not stunned. Poor Chrissy could almost have wished that the news, forced from her unwilling lips, could have had that effect for a time on her mother. That a girl in her senses, and in Chrissy's position, the second daughter of a poor man, who gave away half his living had had a family of younger ones to provide for, could actually have refused a man like Chess Gardner was beyond her comprehension. She rang the changes on it until her poor daughter felt as though almost everything was going beyond her own comprehension. "After encouraging him constantly, too, for weeks and months!" This and kindred sentences were often on the mother's lips, to Chrissy's infinite distress. She had made a careful reply once; she had opened her mouth once or twice since to add to that reply and then had closed it again, with a sense of bitter pain. It was one of those half-truths which have power to sting sensitive consciences. Having settled her own duty in the matter and put down with resolute will and conscience the special interest which she believed she could have felt for this man, clearly she ought not to have acted as though there were no other heart but her own to look after; as though she had no responsibility in regard to his comfort in life. "I did not think he meant anything but friendliness after that one time," she told herself miserably and added with unsparing truthfulness; "in fact, I did not think anything about him after he disappointed me; that is what made the trouble and the shame. I ought to have thought. I was absorbed and selfish."

But so was she absorbed now; never more so in her life. The new Society seemed fairly to possess her. With a humbled feeling that she owed it all the spiritual strength she had, and with a wholesome memory of the fact that in her first absorption it had stolen from her that which she ought not to have given, mainly, the time for study and prayer and home duties, she entered upon the work forewarned and enjoyed it as she had not known that actual work could be enjoyed. That she missed Mr. Gardner she frankly admitted to herself and to her home friends. He went away almost immediately after that last interview; it was impossible not to feel a sense of loneliness, as well as a sense of disappointment over the thought that the Christian Endeavor Society, which he had so kindly helped to form, had been only a pain and in no way a blessing to him.

But it was such a pleasure to her to be taken to and from the meeting by Harmon, to realize his growing interest in the work, to recognize his helpfulness in a dozen little ways which Chess Gardner had never thought, that perhaps it would have been an added humiliation to that gentleman to have known that, after all, his place was almost more than filled by the young lady's brother!

Also, it was such a joy to Chrissy to see her father's joy in Harmon. Half the burden of his life seemed to have been lifted from his shoulders.

Altogether, Chrissy could not but feel that although there certainly had been some hard places, yet after all, the year had been one of growth and happiness.

She stood musing about it that moonlit June evening, quite alone. Mrs. Hollister was dining with her married daughter uptown; the doctor was on his endless round of visits. Harmon had, a few moments before, looked in to say:

"Chrissy, I shall not be at home until midnight, or after. I'm to lead that railroad prayer meeting at the roundhouse tonight; and the men do not get in until eleven. Just mention it to Father, will you?"

"Very well," Chrissy had said, smiling in memory of the time when to give her father a message about Harmon coming in at midnight would have made his heart ache. Such a little time ago, too; and now how easy it was to trust Harmon's comings and goings.

"It is just a year ago tonight," said Chrissy in her pleasant musing, "that I took that strangely written pledge card in my hand, shivering as I touched it. What if I had signed the terrible thing? What if I had not signed the other and had just stayed the half-discontented butterfly that I was? I suppose they are all gathered in the great parlor now. Nellie, too; I'm glad she could go there just now, but it is lonely without her. I suppose Stuart Holmes is there by this time. He was to take his vacation in June, and of course he would spend it there. I wonder when he and Nellie will be married. It seems almost strange that she tells me nothing about it; yet I don't know, I don't believe I should be one to be always telling things, provided I had anything to tell. I don't suppose I shall ever marry," thought this sweet, wise old lady of nineteen. "I shall live with Harmon, perhaps; I do hope he will get me a sister to love. How bright the moonlight is tonight. I wonder if I am just a little lonesome. I should like to be with Grace, and all of them, in Western, just for this evening. That's not the office bell, anyway."

With this abrupt conclusion, she dropped the curtain she had been holding as she looked out into the moonlit world and came forward into the front parlor, ready to receive a possible guest.

"How do you do?" said Stuart Holmes, holding out his hand in hearty greeting.

31

A VOLUBLE HISTORIAN

"YES," said Mrs. Hollister, rocking back and forth gracefully in her large easy chair, a complacent smile on her handsome face; "they have both gone to Western. It is a kind of mecca to them, I believe. It is really amusing to me to see how attached Chrissy is to that little village. I've never seen the place yet, myself; they tell me it is lovely in summer, but the loveliness is largely in their imagination, I fancy. Mrs. Dunsmore, wouldn't you find that large gray chair more comfortable? How pleasant it does seem to have you sitting here again with me. Does it seem possible that it is more than a year since you went abroad?

"Oh! I never had any great expectations of going abroad; I used to think my children would, but I don't know," Mrs. Hollister said. "Louise had quite settled down to housekeeping and motherhood. She had a little witch of a daughter, you know; calls her Christine Hollister—the full name. She says she doesn't know how in the world she ever dared to do it; the idea of having another Chrissy Hollister in the family to manage! But I tell her if she brings hers up as well as I did mine, she may have reason to be thankful.

"Oh, yes; both weddings are to be in June. Chrissy went on for this one, two weeks before the time, then they all come back with her. Harmon is to hover midway between Western and the home of an old classmate of his, a few miles from here; but I don't suppose the classmate will see much of him.

"Grace, the name is—Grace Norton. A lovely girl, not in society much; she is high toned and very dignified. Not at all the sort you would have supposed Harmon would select; not that she is not everything that could be desired, but they are very unlike. He is so merry and full of life; well, she has life enough, too, but a demure way of showing it. The doctor is very fond of her. Chrissy pretends to be jealous because he admires her so much.

"Oh, no! she doesn't live in Western, but she has an aunt there of whom she is very fond, and with whom she has always spent her summers. I think, indeed, she spent one winter with her after she graduated. Her mother is an invalid, and they have always had to board, so I suppose really the aunt's seems the home-like place. Chrissy says it is a charming old-fashioned house. It is where she stayed two years ago when she went away. Don't you remember? We were all at Sea Rest together, and Chrissy was at Western. That is where all this romance began.

"The Society? Oh, dear! yes! She is as eager over it as ever. I presume she will organize six in New York City before she has been there a month. Her enthusiasm knows no bounds. And it is really a wonderful thing, Mrs. Dunsmore. You would be surprised to know how it has developed our young people. Dr.

Dullard says he would not have imagined that less than two years could bring about such changes.

"Yes, my children are all in it. Harmon is the president now. You wouldn't have imagined my boy, Harmon, presiding over an organization like that, would you? Leading its prayer meetings, you know; and leading all sorts of meetings, for that matter; hard at work among the railroad men, he is, and the streetcar men, and all sorts of men.

"Oh, yes! just as much of a fanatic as his sister is. They are very much alike; a comfortable sort of fanaticism it is, too. When I hear mothers worrying about their sons, where they spend their evenings, and who their associates are, and sighing over their bad habits, I can hardly help feeling a little bit vain. We never had but the one, to be sure, but we have succeeded in bringing him up so that his whereabouts and his associates never give us a moment of anxiety. On the contrary, if I can say, as I do to many a mother, 'My son, Harmon, has your boy in charge, I saw them go by together'; or, 'I heard him say he was going with him to the park,' why, I just rejoice with them over the instant feeling of relief that spreads over their faces.

"Oh! indeed it is a comfort. Mrs. Ward said to me only the other evening, 'Dear Mrs. Hollister, do you have any idea what a blessing your son is to this city?' She has two rather wild sons, poor woman; not hard, you know, but frisky; smoke a good deal, and are fond of horses, and that sort of thing. Harmon seems to be peculiarly interested in young men of that stamp, and he really has the most unbounded influence over them! His father thinks he is wonderful; but I don't know. He was brought up with refined tastes, and a love for home, you know, and such young men naturally reach out helping hands when they get where they can.

"Oh! yes, indeed; his wife will sympathize most heartily with all that sort of thing. She is a worker in this same society in Western; a great power, Chrissy says, and I can well imagine it.

"No; they are not going to live with us. They will set up an establishment of their own, on Clark Place; why, that stone house just around the corner from Eustis Avenue is the place. I forget that you have been away so long. Harmon says he selected that one day when he was a boy, because he thought it would be such a convenient center from which to get to all parts of the city; the streetcar lines diverge there, you know. You can see where his sympathies were, even when a boy; his heart is so bound up in work for the railroad men, that even so long ago as that, it seems he was planning for it. He says he is going to have his father and mother come to dinner at his house, as Louise does. It positively makes one feel old to hear them talk.

"Oh, yes! Louise and her husband are both in the church; my children all are, indeed, but Sara. Her time will come, I've no doubt. Religious training tells; I brought up my children from their babyhood to respect the church. Louise isn't as absorbed as her sister, of course; she had her home and her family to look after. I tell Chrissy she will see a difference when she is married, but she doesn't believe it. Well, the temperaments of the two are different; they never will be much alike. Louise resembles me, while Chrissy is all father. We are evenly divided as a family. Harmon and Chrissy are like their father; well, and little Faye, too, all intensity and enthusiasm, you know; while Louise and Sara are more like me; take things quietly and are not tempted to rush into extremes; though I have no occasion to quarrel with the extremes which my children have chosen. Horace, my son-in-law, is rather inclined to be enthusiastic; Louise is a good balance for him. Harmon has a great influence over Horace; he wasn't in the church, you know, until after Harmon took such a remarkable stand. He became interested that very evening, indeed.

"Oh! as to Chrissy, I don't know when the child wasn't different from everybody else; but she became absorbed in this new society that summer at Western and met there the gentleman whom she is to marry. Haven't I told you his name yet? What an idea! And he is to be my son-in-law in three weeks more. Holmes, it is, Stuart Holmes.

"Yes, it is an aristocratic name; he is of a very fine family. Not wealthy, you know; but old and high toned—a family of scholars. Stuart is a banker; he will be a rich man, I think, without doubt. Horace says he is indispensable in the bank. Oh! he is one of the most remarkable Christians I ever knew and a man of marked talent. Dr. Dullard says he ought to be in the church, and that Chrissy would make simply a wonderful minister's wife; but I believe Stuart had an idea that he could do more good as a man of business— with his money, I presume; and I confess that I would quite as soon have Chrissy the wife of a banker as a minister; that life is so hard. Then they are always tied to their churches; unable to get away anywhere. I should not wonder if Chrissy had a chance to go abroad, sometime. Businessmen go over there a great deal nowadays, you know. He has a very pleasant home for her in New York.

"Oh! yes, indeed; I have reason to be entirely satisfied in my children. I have a great admiration for my prospective son-in-law.

"Oh, dear Mrs. Dunsmore! do you remember that fancy of mine? Well, to be frank, I did certainly suppose for a time that Chrissy would be Mrs. Chess Gardner. But there is no accounting for a girl's tastes. Of course I prefer the other one now; but I did not know him at the time, and Chess was so attentive and so unexceptional. Poor fellow; I thought for a while that he was utterly heartbroken.

"No, he is not married, but he is soon to be. Oh, no! there was no break between him and Chrissy—at least not for long. They are intimate friends—quite like brother and sister. He is to marry a friend of Chrissy's; quite a romantic thing it is. She is poor; a schoolteacher and an orphan and quite dependent on herself; and here she is going to be Mrs. Chess Gardner with all sorts of elegancies, and a wedding trip to Naples, and all that kind of thing. Isn't Dame Fortune a queer creature?

"Of all persons to select for a wife for Chess Gardner the last one I should have chosen would have been Nellie Tudor. If my Harmon had fancied her, I should not have been so surprised. She is so merry, childish; Chess is so intellectual, and so stately that one would have supposed his choice would have been very different. Not that I would have cared to have Harmon marry her; but I thought at one time that he would; they were quite intimate friends, and we have become very much attached to her. Still, I confess I was anxious lest Harmon should choose her; it seemed a sort of pity, some way, when he could make a choice where he pleased. To tell the truth, I rather took Chrissy to task for being intimate with her and leading her brother into temptation.

"I think the child got an impression that I didn't like her and stayed away from here; she was living with an aunt on Meridian Street. I never dreamed, you see, that I was cutting the future Mrs. Chess Gardner. She's a pretty creature; and when she comes back from Europe I suppose will be quite the fashion.

"Oh, no! she will never be a society lady; she is too much like Chrissy for that. Chrissy has molded her a good deal; and Chess Gardner, too, for that matter. She has such a remarkable influence over all her friends. I am certainly wonderfully blessed in my children, Mrs. Dunsmore."

Here occurred an interruption in the person of a tall, pale girl in black, who entered quietly, with a note which she gave to Mrs. Hollister and glided away. Whereupon the guest, Mrs. Hollister's seaside friend and special confidante of years, remarked that the girl's face looked familiar some way; yet she couldn't place it and asked where she was picked up.

"Why, it is familiar," said Mrs. Hollister, started at once on a new track. "Don't you remember my Emmeline? She was second girl when you went abroad; a pretty, graceful creature with rosy cheeks and a quantity of fluffy hair.

"Yes, this is the very girl! You wouldn't believe that less than two years could make such a change, would you? She has a sad story, poor thing, and quite romantic, too. She became fascinated with a low fellow who belonged to a traveling circus and married him. We tried in every way to prevent it, of course, but to no purpose. The fellow led her a terrible life; was positively cruel to her, and struck her, and all that. They brought up, don't you think, in London, at last. Think of my Emmeline in London! There the fellow abandoned her, and Chess Gardner met her wandering through the streets alone, and starving, and frightened almost out of her senses. He befriended her and found her miserable husband for her; but the wretch died, fortunately, and then Chess wrote to Chrissy about

Emmeline—romantic, wasn't it? I was inclined to have nothing to do with her; so ungrateful in her to leave us in the first place, you know, and go off with the fellow, but Chess pled eloquently and Chrissy was determined, and the end of it was, he sent her home; paid her passage and saw that she was decently clothed; did everything, in fact, as though she had been a dependent of his, all for Chrissy's sake, I think; he knew she was fond of Emmeline, but Chrissy said it was for Christ's sake; that is her style of sentiment, you know. She manages me with the rest of them, so I took Emmeline back. I must say the girl is a comfort. I'm having my reward for being charitable. She is fond of us all and devoted to my daughter Faye.

"Yes, we are all going to Western the last of next week. That is Chrissy's fancy; that her father is to spend a Sabbath there and to go church with her. I don't know why, I am sure. Then we return and make all haste getting ready for Chrissy's wedding. Chess Gardner and his lady are to be her attendants. Oh! it is all as romantic as possible. I'm so glad you will be here to meet my handsome new son-in-law. He is the finest looking of them all."

This voluble historian reeled out her story as given above toward the setting sun of another June day; perfect as to air, and earth, and sky. Especially perfect far away from the city, in the pretty little village of Western, where, at that particular moment, in a pretty cottage room—exactly the room, by the way, in which you first met her—Chrissy stood by the dressing bureau, her hair all in a wealth of soft disorder flowing over her dressing sacque, and smiling to herself in the mirror. The special occasion of her smiles was that she had at that moment discovered a new decoration on the mirror frame. Winding in among the vines and the birds, with which Grace Norton's hand, you may remember, had decorated that mirror for her friend, were five letters, looking to the unwary like stems of flowers and veins, with merely the semblance of a letter here and there, but taking shape to Chrissy's amused eyes in the old watch cry *YPSCE*.

"Grace!" she called, and that maiden from across the hall responded and came smiling to the door.

"What do these letters mean which I have found roving over this mirror?" began Chrissy, and then broke into sweet laughter, springing back to wind her arms about Grace Norton's neck and say between the kisses: "Oh! Gracie, Gracie; to think that you are going to be my sister! Grace, isn't life wonderful? There! Somebody is going to call you; somebody always did. It is Harmon, though, this time. He will always be calling you after this."

"No, it isn't," laughed Grace. "It is Stuart, and he is asking for you. He always was asking for you in the old days, and he always will be after this."

Chrissy disengaged herself in haste, her face all in a bright flush. "Won't you go, Grace, and tell him I will be down in a few minutes?"

Then the business of dressing went on with much more speed than it had two years before.

In the hall below, they were waiting for her—her brother, Harmon, and Stuart Holmes. Stuart had been for a day or two in Western. Chrissy and Harmon had arrived but that afternoon.

To Harmon Hollister, if one had time, you would need an introduction. At least, some of his old acquaintances found it difficult to recognize him. The slight, delicate form had rounded out, the pallid, pinched look was entirely gone from his face. No trace of the old, almost constant, cough remained. So much had regular hours, careful habits, the rigid banishing of cigars and wine, and the grace of God in the heart done for this almost hopeless invalid.

"We want to advise with you," said Stuart Holmes. "Harmon found a note begging him to go to Carleton this evening to hold a meeting at the Round House and to bring me with him. The men will be in at ten o'clock for an hour, and not again, all of them, for several nights."

"Where is Carleton?" Chrissy asked.

"Seven miles below here; it would necessitate a start soon after supper."

"Oh!" The monosyllable was long drawn out, and the tone, it must be confessed, decidedly regretful. "Just for this one evening—couldn't you both be here? It is a sort of anniversary, you know."

"I know; I had the courage to propose it," said Stuart Holmes, smiling. "But your brother, Harmon, does not at all approve."

Chrissy turned and looked at her tall, handsome brother.

Some memory of a more recent past came floating over her. How she said to him, once, something like this:

"Can you think of what a joy it would be to me to hear it said, 'Harmon Hollister does not approve of it' and to know that thoughtful people would reply, 'If such a man as Harmon Hollister does not approve, it needs thinking about'?"

"His work first, Chrissy," Harmon said gently, a shade of regret for her disappointment in his voice.

"Yes," said Chrissy heartily and smiled.

THE END